ILLICIT TRADE

ILLICIT TRADE

A Valentin Vermeulen Thriller

Michael Niemann

coffeetownpress

Seattle, WA

coffeetownpress

Coffeetown Press
PO Box 70515
Seattle, WA 98127

For more information go to: www.coffeetownpress.com
www.michael-niemann.com

Cover design by Sabrina Sun

Illicit Trade
Copyright © 2017 by Michael Niemann

ISBN: 978-1-60381-589-5 (Trade Paper)
ISBN: 978-1-60381-590-1 (eBook)

Library of Congress Control Number: 2016956980

Printed in the United States of America

For Joanna

ACKNOWLEDGMENTS

———◆———

ALTHOUGH WRITING IS A SOLITARY UNDERTAKING, there are many who contributed in their own way to the completion of this novel. The support of my partner Joanna for my writing endeavors means the world to me. She helps create the environment which allows imagination to thrive. The members my *Monday Mayhem* writing group, Carole Beers, Sharon Dean, Clive Rosengren and Tim Wohlforth, provided ongoing feedback and a critical eye when I needed it most. My buddy Fred Grewe always listened to my latest plot twist while we drank beer and had the good sense to caution me whenever they defied logic. Melody Condon copyedited the first version with her usual skill. Bobby Arellano's keen eyes caught a few typos. The expert advice and editing of Catherine Treadgold and Jennifer McCord at Coffeetown Press made this book much better. I'm grateful to be working with them.

The illicit trade mentioned in this novel is real and growing. This dark side of globalization is the multibillion dollar flow of illicit goods and people based on the exploitation of the weak, and more often than not, for the benefit of the powerful. The trafficking of people is a particularly gruesome part. The work of anthropologist Nancy Sheper-Hughes has been particularly helpful during my research. I recommend her article "Parts Unknown" in *Ethnography* 5(1), 2004 to anyone who want to know more about this illicit trade.

Also by the Author

Legitimate Business

CHAPTER ONE

———◆———

H E SHOULDN'T HAVE COME. HIS GUT had known all along. He'd thought it was just a case of nerves, pretty normal for someone who'd never been in an airplane before. But it had gotten worse, much worse. He bent forward to ease the pain.

"Citizens to the left, visitors to the right." The female officer in a blue uniform looked right through him. "Citizens to the left, visitors to the right."

Like most passengers, Joseph Odinga stepped to the right.

Maybe the pain was hunger. During the flights he'd only picked at his meals.

The line moved again. The passport officers at John F. Kennedy International Airport in New York City were taking their time. He stumbled forward, grateful for the tape that outlined the maze through which the visitors were herded. His passport and paperwork felt slippery in his hand. A kind flight attendant had helped him fill out the immigration forms. On his own, he'd have made a mess of it.

He reached the end of the line. Another officer—lighter skinned than the first—held up her hand. He stopped, wiped sweat from his forehead. The officer directed him to the eighth booth. There were three parties ahead of him.

His seat neighbors, a Kenyan woman and her son, spoke to the agent inside the booth. The woman put her right thumb, then the four fingers of her right hand, on a small green screen. She repeated the process with her left hand. The officer pointed a small round thing at her. If that was a camera, it was smaller than any Joseph had seen.

He could see the officer in the booth asking questions. The woman smiled, nodded, said something in return. She looked confident. They had the right papers. The officer in the booth smiled. He stamped her passport, snapped it shut, and handed it to her. They were in.

"Next."

A white man stepped forward and handed his papers across the counter. The officer said something. The man answered. He didn't smile. Neither did the officer, who typed on a keyboard. There were more questions. Still no smiling. It looked like the kind of trouble that had caused the cramps in Joseph's stomach. A border agent, dodgy papers, and no place to hide.

The alien creature that had been settling inside his gut ever since he left Nairobi began to devour his innards. He wanted to lie down and curl up to ease the pain. But he couldn't do that. Don't attract attention—that's what the white man in Kibera had told him. Sweat ran down his face and stained the collar of his shirt. He shouldn't have come. His stomach's message was clear. He should have stayed home. He already missed the heat and smell of a quarter-million people crammed into five hundred acres of slum just south of the Royal Nairobi Golf Club. He missed taking portraits and passport photos.

"Next."

The man had made it through. He'd disappeared and been replaced by two African girls. Maybe they were exchange students, coming to the U.S. for a year. They were dressed in sharp clothes and bubbled with excitement. He knew they weren't from Kibera. They'd gone to a private high school. They looked like the daughters of government ministers.

The officer in the booth took a long time dealing with the students' paperwork. Was there so much to document just to come and study here? Joseph remembered his own visa application. Good thing somebody else had filled it in. It was too complicated.

The officer took his time.

The delay only gave the creature in Joseph's belly more time to burrow. *Please, let it be over*, he thought. *I don't care anymore.* Anything but standing here, being eaten by fear. He wanted to turn around, go back. What good could be found in a country that so frightened you before you even got inside?

"Next."

The officer looked at him with a stare that went straight down to the creature eating his guts. His name tag read Menendez.

Joseph stood there.

What now?

His shirt clung to his skin like a cold rag.

"Good morning," Officer Menendez said.

"Good morning."

"Speak up. I can't hear you."

Joseph remembered to hand the officer his passport and the other documents.

Officer Menendez took his passport and slid the page with his picture through a slot.

"Are you feeling okay, Mr. Odinga? You don't look so good."

"Yes, uh … no, my stomach is not good."

"Probably that airline food."

Officer Menendez flipped through the paperwork.

"You are here to attend a UN hearing on urban development?" he said.

"Yes."

"Where do you work?"

"Kibera."

"No, who is your employer?"

Joseph tried to remember what the white man had told him to say. UN hearing. Urban development. Slums. Yes, that was it.

"Slums," he said.

"Yeah, I understand that. What I want to know is who you work for."

Joseph saw the furrows forming on Officer Menendez's forehead. This wasn't going well. *Who do I work for?* The white man had told him. But he couldn't remember. Wait, there it was.

"University."

"Okay, what university?"

"University in Nairobi."

"Yes, what's its name?"

Joseph couldn't think. His mind was busy checking the progress of the animal in his gut. It didn't have time for questions.

"You don't speak much English, do you?" Menendez said.

"Some."

"You say you are a professor at a university in Nairobi, but you only speak *some* English?"

Joseph shook his head. "No, not professor. I work at Technical University in Nairobi."

"What are you doing at this UN hearing?" Menendez said.

"Slums," he said again.

It took all the energy he had left. The creature had eaten all his organs. There was a gaping hole where his stomach had been. He looked down, expecting to see blood pour to the floor. There were only gray tiles and a yellow line. The tiles blurred. The line turned into a snake. It smiled at him and said, "You should have stayed in Kibera."

The snake was right.

The white man had made it sound so easy. Go to the U.S. Make a lot of money. Pay for your mother's surgery and your little sister's school fees.

He looked up again. There were two more officers in blue uniforms. They carried guns in their holsters. They grabbed him by his arms and took him away. There wouldn't be any money. He'd let his family down.

He'd failed.

Chapter Two

———◆———

THE WAITRESS AT THE CAFÉ ON Second Avenue and 48th Street was kind of cute. Valentin Vermeulen watched as she wiped the crumbs off a neighboring table that had just been vacated. Her movements were unhurried and precise. When she raised her head to catch him staring, he looked away. Forty-five years old and checking out cute waitresses.

"That's quite the tie you're wearing," the waitress said.

"It is, isn't it?"

The tie's patterns rivaled the latest exhibit at the Museum of Modern Art. It belied the plainness of the rest of his appearance, an off-the-rack dark woolen suit, a white shirt, and gray socks. Like millions of others who spent their days in offices.

"Did you get it in the city?" the waitress said.

"Er … no." He was getting a little hot under the collar. "It's a gift from my daughter. She bought it in Düsseldorf, er, in Germany."

Vermeulen expected the look that said, *you creep, you have a daughter old enough to give you fancy ties and you're checking out my ass*, but it didn't come.

"Germany, huh? I figured it had to be from overseas. Never saw anything like it around here. And I see a lot of different outfits, with the United Nations so close by."

"I bet."

"You want some more coffee?"

He nodded. The waitress left. He breathed easier.

She came back with the coffee. "I bet you work at the United Nations," she said.

"What makes you say that?"

"Well, you have a daughter in Germany. You look European—I mean, your shoes are definitely European. And you were embarrassed when I caught you looking at me. Most Americans wouldn't be."

He had the rugged countenance of the Flemish farmers in his family tree, but he never thought of himself as looking European. She was right about the shoes. He was particular about his shoes. It was the one piece of advice from his father that he'd heeded.

"Well done," he said. "I work for the Office of Internal Oversight Services at the UN."

A new patron sat down at the vacant table and the waitress left to get a menu.

He'd been back in New York City for almost a year. After seven years in the wilderness, hopscotching from one faraway mission to another, he'd finally proven his loyalty to the satisfaction of his superiors at the OIOS. In the end, generating positive headlines for the UN carried enough weight to overcome the legacy of his original faux pas back in 2003. He'd made a terrible first impression by accusing the son of the then Secretary General of profiting from the Iraqi oil-for-food program.

During the first months back in New York City, he was simply content to be back. That blotted out any thoughts about the downsides. He'd moved back into his studio apartment on Gansevoort Street, only half a block away from the High Line. Its owners hadn't yet turned into real estate speculators and had allowed him to sublet it while he was out of the country. Just stretching out in his own bed was grand. Then there were the offerings of a world city: great food at reasonable prices—if you knew where to look; his favorite Belgian beer, De Koninck, available in a store just three blocks away; and a little shop that stocked his favorite cigarettes, Gitane Papier Maïs. It all added up to a blissful half-year.

During the next six months, the sheen wore off. The dress code was just one annoyance. The inane office dynamics and the dull work also weighed upon his spirits. A restlessness he recognized from his days at the Crown Prosecutor's office in Antwerp infiltrated his life. Back then, it was the impending divorce from his wife that made him tap his foot like a teenager. This time it was simple boredom. Back then, his solution was to leave Belgium for the job at the UN the moment his divorce was finalized. This time, he couldn't think of an alternative.

He missed sorting out clues, cornering crooks, and closing cases. Instead, he wrote reports about cases closed by someone else. Yes, there were the memories of seedy hotels, bad food at airports, rarely having time to catch your breath before jetting off to another assignment. He didn't want to go back to that. But the occasional assignment of a big fraud case, with assurances of a return to New York City … that would be nice. He might even get his tan back.

His phone rang. He pushed an errant forelock of blond hair from his forehead. It was his boss, Suarez. Against his better judgment, he tapped the Answer button.

"Where are you?" Suarez said.

"Just finishing lunch."

"At the cafeteria downstairs?"

"No. A little bakery on Second, just a couple of blocks south of the UN Plaza."

"Food at the cafeteria not good enough for you?"

Everybody knew that the food in the cafeteria was subpar. Suarez always sounded like he wanted to pick a fight. Vermeulen knew enough not to take the bait.

"I can be in your office in ten minutes," Vermeulen said.

"Don't bother. Get yourself to the ICE office at 29 Federal Plaza. Fred Sunderland, Special Agent in Charge, is waiting for you."

"The ICE office?"

"Immigration and Customs Enforcement. Apparently someone in the Nairobi office is using fake invitation letters for visas to the U.S."

Vermeulen sighed. That sounded like an errand, not the kind of assignment he'd been daydreaming about.

Fred Sunderland was a portly fellow who could've subbed for Santa Claus. All he needed was a red hat and a white beard. Except he wasn't the least bit jolly.

"Have a seat, Mister …" he studied the card Vermeulen had given him, "Vermoolen."

Vermeulen didn't bother to correct him. There was no sound in the English language that would have approximated the pronunciation of his last name.

"You have a problem," Sunderland continued. "This fake letter from your Nairobi office was used to get someone a visa to the U.S."

Vermeulen noticed the use of the pronoun. As if *he* had personally smuggled an undocumented alien into the country. Sunderland passed a plastic sleeve containing the letter across the desk. It looked real enough. The letterhead was from the UN Human Settlements Program, UN-HABITAT, in Nairobi. It stated that Joseph Odinga had been invited to speak at a conference on slum rehabilitation in New York. The signature was difficult to make out; the printed name below presumably belonged to some program officer.

"How do you know it's fake?" Vermeulen said.

"The Customs and Border Protection officer, who checked his papers at JFK, noted Odinga's suspicious behavior. When questioned further, Mr. Odinga couldn't explain the circumstances of his visit. Doesn't sound like a conference speaker to me."

"That's all? An African man acts nervous at the passport counter and you lock him up? Why wouldn't he be nervous? It's not like international arrival at JFK is a pleasant experience. The conference organizers probably invited slum dwellers to get firsthand insights into the conditions of their existence. I bet it's the first time Mr. Odinga has ever traveled out of Kenya."

Sunderland's eyes turned into slits. He leaned forward. "Listen, Vermoolen. I don't need some flunky from the United Nations telling me how to protect our borders. That man won't be testifying at one of your gabfests. He didn't know why he was here. He's illegal."

"I assume he was confused. Probably doesn't speak English well. And he was scared."

"If I wanted someone to go to bat for Odinga, Vermoolen, I'd have called one of the immigration shysters. I asked the UN to send someone who'd find out who's issuing fake letters in Nairobi and stop it."

Vermeulen already disliked the man enough to challenge him. "I don't believe you've established that the letter was fake."

Sunderland snorted, opened a folder, and pulled out three more plastic sleeves containing letters. Each invited someone to a UN event. Two were issued by UN agencies with offices in Vienna. The third also came from UN-HABITAT in Nairobi.

"The first one showed up three months ago. We only caught those scam artists who didn't have the wherewithal to fake out the Customs and Border Protection officers. We're not sure how many slipped through. For all I know, there are tens or hundreds more who came in and promptly disappeared. You'd better put a stop to it."

"Or what? Spare me the bluster. I'm still not convinced that these are fake letters. Your fair city houses a world organization with many far-flung programs. Not everyone who's invited is a head of state."

"Did any of these conferences actually take place?"

Vermeulen didn't know the answer. As usual, Suarez hadn't told him anything before sending him on this errand.

Trying to suppress his impatience with the entire situation, he asked, "Can I speak to Mr. Odinga? Where is he? Where are the other three?"

"Odinga is probably in Elizabeth. Two of the others are somewhere in the system. The third waived his right to a hearing and was deported."

"Can I have copies of these letters? I'll have to ascertain their origin." Sunderland slipped him an envelope. "And I'd like to make an appointment to speak with Mr. Odinga."

"Does it look like I'm in charge of his calendar? You want to talk to him, you go across the Hudson and stand in line." Sunderland thrust his ruddy face forward so that Vermeulen could smell the onions on his breath. "Just so we understand each other, Vermoolen, until the United Nations cleans up this mess, the officers at JFK will give special attention to UN invitees. We may not be able to prevent the world's dictators from coming here and spewing their venom, but we sure as hell can keep their unwashed rabble out."

Vermeulen got up. At the door, he turned. "Good thing the Statue of Liberty stands in New York Harbor. That way, the passengers arriving at JFK won't see its inscription. They might confuse this country with one that actually cares."

CHAPTER THREE

———————◆———————

IT TOOK VERMEULEN THE ENTIRE AFTERNOON and part of the next morning to locate Joseph Odinga. Nobody at Immigration and Customs Enforcement seemed to have any interest in making his job easier. Maybe Sunderland had told them to give him the runaround. At ten thirty, after umpteen transfers, a woman with a kind voice finally confirmed that Joseph Odinga was indeed being held at the Elizabeth Contract Detention Facility.

He rented a car and set out for the Lincoln Tunnel. The only part of New Jersey he'd ever seen was the Newark Airport and the stretch of the Jersey Turnpike the cab took to get him back to Manhattan. The route to the detention center was the same trip in reverse. After merging onto the eastern spur of the turnpike, he settled into the right lane, maintaining a comfortable distance from the eighteen-wheeler in front of him. There was no reason to hurry. The other drivers didn't feel the same way. Their incessant lane changing would have made a Buddhist monk antsy.

He passed a service area. In the distance to his left, he saw the still-incomplete structure of the new World Trade Center rising into the sky. It was a splendid design, a worthy successor to the original destroyed in the 2001 attacks. He'd visited the site upon his return to New York. The two memorial pools in the footprints of the old towers invited reflection and empathy. He couldn't say the same about the politics of the last decade. Everything was touched by the global war on terror, including immigration policy. For all he knew, this drive to Elizabeth wouldn't have been necessary before all the new rules and laws were enacted.

The Meadowlands rolled by, then the Passaic River. The massive steel bridge of the Pulaski Skyway followed. The vegetation of the marshland gave way to oil storage tanks, the iconic landmarks of Central Jersey. An exit sign announced the Newark Airport. The oil tanks were replaced by a forest of billboards. To the left loomed the massive container cranes of the Port of Newark. He thought that this particular spot had to be the acme of transport evolution in human history. A jet taking off, a twelve-lane highway choking with traffic, an endless freight train chugging along, and a huge cargo vessel being unloaded—all of it happening at the same time in the same place.

The blue IKEA store inched into view. Easing right at exit 13A, he paid his toll, dove into a sea of warehouses and off-airport parking areas, and passed a FedEx sorting facility. The traffic, mostly trucks, barely eased forward. The detention facility was a low-slung yellow brick warehouse structure. The only interruptions in its monotonous brick wall were a row of windows just below the flat roof and four wide loading doors. A sign warned him that double parking was prohibited and that his car would be subject to towing. Another sign pointed to the entrance. He parked in the visitor lot across the street.

Ten people were standing near the wire mesh fence and gate. They'd bundled up against the chilly March air. Over their jackets, they wore white T-shirts with the words "Not One More Deportation." When they saw him approach, they began shouting that slogan.

He raised his hands. "I'm just here to visit a detainee."

A woman in her late twenties with thick black hair and a café-au-lait complexion motioned for the others to quiet down.

"Are you a lawyer?" she said.

"No." He hesitated a moment. "Well, yes, I am, but that's not why I'm here."

"Then you must be a consular official."

He shook his head. "No."

"Then you won't be visiting anyone for another three hours."

"What?"

"Visiting hours don't start until five p.m. on weekdays."

It had never occurred to him to check for visiting hours.

"I work for the United Nations," he said. "I think they are going to let me in."

She eyed him with curiosity.

"The United Nations? Are you finally investigating Obama's deportations?"

"I'm afraid not. I'm here for a different reason."

Her disappointment lasted only a second. "Well, you should. What's going on here is totally in violation of the Refugee Convention and other human rights treaties."

"That may well be," he said. He liked the fire in her eyes. "Unfortunately, it's not my job. You should contact the Human Rights Council. I'm sure they have a special rapporteur for this."

He passed through the gate and headed for the entrance, a fake porte-cochère flanked by poles flying the U.S. and American Prisons Corporation flags. The reception area was bisected by a glass-enclosed counter and a barred metal door. Nobody was in the waiting area.

He stated his case to a heavyset white woman behind the window. She listened for a moment and interrupted him.

"Visiting hours start at five p.m. No visitors before that."

"I'm trying to tell you that I'm not a visitor. I'm a United Nations representative, here to follow up on a case brought to us by the immigration authorities."

"Are you the attorney for one of the inmates?"

"No, what I'm trying to tell you—"

"Are you a consular official?"

"No, I'm with the United Nations. There's a man here—"

"Visiting hours start at five p.m."

He'd tried to keep calm, but the stubbornness of this woman was getting to him.

He raised his voice just a little. "Listen, ma'am. There is a man in this facility who supposedly used a forged United Nations letter. Immigration and Customs Enforcement called us and I'm here to investigate that claim."

"If you aren't an attorney or consular official you'll have to wait until five."

He swallowed and reminded himself that the little bit of power her position behind the window gave her was all the power she'd ever have in her life.

"Can I speak to your supervisor, please?"

"He isn't going to say anything different. Leave the building and wait till five or I'll have to call security."

He'd dealt with enough petty bureaucrats to know that the next round would result in his not getting to see Joseph Odinga. So he turned and left the building.

"Didn't get in, did you?" the woman with the black hair said.

He shook his head.

"Are you really with the United Nations?"

He nodded and stretched out his hand. "Valentin Vermeulen, Office of Internal Oversight Services."

The woman shook his hand. She had a soft grip. "Alma Rodriguez, *Unidad Latina*. I've never met anyone working for the United Nations."

"And I've never met anyone working for *Unidad Latina*."

Alma Rodriguez smiled. "I think there might be a slight difference. Listen, we're about to wrap up. You want to get a cup of coffee? I'm guessing you're not driving back to Manhattan to come back at five."

"You're right. Are you done protesting?"

"We're here to bear witness to the deportations. Those usually happen before two. There's a diner up the road. I'd love to pick your brain on what the UN can do to help us."

"I'm afraid you overestimate my knowledge and influence, but yes, I'd love a cup of coffee."

CHAPTER FOUR

———◆———

Fᴿᴏᴍ ᴛʜᴇ ᴏᴜᴛsɪᴅᴇ, ᴛʜᴇ ᴅɪɴᴇʀ ʟᴏᴏᴋᴇᴅ like a repurposed fast-food franchise. Not like the chrome-sided classics he'd seen in photographs. Inside, a brown Formica counter with a copper-clad espresso machine and a pie case ran along one wall. A row of old bar stools were bolted to the floor in front of the counter. Brown vinyl booths occupied the other side of the room. A handful of tables with chairs filled the space in between.

He pulled out a chair for Alma, which earned him another smile.

"A real gentleman," she said.

Vermeulen felt a flash of embarrassment. Was he really so old-fashioned? Rodriguez must have noticed the reaction, because she said, "It's very nice, don't get me wrong. I'm just not used to it."

A fiftyish waitress approached with a menu the size of an unfolded highway map. Her name tag read 'Sandy.'

"Coffee, hon?" she said to Rodriguez.

"Please."

"And you?"

"Yes," Vermeulen said. "What kind of sweets do you have?"

"We got apple pie, pecan pie, Boston cream pie, and blueberry pie."

"I'll have the blueberry pie. Anything for you, Ms. Rodriguez? It's my treat."

Rodriguez hesitated a moment. "Sure, I'll have a piece of apple pie. And, please, call me Alma."

"Sure, if you call me Valentin."

"À la mode?" Sandy said.

They both nodded without hesitation, which made them laugh.

"When I was a kid, we only got ice cream in the summer," Vermeulen said. "One of my pleasures as an adult is eating ice cream even in the winter."

"I grew up in Guadalajara. It seemed like there were ice cream vendors everywhere pushing little carts down the streets. My *abuelita* used to buy me frozen treats. Got me hooked for life."

Sandy came back with two industrial-grade mugs, a carafe of coffee, and a pitcher of cream.

"So, are you protesting at the detention center every day?" Vermeulen said.

Rodriguez took a sip of coffee. "Ahh, it's nice and hot. Yes, we try to have a presence there every day from ten to two. To be honest, we don't manage to cover every day. Our volunteers have to make a living. Since I work part-time for *Unidad Latina*, I can be here more often, but I also go to college, so I have to juggle my schedule."

She noticed his raised eyebrows. "Yes, I know I'm a little old for college, but it's the soonest I could afford to go."

"What are you studying?"

"Human resources management. But enough about me. What do you do at the United Nations?"

"I work for an agency that audits and investigates fraud. The UN is a large organization, and my agency's job is to make sure that nobody defrauds it."

"Why does that bring you to an ICE detention center?"

Vermeulen hesitated. There wasn't really anything secret about the case, but that didn't mean he should be telling everyone about it.

Sandy came and brought the pies, a welcome interruption. He took a bite and savored the blending of the blueberry and vanilla flavors. Pie was such a unique American treat, and this one was well made with a flaky crust and a filling not too sweet. He took another bite before coming up with an answer.

"There's an allegation that a man detained there used UN materials without authorization. I want to find out if that's the case."

Alma seemed to be enjoying her pie, too, but not enough to have missed his calculated phrasing. "You sound like a bureaucrat, hiding rather than revealing things."

That barb stung. Vermeulen didn't think of himself as a bureaucrat. If anything, bureaucrats were his adversaries.

"That's not fair," he said. But he knew she was right. She took another bite and washed it down with more coffee.

"Don't worry. I won't hold it against you. Because you said a lot more than you thought you did. The man in question was detained by Immigration and Customs Enforcement, so there was something wrong with his paperwork. But he made it to JFK, so he must've had a visa. They wouldn't have let him on the plane otherwise. That means he probably used fake documents to get the visa. Since most Europeans can get visas without having to supply supporting documentation, my guess is he came from a third-world country. Most arrivals here are from Africa and the Middle East, places where the UN is active. Did he use a fake UN letter?"

Vermeulen tried to hide his surprise. "I didn't say he came through JFK."

"Listen, obviously the person isn't Mexican or Central American. There's not much of a UN presence there. So he must've come from elsewhere. JFK is the place where people from elsewhere arrive. There are no international flights to La Guardia. Newark is possible but not as likely as JFK."

He raised his eyebrows. "You are very good."

"I've been an immigration activist since before I became legal. I've heard so many stories. Desperate people choose desperate strategies."

"I don't even know if the letter was fake or not. It could all be above board. That's why I need to talk to him."

"I know," she said. "I can't get over the power individual officers at the border have in deciding who's allowed in and who isn't. Even if all your paperwork is in order, you can still be denied entry if some guy doesn't like your nose. Once you disappear into the system, it's really hard to be heard."

"Is that why you are out there?"

"Yes, we think it's important that we bear witness to the daily toll of this country's messed up immigration policy. Obama is worse than any of his predecessors. Since his 'Safe Communities' program started, his administration has deported four hundred thousand people a year." She took a bite of pie and chewed for a moment. "ICE says they only deport hardened criminals, but that's a lie. The last case I know of is a mom from Hackensack whose blinker was broken. The cops pulled her over. Since she was undocumented, she didn't have a license. They took her in and notified ICE. A day later she was picked up by ICE and is now detained at the center. Her two kids are citizens. So is her husband. They are going crazy doing what they can to keep her from being deported. Once she's out of the country, she can never come back legally."

"What are her chances?"

She gave a weary shake of her head. "Not good. Worse than fifty/fifty. We found a good lawyer—pro bono, of course—who's filed the necessary paperwork to make sure she stays in Elizabeth and isn't transferred elsewhere. During the hearing he's going to make the case that she doesn't qualify for expedited removal, because she has no criminal history and hasn't repeatedly entered the country without proper documents."

Although he'd entered the U.S. more often than he could remember, he'd never considered this aspect of U.S. law. "Do detainees get transferred a lot?"

"Yeah. Sometimes it feels like they transfer them to keep them from getting legal representation. We've had lawyers show up here only to find out that their clients had been moved to Pennsylvania or even Georgia. That makes it even harder to get them legal advice."

He looked at this watch. "Then I'd better finish my pie and get over to the facility. I wouldn't want Mr. Odinga to disappear."

CHAPTER FIVE

———◆———

JOSEPH ODINGA, WHO HAD NEVER BEEN to a prison, didn't know how to behave in one. He stayed silent and avoided conversations. They had just returned from dinner, if you could call four in the afternoon dinnertime. But that schedule suited the corrections officers, so that's when they got dinner. Besides, visiting hours started at five, and the detainees would rather visit than eat bad food.

Dormitory B was buzzing with anticipation. Some had regular visitors—they'd lived in the area for fifteen or twenty years, put down roots, and were caught with a broken tail light. The ones who didn't were the tattooed gangbangers on their way back to El Salvador or Honduras and the folks nabbed at JFK.

Joseph could tell the difference between the men torn from families—heartbroken and consoling each other—and the men with that predatory look in their eyes. Much of the talk around him was in Spanish. The jokes, the stories, the shouted encouragements were lost on him. What little English he spoke was enough to go to chow, the bathroom, and the showers and to stay out of the way of the tattooed guys.

He spent most of his day lying on his bed, number 39. There were ten beds on the loft, five each on either side of a waist-high partition. His bed was next to it. Even though he could see right through it, it gave him a sense of privacy. He'd never have thought that he'd value privacy. Kibera was a huge slum. People lived on top of each other, sometimes literally. But that closeness didn't mean they'd be in your shack. You could always close the door.

The open toilets at the detention center bothered him the most. Even in Kibera, you did your business in private. Here, you had to do it in front of anyone who walked by. That's why he waited until after dinner, when everyone had settled down or was off to the visiting room.

He lay on his bed until the shuffling sounds of people milling about had stopped and the voices quieted. He got up, inched past the partition and the other five beds, and walked down the stairs to the main level. Thirty beds stood there in groups of four, also divided by partitions. A few men were lying on their beds. Three guys were playing cards at the tables near the entrance. Most stood by the door waiting to be called for visits. Some Spanish TV show droned from an ancient TV hanging above the door. Five of the six tattooed guys were dozing on their beds.

The first toilet wasn't working. The next was too disgusting. He chose the last of the four. A shuffling sound behind him made him turn around. The sixth gangbanger, the one he'd called "Thirteen" because that number was tattooed across his cheek, stood by the wall that separated the sinks from the toilets.

"*Hola*," he said with a broad grin on his face. He said something else.

Joseph couldn't even guess the meaning and shrugged. Thirteen was shorter than he, but built like a truck. His arms looked like braided ropes. He came closer. Joseph sighed. There went his plan. Thirteen would just sit on the toilet next to him. He turned to go back upstairs.

"*¿Adónde vas?*" Thirteen said and held out one arm to keep Joseph from passing.

"Okay," Joseph said, hoping that the universal word of agreement would make the arm drop down again.

It didn't.

Instead, Thirteen grabbed Joseph's shirt and pulled him closer.

Joseph's first thought was that Thirteen wanted to give him a hug. But that made no sense at all. Thirteen wouldn't even hug his mother. He considered resistance. He was taller. Shouldn't he use that to his advantage? Before he could develop a plan, he found himself chest to chest with Thirteen.

An odd smell entered his nostrils. Was that Thirteen's? Or his own? He decided it was Thirteen's, probably that stuff he put in his hair. He raised his own arm, intending to separate Thirteen's hand from his shirt. He succeeded and pushed the other back. Thirteen let go of his shirt. That was a surprise. Maybe he needed to be a little more assertive. His confidence lasted ten seconds. That's how long it took for Thirteen to hook his foot around Joseph's right leg and jerk it forward. Joseph, unprepared, fell back.

He tried to break the fall with his left elbow, which made a terrible cracking sound when the joint hit the tile floor. The pain shooting through his arm was excruciating. He opened his mouth to let out a scream. Only a muffled sound came from his mouth. Thirteen had clamped his large hand over it. He started to hyperventilate. Except Thirteen's hand didn't let him open his mouth. Joseph sucked air through his nostrils, snorting like a horse in distress.

He felt Thirteen's knee on his chest. And not just the knee. Thirteen's entire weight bore down on that knee. The hand stayed clamped over his mouth. He couldn't breathe through his nose anymore. His chest couldn't move with all that weight on it. He gasped. His lungs screamed for air. None was coming in. He bucked like a zebra, trying to shake off Thirteen. It didn't work. Thirteen had stretched out his other leg and used it as a lever against any effort to dislodge him. He tried squirming, hoping to slip out sideways. Thirteen's weight kept him pressed down. The tips of his fingers began to tingle. His toes did the same thing. The tingling moved from his extremities to the core of his body. The pain from the elbow didn't seem to matter anymore. His bucking and squirming became more feeble. His body didn't want to struggle against Thirteen anymore. It was too hard.

He closed his eyes. His little photography studio, if you could call it that, was suddenly there. The chair, the different colored pieces of cloth he used for the backdrop, the old tripod and the Minolta camera. He'd taken good pictures. None of his customers ever came back to complain that the size was wrong for the passports or IDs. Oddly, everything looked blue. He felt his muscles relax. There was more blue light. He forced his eyes open one more time. Thirteen's mouth was close to his ear. The ugly "13" tattoo hovered right over his left eye.

"Hello from the Broker," Thirteen whispered.

Joseph had never met anyone called 'The Broker.' It didn't matter anymore. He closed his eyes and never opened them again.

CHAPTER SIX

---◆---

VERMEULEN WAS BACK AT THE DETENTION center at five o'clock sharp. Alma's account of random transfers worried him. Once Joseph Odinga disappeared into the system, it would be difficult to find him again. The chairs in the reception area were still empty. Which didn't make sense. Why wasn't anyone waiting to visit the inmates?

The hostile female guard had been replaced by a black man with grizzled hair and white stubble. As Vermeulen approached the window, the man pointed to a hand-scrawled sign taped to the inside of the glass: NO VISIT'S TODAY!

He stepped up to the window.

"No visits today," the guard said.

"The sign outside says that visiting hours are five to ten."

"That's true. Can't argue with that."

"So why are there no visits today?"

"Lockdown."

"What?"

"Lockdown. All inmates are in lockdown. They can't leave their dorms."

"I have to talk to one of the detainees."

"Not today. Gotta come back tomorrow."

"I can't come back tomorrow. This is an official visit." He presented his UN ID.

The man seemed duly impressed. He'd heard of the UN somewhere. "Is that like an embassy or consulate?" he said.

"Exactly," Vemeulen said, remembering his earlier experience.

"Never seen one of those. But you know what they say ...."

Vermeulen shook his head. "No, what do they say?"

"Hang around long enough and you'll see everything."

Vermeulen nodded and waited.

It took the guard a moment to understand.

"Oh, you still ain't gonna visit today. Lockdown means no visits, not even consular or lawyers."

"Why is there a lockdown? I was here three hours ago and nobody said anything about a lockdown."

The guard gave him a pitying look. "You don't know much about prisons, do you?"

As a matter of fact, Vermeulen did. When he was a Crown Prosecutor in Antwerp, he visited prisons all the time, just never one that had a lockdown.

"Lockdown ain't something you schedule," the guard said. "It happens when there's trouble. And you don't know before when trouble's gonna happen, now, do you?"

"So there was trouble here in the last three hours?"

"Just a half hour ago."

"What kind of trouble?"

"I don't know. They never tell me nothing. Just got the word, lockdown. No visitors."

"How can I find out?"

"You can't. Hell, if I don't know, how are you gonna find out?"

"Isn't there a supervisor I can speak to?"

"They're busy with the lockdown. This here's a private prison. They gotta make money, and they do that by not hiring enough people to run it. Best come back tomorrow."

The telephone on the guard's desk rang. He reached for the receiver and answered. Vermeulen shuffled to the side. What was he supposed to do now? There was no way around the guard. Asking for a supervisor didn't seem to have any effect. He could feel his anger over a wasted afternoon rising. But he'd eaten pie with Alma. So it hadn't been a complete waste.

The guard said, "Yes, sir. Will do." He hung up the receiver. Before he could ask Vermeulen why he was still standing there, another guard came running into the glass cage.

"Man, you're not gonna believe it," he said. "One of the guys is dead."

"Somebody kill him?" the guard said.

"I dunno, they found 'im by the johns."

"What happened?"

"I dunno. Coulda been a heart attack."

"Was it one of the Maras?"

"You wish. It was the quiet guy who came couple'a days ago. From Africa, I think."

That got Vermeulen's attention. "Was his name Joseph Odinga?" he said through the window.

The second guard did a double take.

"Oops, didn't even see you there. You didn't hear nothing, did you?"

Vermeulen didn't play along. "Was his name Joseph Odinga?"

"Sorry. I can't tell you nothing. Lockdown."

"Listen, I came here to talk to that man. I need to know if he's dead or not."

"The company won't let us say anything. We could lose our jobs."

"How can I find out? It's really important."

"You got a card? I can give it to the supervisor."

Vermeulen pulled out a card and scribbled his cellphone number on the back. "Please make sure he gets it."

The trip back to Manhattan was dreary. The fading daylight turned the Jersey landscape into a monochromatic tableau with nothing worth looking at. Vermeulen was certain that the dead man at the detention center was Joseph Odinga. How many quiet men from Africa could there be in Elizabeth? Odinga's death caught him by surprise. After listening to Alma, he'd considered the possibility of a transfer, but death? Poor man. Maybe he did have a heart attack. The man must have been stressed out, traveling for the first time in his life and ending up in prison, without having done anything wrong.

Vermeulen didn't buy the fake letter story Sunderland had spun. ICE had a siege mentality—us versus the brown hordes of the Third World. He'd seen it often enough at JFK. And it had gotten worse since 2001. But just to make sure, he'd follow up with Bengtsson, head of the Nairobi OIOS office, and run the scenario past him. Since the Darfur audit a year ago, they got on well. Bengtsson would ask the people whose names were on the letters. They'd explain that it was a legitimate invitation, and he could wrap up the case.

His phone rang. He answered. "Vermeulen here. I'm driving. I'll call you back as soon as I can."

It had taken him a while to resist the urge to conduct a phone conversation while driving. But rules had gotten stricter, and he didn't need a ticket for something that was better done while stationary. He pulled into the Alexander Hamilton Service Area, stopped, and dialed the last caller's number.

"Yeah," a man answered. "Are you the embassy fellow who was just at the detention center?"

"Yes, I am. Who's this?"

"It doesn't matter."

The voice didn't sound like that of the old guard behind the window. It could be the guy who'd come in later.

"You still wanna know the name of the dead man?"

"Sure."

"It was Joseph Odinga."

"Thanks. Why are you telling me?"

"The company I work for is shit. They treat their employees like shit and they treat the inmates like shit. I hate them. You seemed like an okay guy. So I called you."

"What's going to happen to him?"

"They're gonna do an autopsy. Maybe you can get those results."

Vermeulen doubted that. "Yes, maybe. Have you heard anything else?"

The man was quiet for a moment. "Mind you, this is just gossip. I was passing by Dormitory B, getting ready to go home. One of the Mexicans pulled me aside and said that he saw Odinga and one of the Salvadorian gangbangers go at it near the johns. The other guy was on top of Odinga. The Mexican didn't see what happened. But the gangbanger came back into the dorm and a little later someone found Odinga dead."

"Are you saying that Odinga was murdered?"

"That's what the Mexican fellow was implying. I'm just passing it on."

CHAPTER SEVEN

———— ◆ ————

VERMEULEN GOT BACK TO HIS APARTMENT at ten that evening. An accident at the Lincoln Tunnel, an argument with the car rental clerk, and the search for a cab took time and a toll on his patience. He'd picked up some Chinese takeout for dinner and was ready for a quiet evening. As soon as he shut the door to his apartment, he opened a bottle of De Koninck and lit his first Gitane of the day.

He'd been thinking about quitting. There were fewer places to smoke now. The office, restaurants … pretty much everywhere was off limits, except the street and his apartment. And his daughter Gaby had been on his case. She was stubborn and mentioned it every time they talked. Still, a beer and a smoke after a crazy day were his preferred way to relax.

The Clash, his favorite band, were playing via the set of Bluetooth speakers he'd bought at the Düsseldorf airport duty-free before his trip to Darfur. Lately, he'd been listening to the album *Sandinista!,* the band's experiment with rhythms from around the world.

He'd just dumped the rice and General Tso's chicken on a plate when the Clash played "Somebody Got Murdered." It startled him. Odinga had been murdered? Prisons in the U.S. were dangerous places. But a detention center for undocumented aliens? That seemed unlikely. The guards described Odinga as a quiet man. A quiet man wouldn't pick a fight with a gang member. And Odinga didn't have anything anyone might want to take from him.

A thought he hadn't entertained startled him. He put the fork down. The chicken didn't live up to General Tso's reputation anyway.

Odinga's death didn't make sense unless the invitation letter was fake. So far, he'd assumed the letter was real. Call it prejudice against Sunderland and ICE.

If the invitation was forged, Odinga's death made a lot more sense. He became a liability the moment he was detained. He knew who was involved. Maybe not everyone, but certainly those who helped him get the visa. Whatever scam Odinga got involved in was big enough to require his elimination.

But why? He was likely to be deported. Maybe he had applied for asylum, but Vermeulen was pretty certain Odinga would have difficulties proving a credible fear of persecution in Kenya. So, in a month or two, he'd be back in Nairobi. What was the big deal? According to Sunderland, he didn't speak much English. He wasn't likely to blab the story of how he got the letter.

Vermeulen stirred some rice into the sauce and raised the fork. When it was halfway to his mouth, he stopped. He knew why Odinga had to die. It was his visit to the detention facility that set the wheels in motion. He showed up at two, was told to come back at five. In those three hours, while he had coffee and pie with Alma, someone made sure that Odinga wouldn't speak to him.

He put the fork down again. His appetite had disappeared. He got up, lit another Gitane, and paced up and down his narrow kitchen.

He took a long swallow of beer. This was crazy. There was no evidence that Odinga was even murdered, just rumors relayed by an employee who probably had an ax to grind. Even if the letter were fake, it wasn't something so extraordinary that it would have gotten Odinga killed.

AT ELEVEN, HE CALLED BENGTSSON IN Nairobi. It was seven the next morning there, and he hoped Bengtsson wasn't sleeping in. He answered reassuringly fast.

"Hey, Arne. Valentin here. I hope I didn't wake you up."

"You'll have to call earlier than that. Good to hear from you. When are you going to grace us with your presence?"

"I have no idea. Right now I'm chained to my desk at headquarters. A dubious reward at best."

"That just doesn't sound like you."

"You're right. I'm realizing that myself. But, on the upside, I don't miss cheap hotels and lousy food."

"There's that. Just know I'd love a visit. It doesn't have to be official. Kenya is a wonderful place."

"Thanks, I'll keep that in mind."

"So what's up?" Bengtsson said. "You didn't call just to hear my melodious voice."

The quip made Vermeulen smile. Bengtsson's voice, with its nasal Scandinavian accent, was anything but melodious.

"No. I didn't. We have an issue here. U.S. Customs and Border Protection have detained two Kenyans who they claim obtained visas using forged invitation letters issued by UN-HABITAT. I have copies. They were both signed by a Salif Traoré, at least that's what the printed name is. There's no title or anything else. Could you check out Mr. Traoré? Does he exist? If so, did he sign these invitations?"

"Anything else?"

"Well, there are two more letters that came from the UN Environment Program office in Vienna. Do you know who runs the Vienna office of OIOS?"

"Sure, that's Pierre Dufaux. Do you want his number?"

"If you have it, please."

Bengtsson took a moment and then rattled out a number. Vermeulen noted it on a scrap of paper.

"Thanks, that was really helpful. Please call me when you find out something. Anytime."

Vermeulen ended the call. A familiar sensation coursed through his body. The dull errand to New Jersey had turned into just the kind of case he'd been hoping for.

CHAPTER EIGHT

———◆———

O KEYO ABASI FELT TERRIBLE. HIS LEGS didn't want to support him anymore. It was ten in the morning and he stood outside Broad Street Station in Newark, waiting for a bus to take him back to JFK. All the seats at the bus stop were taken. He leaned against the support column, hoping that taking a little weight off his legs would make the pain bearable. It didn't.

"Please God, let the bus come," he mumbled to himself. "If I can just sit down, I'll be okay."

He had no idea when the right bus was supposed to arrive. He needed to sit. The stairs to the elevated train were the only option. He dragged his aching body across the sidewalk. His legs had no strength left to lower his body gently. The concrete was hard when his backside hit it. A flash of pain shot through him. He almost toppled over. Once the pain subsided a little, he worried about getting up again, but decided to face that challenge when his bus arrived.

He felt inside his pocket. It was still there—the envelope with twenty-five hundred dollars. Only a fraction of what he'd been promised. But he hadn't been in any condition to fight back. He was lying on a gurney, his brain swimming from the drugs they had injected and his left side pulsing with a dull pain. The man who gave him the envelope said that cost and transaction fees had been deducted. Back in Kibera, nobody had mentioned cost and transaction fees.

If only the bus would come. He wanted to be on the airplane and sleep, sleep until he was back home. His sister would care for him if he didn't feel better by then. But he would feel better. He knew it.

* * *

EARLE JACKSON LEANED AGAINST THE OLD clock tower of the Broad Street Station in Newark. It was a casual pose. Just a black dude, waiting. He was tall, but not in an intimidating way. He didn't sport fancy cornrows or dreads, no gold chains or teeth, and certainly not pants halfway down his ass and some loud big jacket that would've done well in the arctic. No, Jackson was a businessman, and a businessman had to project a proper image. Especially when looking for clients.

Broad Street Station was a good place to scout. The hospital was just a few blocks away, there were plenty of doctors' offices around, and his marks were looking for doctors. In the olden days, Jackson would have been called a 'tout.' He'd looked that word up when some irate senior citizen called him that. Jackson preferred 'liaison.' It sounded professional, exactly how he felt about his role, connecting old folks on Medicare with two doctors who were looking for patients.

Jackson had a good eye for the right kind of old folks. They got off the train or the bus at the station and looked lost. They hadn't been to a doctor in a while. They figured whatever ailed them would just go away. But it hadn't and their kids finally sent them off to a doctor, thinking they'd take a cab. But Jackson knew those folks. They wouldn't spend good money on a cab. They'd walk. That's why God gave them feet. Except their feet didn't work so good anymore. They were tired and ready to take a load off.

He'd put on a nice smile. Talk to them. *How ya doin', auntie?* Ask them if they needed help. They'd show him a paper with some address. He'd look at it and say that it wasn't far, that he'd walk them there. He'd offer the ladies an arm to lean on and talk about the weather.

Sometimes, when he got them to the medical offices of Mulberry and Patel, they said that it wasn't the doctor they'd come to see. He told them that these days doctors all got consolidated, you know, put their offices together to save money, be more efficient. They nodded. Nobody ever refused to go inside. The receptionist, Marcia, checked their Medicare card. If it was okay, she nodded, took him into the X-ray room, and gave him his referral fee.

It was a way to make a living. The old folks got taken care of—he'd made sure of that. Ripping off old folks really wasn't his thing. Marcia had told him that the doctors did right by them. Okay, they billed the government for a lot more procedures than they actually performed, but that didn't hurt nobody. These days, everybody had to have an angle. Besides, the government was wasting money left and right. Compared to that, this scam was nothing.

Lately, he'd been thinking about his fee. It really was nothing, what with the cost of living going up and his having to think about the future. He wanted to ask the doctors for more money, but Marcia told him to be careful, not to kill the goose that laid the golden egg. Except he only got fifty bucks for a referral, and that wasn't a goose egg, more like one of those itty birds' eggs, and definitely not golden. So he'd been thinking about new revenue streams. He'd heard that phrase on TV and liked it. There was plenty of money in the medical field—insurance companies, Medicare, Medicaid. He just needed new ideas to see that some of that money ended up in his pocket.

As he considered his options, he saw a man almost fall over, trying to sit down on the stairs. The man didn't look very old, definitely not a candidate for his doctors. He wore cheap clothes. They weren't dirty or anything, more like that old-guy stuff you'd find at Goodwill.

Jackson pushed himself from the wall and sauntered toward the stairs. As he came closer he could see that the man was in bad shape. His dark skin was ashen. Sweat shone on his forehead. He could barely keep himself straight on those steps.

"Hey bro," Jackson said, sitting down on the stairs next to the man. "You don't look so good. Need any help?"

The man looked at him with difficulty. His face was all knotted with pain.

"Man, you in trouble. What's your name?"

"Okeyo," the man said.

"Okeyo? That some kind of African name?"

The man nodded.

"You from there?" Jackson said.

"Kenya."

"Whatcha doing in Newark, looking like hell warmed over?"

"JFK."

"You wanna go to the airport? Fly home to Kenya?"

The man nodded again.

"Man, you ain't gonna make it there. Not the way you look. Lemme take you to a doctor."

Jackson figured he'd drape the man's arm over his shoulder and get him up, lifting from the knees. He got as far as putting the arm on his shoulder. It fell right down again.

"Come on, man. Work with me. We gotta get you to a doctor."

Okeyo didn't say anything.

"Okay, here we go again."

The second attempt wasn't any more successful. He'd put his left arm around the man's waist to hold him while they were getting up. Okeyo's left side was wet. Jackson pulled his hand away and stared at it. It was all red.

"Man, you're bleeding. You got shot or something?"

Okeyo remained silent. Jackson looked into his face. There was no recognition. Something that sounded like a sigh came from his mouth and Okeyo's eyes froze in place.

"Shit, man, did you just die on me? I don't need that."

Holding a dead man was bad news, especially with his priors. It didn't matter that he just wanted to be a Good Samaritan. He wiped his hand on the man's jacket. Better get away, now.

Before taking off, he checked Okeyo's pockets. The man was dead; he didn't have any use for the stuff in his pockets. Especially not for the envelope with the wad of bills and the passport. They disappeared in Jackson's back pocket. He got up and sauntered to the underpass. Before he headed under the railroad tracks, he looked back one more time. Okeyo had fallen across the stairs. Two passersby stood by him and a third knelt next to the prostrate body.

CHAPTER NINE

───────◆───────

JACKSON FOUND HIMSELF A QUIET SPOT in Branch Brook Park, a safe distance from the dead man, before he opened the envelope and counted the bills. Twenty-five hundred dollars. Man, that'd be like, what? Two, three months' worth of hustling old folks for his doctors? It was his lucky day.

The envelope also contained an e-ticket receipt for a flight from JFK to Nairobi dated five days later and a blue passport. The second page had Okeyo's photo and said that his last name was Abasi. The photo was pretty bad. Almost any black man, hell, Jackson himself, could have passed for Abasi. He paged further and found the visa for the U.S. and the immigration stamp. It looked like Okeyo had another week before he had to leave. Jackson didn't know what use he had for the passport, but you never knew. It might come in handy later. On a slip of paper stuck between the last two pages was an address not too far from Broad Street Station, close to the hospital.

Jackson noticed dried blood on his left hand. He'd better find a restroom and get that washed off. If the police stopped him with the man's money and passport and saw blood on his hand, he'd be in a load of trouble.

On the way to washing his hands, he thought about the odd encounter. All that blood on Okeyo meant that the man had been stabbed or shot. But he still had that money. So whoever hurt him didn't finish the job. But why? Okeyo didn't have any fight left in him when Jackson found him. Did he kill the attacker? The man didn't carry a knife or a gun, so that didn't seem likely. Maybe the attacker was interrupted.

He found a bathroom and washed his hands carefully, even scraping under his fingernails with a little twig he'd picked up. He stared into the clouded stainless steel mirror. How did a man from Kenya who looked piss poor get all those dollars? Had he brought it from home, like his family pitching in a few bucks each so he'd have a good start here? But the visa was only for a couple of weeks. If he was planning on staying, he'd be illegal. Maybe he came here to earn that money. But twenty-five hundred dollars in a week? Damn, he'd sign up for that job himself. He took the slip with the address from the envelope. Maybe he should check that place out.

JACKSON HAD A NICE LUNCH AT a little café on Bleeker Street, close to the address on the piece of paper. A BLT with plenty of bacon, a soda, and then a cup of coffee and one of them Italian cookies. Having the extra bills in his pocket made him feel confident. The waitress, Tami, was kinda cute, too, and they flirted a little. After an hour, he got up to leave. Tami didn't give him her phone number. He made a disappointed face, but it was okay. He might come back. She wanted to see him try a little harder, and he appreciated that in a girl. Besides, she was probably a student and wasn't gonna fall for the first guy who walked in the door.

The whole area was full of students, what with the hospital and the New Jersey Institute of Technology and Rutgers all bunched together. There had been moments when he thought he should go to college—maybe not Rutgers, but community college—get some credentials and have a career. But then he needed to earn some money. And he was better off. Take his cousin, Jimmy. He was a student and didn't have a pot to piss in. When he wasn't studying, he was making sandwiches at Subway. Nah, Jackson was better off making fifty bucks for a referral. And who knew, maybe that address in his hand was his first step to making twenty-five hundred in a week like that dead man from Kenya.

He crossed from Bleeker Street to Central Avenue to Martin Luther King Jr. Boulevard. On one side of the street were hospital buildings with all kinds of specialized offices. The address on the slip led him to a three-story brownstone on the opposite side. It was a worn-looking building next to a freshly painted blue house with some Greek fraternity letters across the façade. Next to the door hung a white sign telling everyone that it was Dr. Rosenbaum's office and that the doctor's specialty was surgery.

Jackson kept walking until he found a little bodega with a couple of chairs outside. He got himself a soda and sat down.

A surgeon's office. That wasn't what Jackson had expected. Why would a guy from Kenya get twenty-five hundred dollars at a surgeon's office? Doctors didn't pay you; you paid them. He knew people were getting paid for having drugs tested on them. But the pay wasn't anywhere near what Okeyo had in his pocket. That's why Jackson never did any of that. People putting who knows what kinda shit in your body and paying you peanuts. Hell, you had to be desperate.

Maybe he had it all wrong. Maybe Okeyo had all that money in his pocket because he was going to see the surgeon. But why was he full of blood, like he'd already been cut open? Had the doctor screwed up and figured that a poor Kenyan wasn't going to complain? There was a way to find out.

"You got a phonebook here?" he asked the man behind the cash register.

The man nodded and handed it to him. A minute later, Jackson had Dr. Rosenbaum's number.

"You sell phones?"

The man pointed to the wall behind him. "What kind do you want?"

"The cheapest kind."

The man got one from the rack. "Twenty bucks. You wanna buy minutes too?"

"Sure, gimme a ten dollar card."

It was good to have money in your pocket. It let you do things, make plans, move ahead. He unwrapped the phone and left the plastic packaging on the counter. Outside, he slipped the SIM card in and activated the phone. Once the minutes were registered, he dialed Dr. Rosenbaum's office. A receptionist answered.

"Dr. Rosenbaum, please," Jackson said.

"Do you want an appointment?"

"No, I want to talk to Dr. Rosenbaum."

"Are you one of his patients?"

"No."

"I'm afraid the doctor is busy."

"Tell him to get unbusy."

"Sir, I don't like your tone."

"Ask Dr. Rosenbaum why a dead man from Kenya has twenty-five hundred dollars and the doctor's address in his pocket."

CHAPTER TEN

———— ◆ ————

BENGTSSON IN NAIROBI AND DUFAUX IN Vienna called Vermeulen within a half hour of each other. Both had spoken to the people whose signatures were on the four invitation letters. The reports confirmed what Vermeulen had already assumed the evening before. The letters were fake. Neither Salif Traoré in Nairobi nor Frank Wilmot in Vienna remembered sending any invitations. They didn't know how their signatures ended up on the letters.

Vermeulen suspected that someone had slipped them into a stack of documents needing signatures. People who ran UN divisions had to process so much paperwork, they probably didn't bother to inspect every piece of paper before signing. The good news was that the conferences and hearings specified in the letters were real events. It confirmed to Vermeulen that someone inside the UN was involved in the scam.

Finding those people was the first step of an investigation. Of course, he still had to convince Suarez that all this required his involvement. That shouldn't be too difficult. Just the threat of Sunderland holding up UN visitors would be enough. Relations with the host country were always a top concern. Sure, people grumbled about the U.S. and its heavy-handed bullying of the UN, but they all knew to keep their mouths shut and play nice.

He'd been meaning to call Sunderland and tell him that the letters were indeed fake and that Odinga had been killed, but wasn't looking forward to that task. The decision was made for him when the man called him that afternoon.

"We got another one, Vermoolen," Sunderland said.

"At JFK?"

"No. In Newark. Today, around eleven, a Kenyan man collapsed and died at the Broad Street Station."

Another dead man? There had to be something else going on besides getting visas.

"Did he also have a letter of invitation?" Vermeulen said.

Sunderland didn't answer.

"Well, did he?" Vermeulen said.

"He was part of the scam. We know."

"Would you care to elaborate? Because I have some news, too."

"No, I would not. What's your news?"

"Joseph Odinga was murdered yesterday, about a half hour before I could speak with him."

"Did you say 'murdered'?"

Sunderland didn't sound surprised.

"Yes, that's what I said."

"I heard only that he died. Cardiac arrest or something."

"That's probably what the company wants you to believe. I have it on good authority that he was murdered."

"Who told you?"

"I'm not at liberty to say."

"Fuck you, Vermoolen. You think you can play with me? I'll get a judge to force you to tell me."

"That won't work. U.S. judges can't send subpoenas to the UN. Remember, it's extraterritorial. Besides, as a UN investigator, I have diplomatic status. So you can forget about the judge."

That last part wasn't true. The moment he left the UN building, he'd be subject to whatever any judge ordered him to do. But it was worth a try. Sunderland must have bought it because he was quiet again.

"Listen, Sunderland. We should be working together rather than getting into a jurisdictional pissing contest. Given the new information I have, I now concur with you that these were indeed fraudulent invitation letters. I'm as interested as you are in getting to the bottom of this."

There was more silence. Vermeulen could hear the man breathing.

"Good," Sunderland finally said. "I can accept that. Tell me what you know."

"Why don't you start by telling me why you believe that this Kenyan was part of the same scam? Did he also have a letter of invitation?"

"No, he had nothing. His pockets were empty."

"So how do you know he's part of this?"

"The Newark PD ran the fingerprints. Nothing showed up in the usual databases. The guy's clothes looked kind of foreign, so they had the bright idea of running the prints through the immigration database. Sure enough, they belonged to a Mr. Abasi. He was printed at JFK three days ago and made it through without a problem. The Customs and Border Protection officer who checked him didn't remember much, but there was a notation in Abasi's admission record that he had been invited to a hearing. Just like Mr. Odinga."

"So he wasn't detained?" Vermeulen said.

"No. Just as I told you, for everyone we catch, who knows how many make it through?"

"How did he die?"

"We don't know yet. The police report says that he was found lying on the station's stairs with a bleeding wound. Probably from a knife. He might have been stabbed during a robbery. That'd explain why his pockets were empty. They'll do an autopsy. I've asked them to keep me informed. Tell me about Odinga."

"I went to the Elizabeth detention center yesterday. They wouldn't let me in at two when I got there. When I came back for visiting hours at five, the place was under lockdown. While waiting for an explanation, I overheard two guards talking, saying that the quiet African man had been found dead. I pressed them for more information, but they clammed up."

"Why did you say he was murdered?" Sunderland said.

"As I was driving home, I got a call from someone working there. He heard from one of the detainees that Odinga had been in an argument with a gang member. The detainee didn't see what happened after that."

"That's pretty thin. It sounds more like some disgruntled employee wants to get the company into trouble."

"I've thought about that, but the man didn't sound like a complainer. He was more worried that the death would be swept under the rug as heart failure or something like that. It made sense to me, since at two o'clock there was no indication of trouble. I asked to see Mr. Odinga. I was turned away. I came back three hours later and the man was dead. He could have told me who provided the letter. That's just a little too convenient."

"So what you're saying is that you're asking to speak with him caused his murder? Don't you overestimate your importance just a little bit?"

Vermeulen bit his tongue to keep from hurling a few choice words at Sunderland. "I'm going to ignore that," he said. "What really matters is that in two days, two Kenyans who came to the U.S. using similar means are dead. I want to know why. Don't you?"

"Not really. They shouldn't have come here illegally in the first place."

Vermeulen shook his head. "Could you, even just for a moment, leave your prejudice aside? These men didn't cook up the invitation letter scheme on their own. Somebody is behind this. Aren't you supposed to guard the borders? Well, do your job."

CHAPTER ELEVEN

---◆---

CAMILLE DELANO SIPPED HER SNOW QUEEN. The ice-cold liquor flowed down her throat and warmed her body. Leave it to the Azure Lounge to stock a vodka from Kazakhstan, a country that most people hadn't heard of. Made sense. Exotic liquor was a surefire way to attract Newark's hipsters. And the Azure was the new bar in downtown. They had to try extra hard.

The glass of Snow Queen was Delano's ritual. After every successful transaction, she treated herself to one. Most people knew her as 'The Broker.' She arranged deals between people who needed something not legally available and those who had it or were willing to procure it. The last one had netted almost a hundred grand. Definitely worth a celebration. Maybe take some time off. Leave Newark's dreary March weather behind and go diving in Bonaire. She could stop over in Cockburn Town on Grand Turk Island and check on her investments.

The phone interrupted her dreaming. It was the doctor. She had half a mind not to answer. The doctor was a fussy client, always worrying, always second-guessing her choices. If his deals weren't so lucrative, she'd have kicked him to the curb a long time ago. But the transaction she was celebrating had been with him. She got up and walked outside before answering.

"Somebody just called my office." He sounded shrill with panic.

"Isn't that your basic business model—people calling and making appointments?"

"Don't be cute. Somebody who knows about Abasi."

"Saying what?"

"I don't know for sure. He talked to my receptionist. According to her, he said, 'Ask Dr. Rosenbaum why a dead man from Kenya has twenty-five hundred dollars and his address in his pocket.' "

"Hmm."

"Is that all you have to say? I checked the news and they said a dead man was found at Broad Street Station. How did Abasi even get there?"

"I guess he walked down the stairs and then followed MLK Boulevard," she said.

"Did you hear my question? Why was he even outside?"

"Why are you asking me? He was in your practice, which is in your brownstone. Not my problem if you can't make sure the doors are locked."

"You were supposed to get him out of the country."

"That wasn't scheduled until tomorrow at the earliest. Until then he was in your care. You should have done a better job sewing him together."

The pause on the other end told her the gibe had worked. Whenever the doctor forgot that his medical degree and his upper-class attitude didn't mean shit, she had to put him in his place. Challenging his medical skills usually did the trick.

"Nobody speaks to me that way," he said in strangled voice.

"I just did." She ended the call. Let him stew a while. He'd be back, singing a different tune.

Growing up in the New Jersey mob had taught her to act from a position of strength. Getting her MBA from NYU had taught her how to deal with people. Not getting to take over her father's position after his untimely death had taught her never to rely on others.

The doctor was a case in point. He was greedy. That made him work with her. But he still thought she was the criminal and he was somehow above it all. Funny thing was that if the shit ever hit the fan, he'd have to do a lot more explaining than she. For one, she wasn't planning on being around when that happened. Her go-bag was always ready.

She went back into the Lounge. Taking the doctor's call outside meant that the ice in the vodka had melted. She ordered another glass.

When the phone rang, she ignored it and took a sip. The phone rang again. She glanced at the screen. The doctor. Better let him stew a little longer. It'll help him come to his senses. She finished her drink and left the Lounge.

Outside, the phone rang a third time. The doctor, again. Probably ready to eat crow.

"Hello," she said.

"What took you so long?"

"Last thing I knew, you weren't in charge of my schedule."

"You're right. What are we going to do about the man who called?"

"I'm thinking. How does he know Abasi was Kenyan and had the money, unless he went through his pockets? Which means he found the guy before anyone else did and took his things."

"Why was my address in his pocket?"

"To tell him where he had to go. It's not like I have a reception committee at JFK."

"I can't have that kind of information out there."

"Oh, get real. It's not like people don't know where your office is. You are in the phonebook. So what if he had your address? Lots of people have it." Then, more to herself, she said, "I wonder why the guy called you. I bet he's figuring out an angle. He had no problem taking the dead man's money."

"What do you mean?"

"Look at it from his perspective," Delano said, continuously rearranging the bits of information in her mind.

"Whose perspective? Abasi's?"

"A dead guy hasn't got a perspective. No, the caller's perspective. He finds a dead man with an open wound, a wad of bills, and a doctor's address. There's something off about that whole scenario. What would you do if you found a dead man?"

"I don't find dead men."

She rubbed her left temple. Why didn't the caller just take the cash and split? *I would have,* she thought. *But then again, maybe not.*

"Are you still there?" the doctor said.

"Yeah, I'm still here. I think I figured the caller out. He's thinking that whatever happened to Abasi wasn't above board and he's looking to cash in on that."

"Blackmail me?"

"Maybe, or maybe get in on the action. Think about it. Would you take two-and-a-half grand from a dead man you found on the street?"

"Of course not. I'd call the police."

"Right. And so would most upright citizens. Your caller didn't. What does that tell you?"

"He's a crook?"

"Let's just say he's looking out for himself."

"So what should I do? I can't call the police."

"No, that you can't. Don't do anything. See if he calls back."

"What if he does?"

"Then we'll consider what to do next."

"I can't just sit here waiting for a call."

"Then don't. I assume you have patients to see."

"We have to do something before it becomes a crisis."

"So now it's *we* again. Let me remind you, Doctor, that man is your problem, not mine. You screwed up, so don't try to put that on me. Just sit tight and don't be stupid. Remember, if this thing goes sideways, my risk increases. And you know how it is—higher risk requires a higher return."

CHAPTER TWELVE

———◆———

V ERMEULEN RESORTED TO HIS USUAL METHOD of sorting out where he was in a case. He drew boxes on two pieces of paper, one for Odinga and one for Abasi. In each box, he wrote the facts he knew for sure, what he surmised, and finally, wild guesses.

So far, it hadn't helped. His facts were few, and everything else was too vague to allow for conclusions. There were two men from Kenya who'd made their way to the U.S. using fake paperwork to obtain visas. One is caught at the passport control and detained. The other makes it through. Within a day of each other, both men end up dead—one killed in detention, the other on the street.

Maybe Sunderland was right and it was a coincidence. Odinga might have insulted the other man and paid for it with his life. Prisons were dangerous. The second Kenyan could have been robbed at knifepoint. Newark was a rough city, and foreigners don't know what areas to avoid.

He needed to speak to the other detainees who'd been caught with the fake letters. Only they could shed light on what was going on. Alma could help him find out where they were. He picked up his phone and dialed her number.

"Alma speaking," she said when the call connected.

"Hi, this is Valentin Vermeulen." There was a moment of hesitation. "Apple pie and ice cream," he said.

"Oh, of course. Sorry. How are you? Thanks for the treat yesterday. Did you find out what you wanted?"

"No, it turns out that Mr. Odinga was killed just before I got back to the detention center."

"Oh, it was him! What a tragedy. We'd heard that there had been a death, but nobody at the center would say anything. Our office has been getting calls all morning from anxious family members wanting to know what happened."

"Well, you can tell them their relatives are okay. I wonder if you can help me. I'd like to speak to one of the other detainees who came to the U.S. the same way. Do you know how I might find out where they're being held? I really don't want to play phone tag with ICE again."

"Sure. Do you have their names and A-numbers?"

"What numbers?"

"Their alien registration numbers. Homeland Security assigns each person a number. It starts with an 'A' followed by eight or nine digits."

He looked over the paperwork he'd gotten from Sunderland.

"I'm afraid I can't find any A-numbers."

"Okay, give me the names and countries of origin. The ICE web search doesn't work as well with that, but it's worth a shot."

"There's an ICE web search?"

"Yes. You didn't know?"

He'd spent hours on the phone, trying to find Joseph Odinga. Not one of the ICE people had mentioned the web search. He shook his head.

"No. I'm sorry to bother you. I could have done that myself."

"That's okay. I don't mind. It's probably faster if I do it."

He gave her the three names he'd gotten from Sunderland. The clicking of a keyboard came over the phone.

"I found one of them—Mihaly Luca. He's being held at the York County Prison."

"Where's that?"

"York, Pennsylvania, about three hours from here."

"Are any of the others closer?"

"There are multiple listings for one of them, so we don't know who's who, and the other is listed as 'not in custody.' That could mean anything—he might have been released or deported. So Mihaly in York is your best bet."

"Thanks a lot. I owe you another slice of pie."

"That sounds lovely, but I'd better stop helping you. I'll put on too many pounds."

The conversation with Suarez was far less pleasant. Vermeulen informed him that at least five people had obtained visas using fraudulent letters issued by UN offices in Nairobi and Vienna.

"Are you still dealing with that?" Suarez said, scanning a report on his desk.

"Well, yes. The Immigration and Customs Enforcement people are pretty upset that UN letters are used to obtain visas."

"Just tell Bengtsson and Dufaux to put a stop to it. We're not going to waste investigator hours on such trifling matters."

"Two of the men involved have turned up dead."

Suarez looked up.

"One was killed in the detention center and the other was apparently the victim of a robbery."

"What does that have to do with us?" Suarez said.

"It seems like more than a coincidence that two men who could've told us how they got the letters turn up dead the moment I begin to investigate."

Suarez shook his head. "There you go again. How often do I have to tell you that you are not a detective? We investigate fraud at the UN; we don't investigate murders. And most certainly not murders in the host country that have no connection to our work."

"It's clear that those letters were fraudulent. They were issued by someone working for the UN. There's your fraud."

"Yes, and we have people in Nairobi and Vienna to take care of that. It's not your job."

"Doesn't it disturb you that two people are dead? And that they died before I could talk to them about how they got the letters?"

"Not at all. You know as well as I do that U.S. prisons are hellholes where people get killed. And everybody knows that Newark has a high crime rate. I don't see how it has anything to do with the letters."

Vermeulen was getting hot under the collar. Suarez was being deliberately obtuse. The connection between his investigation and the deaths was too obvious to overlook. But he knew his boss well enough to keep a calm façade.

"I've located one more person identified by Immigration and Customs Enforcement. A man from Moldova. He's being held in York, Pennsylvania. I'd like to talk to him and find out what he can tell us about the letters. At a minimum, he could give me a name that I can pass on to Dufaux to help him shut this letter business down. Besides, Sunderland at ICE is livid. He has threatened to hold up any and all visitors coming here to attend UN events. You don't want to be responsible for that, do you?"

It was his trump card. Increased scrutiny of visitors coming to the UN would cause the leadership to ask questions, questions that could eventually end up on Suarez's desk.

"Sunderland threatened to hold up arrivals destined for the UN?"

"Yes. Of course not the diplomats—they have immunity—but everyone else is fair game for him."

"That's not good. Can't you talk to him? He can't hold the whole organization responsible for a handful of fake letters."

"He's serious about the holdups. His point is that the handful of letters is just the tip of the iceberg. I might be able to convince him otherwise, but only if I can show him that we are serious about this investigation."

Suarez shook his head again. For a moment, Vermeulen thought he'd overplayed his hand. "All right," he said. "Go to York and talk to that man. And make sure Sunderland knows you are going. The last thing we need is to have our legitimate visitors hassled at JFK."

"Good. I'll go in the morning. I'll have to rent another car."

Suarez nodded with a glum expression. Vermeulen got up to leave. When he opened the door, Suarez said, "I'm watching you, Vermeulen. You may have gotten a commendation for your antics in Darfur, but I won't stand for a repeat. Go to York, get what you can from that man, and pass it on to Dufaux. That's it."

CHAPTER THIRTEEN

———— ✦ ————

THE NEXT MORNING, EARLE JACKSON PICKED up his new phone to call Dr. Rosenbaum's office again. He'd spent the night thinking about his next move. The doctor hadn't called back. That surprised Jackson. He'd thought the message would be enough to cause alarm. Maybe the receptionist thought it was a crank call and didn't even tell the doctor. But that didn't seem likely. A dead man on the street with a wad of cash and a surgeon's address. If it sounded iffy to Jackson, who'd seen his share of crooked deals, it should've shocked the doctor.

Jackson didn't know any doctors, except for Mulberry and Patel, his business partners. They were obvious crooks, ripping off Medicare and all. He'd always figured they were an exception. Rosenbaum was a surgeon. He cut people open and sewed them back up. Jackson had always thought surgeons were the rock stars of the medical profession. They didn't have to resort to bilking Medicare for tests and procedures they didn't perform. People like that should be alarmed to get the kind of message Jackson left with the receptionist.

Maybe Rosenbaum was scared. Or he'd called the police and they were waiting in his office ready to trace the phone and grab Jackson. Or Rosenbaum was a crook after all and was waiting for his next move. Jackson decided he'd better call and find out. He promised himself he'd hang up the moment it sounded like the doctor was stringing him along. That was a sign the cops were there tracing his phone. If anything sounded fishy, he'd just hang up and toss the phone. He still had his twenty-five hundred dollars, or what was left after he'd gotten himself some new clothes and a nice dinner.

He dialed the number. As on the day before, the receptionist answered.

"Yeah, I want to speak to the doctor about the dead man from Kenya," Jackson said.

Without a word, the receptionist transferred the call. That was suspicious. Were they already tracing him? He listened for suspicious clicks on the line. But that was probably something from the movies. These days everything was digital.

"This is Dr. Rosenbaum," a voice said.

"Good morning, Doctor. How are you on this bright morning?" Jackson figured it wouldn't hurt to speak nicely.

"What do you want?"

"Well, Doctor, I'm just curious how it was that a man from Kenya died in my arms on the stairs of Broad Street Station with a wad of cash and your address in his pocket."

"I don't know what you are talking about." The voice sounded agitated.

Jackson smiled. Something might really come out of this.

"Doctor, let's cut the crap. I'm just curious what happened. Did you botch a surgery and get rid of the evidence? That's not a nice thing to do. Think of the man's family."

There was silence at the other end.

"I'm curious why the man had twenty-five hundred dollars in his pocket. He didn't look like the kind of man who'd walk around with that much cash. So I figured you must've given it to him. To shut him up. Well, since I'm in the picture now, I figure I also deserve some cash for keeping quiet."

Still no answer. The man was stalling.

"You know what, Doctor? I think you need a little time. I'll call back in a while."

Before he ended the call, the doctor's voice came through. "I did not botch an operation. I never botch an operation."

"Good for you, Doctor," Jackson said and pushed the End button.

TWENTY MINUTES AND SEVERAL BUS STOPS later, Jackson found himself a bench overlooking the track oval and football field at Nat Turner Park. He didn't exactly know how cell phone tracing worked, but he'd taken the battery out of the phone the moment he'd ended the call and kept it out until he settled on the bench. Once again connected to the wireless network, he pressed the redial button.

This time, Rosenbaum came on the line immediately.

"Do you want money?" he said.

"I like people who get to the point," Jackson said. "Yes, I'd like to get a share of whatever racket you are running, Doctor."

"I'm not running a racket. Mr. Abasi's death was very unfortunate and entirely his own fault. He should have stayed in the recovery unit. But he didn't want to wait and just walked away. I'm very sorry, but it's not my fault."

"Yeah, I get that, Doctor. He wasn't following doctor's orders. But I'm still curious about that money in his pocket. If you did right by him, he shoulda paid you. So why did you give him that cash?"

"It was a simple transaction and the money was his reimbursement. He would have been fine if he'd stayed even a half day."

"A simple transaction? So he gave you something and you gave him cash for it?"

"No, I didn't."

"You didn't what?"

"I didn't give him the cash."

"You're losing me here, Doctor. You just said it was a simple transaction and the money was the man's pay. But if you didn't give it to him, who did?"

There was silence.

"There's another party involved," Jackson said. "I see."

Just as he thought. There was some racket going on. Poor Abasi got twenty-five hundred for whatever he contributed. That meant the total money involved was way more. Way, way more. Because Jackson had been around the block enough times to know that if a poor brother from Africa got paid twenty-five hundred, then the white folks who ran the thing made a hundred times as much.

"You know what, Doctor? I don't want to be paid off. You got something going that generates a lot of cash. I have a bit of experience in the medical field and I'm sure I can be useful to you. What do you say we meet somewhere and discuss terms?"

"That's not going to happen, Mister ...."

Jackson didn't fall for that trick.

"Why not, Doctor? You need help. I know it. If you have more people from Africa coming, and bringing you whatever it is they bring, it helps to have someone who can relate to those folks. And, let me assure you, I can. It would avoid the kind of mishaps that happened with Mr. Abasi."

"I'd have to talk to someone first."

"Ah, yes, the other party. The one with the money. You do that. I'll call you back tomorrow."

CHAPTER FOURTEEN

———◆———

THE THREE-HOUR DRIVE TO YORK HAD turned into four hours by the time Vermeulen had stopped for a bathroom break and a cup of coffee. Listening to the *London Calling* album made the New Jersey and Penn Turnpikes bearable. When the player came to "Death or Glory," he thought of the men who'd ended up dead. Had they come for glory? Probably not. Who'd leave their home for a foreign land? Those running away, like he had, and those in desperate need. He was sure Abasi and Odinga fell into the 'need' category.

The prison lay on the outskirts of York, near warehouses and a large shopping mall. It was a vast concrete structure, all white like a Richard Meier building, but at the same time forbidding and fortress-like. A tall fence topped with razor wire surrounded everything but the parking lot.

Vermeulen had wondered why a county prison would house ICE detainees. Once he saw the structure, he understood. The prison was far too large for a county. They'd have to jail people for jaywalking to fill up this place. So the empty beds were filled with ICE detainees, with ICE paying the county for the service. A different way to make money from prisons. Vermeulen couldn't imagine anything like it in Belgium, or elsewhere in Western Europe.

He'd checked the visiting hours and rules the day before and knew he had enough time to speak with Mihaly Luca. The trip was labeled an official visit and his office had faxed the particulars to the prison authorities. After having driven this far, he didn't want a repeat of the Elizabeth experience.

There was a line of visitors waiting to be checked in and searched. It took almost a half hour before Vermeulen reached the window. The check-in went smoothly. He followed a guard past a gate and through a series of automatic doors, each sliding shut with a clank that said, "You're not getting out. Get used to it." The clanks made the walls seem to close in even more.

His visit, like most at York County Prison, was specified 'no contact.' The guard pointed to a chair in front of a plexiglass barrier. He sat down and waited.

Luca arrived shortly afterward. The tan pants and shirt were cut too large for his slim body. He looked fifty, but on second glance, could have been as young as thirty. A profound sadness radiated from him. The furrowed forehead, the dull eyes sunk deep in their sockets, the beakish nose, and the thin lips that didn't look like they would ever smile again. It was a face from which any hope of happiness had been excised.

"Good morning," Vermeulen said through the holes in the partition. "I hope you are well."

What an inane thing to say, he thought. It was obvious the man wasn't well.

"Do you understand English?" he said.

An almost imperceptible nod.

"I'm with the United Nations. I'm here to ask you a few questions about how you got your visa."

Silence.

"I want to assure you that I don't mean to cause you any more trouble. I'm not with immigration or any U.S. authority. I believe you are a victim of a scheme in which you had no part."

Another nod.

"Who did you talk to in Moldova?"

Silence.

"Did they promise you money?"

Luca nodded.

"What were you supposed to do for the money?"

More silence.

"Did they promise you work?"

Luca shook his head.

Vermeulen couldn't think of any other reason why someone would help smuggle people into the U.S. There was sweatshop work and sex-trafficking, and Luca obviously wasn't a candidate for the latter.

"How much money did they promise you?"

The man frowned and leaned forward.

"How much?" Vermeulen rubbed his right thumb and index finger together in the global gesture of money.

Luca said something that sounded vaguely Italian, a language Vermeulen did not speak. There was no way to pass a piece of paper and a pen to the man so he could write the number down. Vermeulen made a writing motion with his index finger. Luca nodded, raised his right index finger and started to draw numbers on the plexiglass between them. One. Zero. Zero. Zero. Zero.

"Ten thousand what? Dollars?"

A nod.

Ten thousand dollars. A tidy sum.

"What did you have to do?"

The man was struggling. Something kept him from answering.

"Are you afraid?"

A hesitation, then a nod.

"Are you afraid for yourself?" He pointed to the man's chest.

Luca shook his head again.

"Are you afraid for your family?"

A vigorous nod.

So whoever promised ten thousand dollars to Luca had threatened his family. Probably the most potent threat anyone could make, particularly when the victim was traveling abroad unaccompanied. But Vermeulen still didn't know what it was Luca had to do to earn the ten thousand dollars.

"Where are they?"

Luca slowly recited what turned out to be a name and an address in Orhei, Moldova. Vermeulen wrote it down and held it up for Luca to check. He nodded.

"Listen, Mr. Luca," Vermeulen said. "I can't help you unless you tell me who got you the visa. If you give me the name, I can investigate and help your family."

"You no help," Luca said. "Write them. Please."

"I will," Vermeulen said. "But you have to help me. You know what's going to happen to you?"

Luca shrugged.

"You are going to be deported back to Moldova. You won't be able to come back here. It's the end of the line for you. But there are other people who'll become victims just like you did. If you tell me, I can help them."

Another shrug. He wasn't going to say anything that might endanger his family.

"Did you have an address in the U.S.?"

A nod instead of a shrug.

"Do you still have it?"

Luca spelled out another address, this one on Martin Luther King Jr. Boulevard in Newark, New Jersey. A lead, but not the one that he'd hoped for or that Suarez expected. His job was to find out who forged UN letters.

He looked at Luca's sad face. Whatever he'd gotten himself into, all he ever wanted was to do right by his family. Now he sat in prison, scared out of his wits and without any hope. A familiar anger rose in Vermeulen's gut. Two men dead and one scared to death. This had to stop. To hell with Suarez and his bureaucracy.

CHAPTER FIFTEEN

———◆———

JACKSON BOUGHT A NEW PHONE. HE figured it'd be the safe thing to do. Maybe a bit paranoid, but safe. He'd spent most of the day just walking and thinking. Squeezing a surgeon was already way beyond his usual MO. But it turned out to be a surgeon who had to discuss matters with someone else. Now *that* was troubling.

Doctors always had a racket going. Who asked their doctor what they billed their insurance? Nobody. You might get an insurance statement and say, "Damn, that cost a lot of money." But you weren't going to ask your doctor if he billed right or if an item on the bill should've been there in the first place.

So Jackson wasn't surprised that Dr. Rosenbaum had his own thing going. What surprised him was the fact that the doctor had to talk to somebody else and that he sounded worried, even scared. Somebody more powerful had to be calling the shots. That could mean a world of hurt or it could mean a serious bump in Jackson's income. He was ready for that bump. Hustling old folks for fifty bucks a pop was yesterday's one-at-a-timing. The downside— he had to be honest with himself—was that he might end up dead like that Kenyan fellow at the Broad Street Station.

Jackson had always known his limits. No shooting or knifing. Once a gun was involved, everything got a lot more complicated. It got the police involved, for sure. The same was true for knifing. He wasn't opposed to killing. Sometimes, a man's got to do what a man's got to do. But if you excluded the doped-up brothers who couldn't think straight, shooting and stabbing were just signs of bad planning, a way to cover up the fact that you hadn't thought through all the shit that could happen.

Anticipation. He liked that word. That's how he went about his work.

What would happen when the old auntie stepping off the bus turned out to be a lot feistier than she looked? Or when the old man used his cane to deck him? Just like the Boy Scouts, his motto was "Be Prepared." He grinned. *Like a Boy Scout. Yeah, right.*

Anticipating what would happen the next day was foremost on his mind. He'd call the doctor in the morning, say about nine thirty. Since he got a new phone, he wasn't worried about the call being traced right away. Best case, the doctor'd say, "Sure thing, let's meet and sort things out." Worst case, he'd say, "Get lost. You come near me and I'll sic the boss man on you." And Jackson was certain the boss man had ways of getting rid of him. Of course, even the best case could just be a setup for the worst case. So he had to play it smart. And playing it smart meant preparing for the worst case.

That's why he went back to Martin Luther King Jr. Boulevard. *Good preparation starts with learning the lay of the land.*

* * *

VERMEULEN REACHED NEWARK AT FOUR IN the afternoon. As he cruised past the airport, he wondered if Alma and her colleagues were out protesting at the detention center. There'd been no protesters at the York prison. Crossing the Passaic River, he saw the green turnpike sign announcing the junction with I-280 heading into downtown Newark. He had the address Luca had provided. Giving it no further thought, he exited.

He crossed the Passaic again and took the first Newark off-ramp near the Riverfront Stadium. Once in the city, he stopped and programmed the GPS in his rental car with the address. It was surprisingly close. Following the voice instructions, he drove past a brick building with a tall clock tower. When he saw the sign reading Broad Street Station, he pulled over and stopped. This was where they'd found the dead Kenyan, Abasi. According to the GPS, he was only three blocks from the address. That couldn't be a coincidence.

The address was a nondescript brownstone right across from a series of specialized medical offices that were part of the hospital. Vermeulen parked a few houses down. He got out, locked the car, and sauntered back toward the brownstone. The sidewalks were busy. People getting off work. He matched their pace, slowing only enough to read the sign next to the entrance. All it said was 'Dr. Rosenbaum. Surgeon.' No office hours, no telephone number. He kept walking.

At the end of the block, he crossed to the hospital side of the street and walked back. There was no sign of life in the brownstone. He wondered if Dr. Rosenbaum saw patients there or if he used it for an office and did his surgery at the hospital across the street.

Caught up in his thoughts, he barely managed to avoid bumping into a tall black man heading in the opposite direction. He muttered an apology and went back to his car.

This was the moment of decision. If he got in and drove back to the city, it'd be the end of this case. Luca had told him nothing that could persuade Suarez to continue the investigation. He'd assign Vermeulen to whatever came next. If he turned around, went back to the house, and rang the doorbell, there'd be no knowing what kind of mess he'd step into.

He leaned against the car and glanced back toward the house. He thought of Odinga, Abasi, and the fear in Luca's eyes. It wasn't really a difficult decision. He pushed himself off the car and headed back to the house. Before he got there, he saw the black man he'd almost bumped into heading toward him. Even though the man looked straight ahead, Vermeulen couldn't shake the feeling that he was being checked out. His right hand slipped down and covered his back pocket. They passed each other. Vermeulen kept walking until he reached the house.

It was a little after five.

He rang the doorbell.

CHAPTER SIXTEEN

———◆———

THERE WAS NO RESPONSE. VERMEULEN STEPPED back down to street level and peered in the windows. No lights, no movement. He climbed back up to the door and pushed the button again. It sounded like a buzzer. Something one would install in an office as opposed to a home, which made sense. Dr. Rosenbaum wouldn't live across from the hospital. Not in Newark. There were far nicer suburbs.

He rang again, this time a little longer than seemed polite. Still no reaction inside. He turned to leave. Scanning the sidewalk, he noticed the black man from his earlier encounter loitering by a lamppost. He stopped. The man was looking in the opposite direction. Vermeulen wasn't fooled. He'd learned the basics of how to spot a tail. Seeing someone three times on such a short stretch of street was not random anymore. It couldn't be related to the visa question. Nobody knew he'd be coming here. Unless he'd been followed from the very beginning. And that meant he was in way deeper than he imagined.

The hesitation turned out to have its reward. Steps sounded from inside and a moment later the door opened. Vermeulen turned and faced a plump little man who spent a lot of money on clothes that didn't suit him at all. He had a comb-over that failed to achieve its purpose, a fleshy face with sagging cheeks, and a full mouth. The face, probably unpleasant in ordinary circumstances, looked even more disagreeable because the jaw dropped at seeing Vermeulen, leaving its owner with the expression of a half-wit from a Bruegel painting.

"Who are you?" the man said.

"I'm Valentin Vermeulen. Could I speak to Dr. Rosenbaum?"

Vermeulen could almost see the gears spinning in the man's brain.

It took a few moments before the answer came. "I'm Dr. Rosenbaum. What do you want?"

"I'm with the UN Office of Internal Oversight Services. We had a small problem crop up in the last week and one of the people connected to that problem had a piece of paper with your address. I'm just following up."

He handed Rosenbaum his card.

Rosenbaum's reaction was immediate and the exact opposite of what he'd expected. Panic distorted the man's face, making the earlier slack-jawed expression almost endearing. Clearly Rosenbaum wanted nothing more than to slam the door in his face. But Vermeulen had already slipped his foot forward far enough to keep that from happening.

It took visible effort for Rosenbaum to pull his face back into what could pass for a normal expression.

"Are you the man who called?"

Now it was Vermeulen's turn to be surprised. He only hoped his face didn't look like Rosenbaum's.

"Uh, no. I didn't call. Should I have?" Vermeulen smiled.

Rosenbaum only managed a series of twitches, as if whatever was going on inside him had decided to fight it out on his face. Eventually one side, apparently the side advocating for continued conversation, won.

"No, of course not. What can I do for you?"

"Well, I'd like to know why a poor man from Moldova, sitting in prison in Pennsylvania, has your address in his pocket."

"I have no idea." Rosenbaum had finally gotten himself under control.

"He came to the U.S. using doctored documents. They nabbed him at JFK. He seems terribly afraid, but wouldn't tell me why. This address was all he gave me. Can I come inside?"

Vermeulen stepped up, expecting to enter the house. Rosenbaum moved back but didn't invite him in. He ended up standing between the jambs.

"It must be a mistake. I don't know anyone from Mol .... What's it called again?"

"Moldova."

"No, I don't know anyone from there."

"Have you had a patient from there in the past? Maybe the man was sick and someone recommended you."

"I don't keep track of my patients' nationalities. How would I even know?"

"Don't you talk to them before you cut them open?"

"Of course, but I don't go into those kinds of details."

"What's your specialty?"

Rosenbaum hesitated. "Heart surgery, liver, kidneys, anything related to internal organs."

Vermeulen nodded, but none of this made any sense.

"Maybe you saved someone's life …."

"I save someone's life every day. I can't keep track of where they come from."

The combination of hubris and disdain made Vermeulen want to smack the man.

"So you don't recall any foreign patients?" he said.

Rosenbaum hesitated a moment before answering that he didn't, but the moment was long enough for Vermeulen. Maybe the doctor hadn't seen anyone from Moldova, but he'd definitely seen foreign patients.

"If you'll excuse me," Rosenbaum said. "I'm expecting another visitor."

"Any idea why your address ended up in that man's pocket?"

"None whatsoever. If there's nothing more, I'd appreciate your leaving now."

Rosenbaum had transformed himself from a nervous wreck barely in control of his twitches to the kind of person Vermeulen expected to see in an intensive care unit—in charge and used to issuing orders. While that might have been reassuring if Vermeulen were a patient, it didn't serve his purpose right then.

"I'm not quite done yet. You see, that man didn't have your address by accident. It's not like you're in the Moldovan phone book. He couldn't have gotten it in the U.S. because he never made it into the country. That means someone must have given it to him before he left Moldova. And I'm pretty certain you have an idea about how or why that happened."

Rosenbaum's face began twitching again. Vermeulen almost pitied the man. Fear and resolve seemed to be at war with each other in Rosenbaum's psyche. Such mood swings had to take their toll.

"I have no idea what you are talking about. If you don't leave now, I will call the police."

"What do you know about the Kenyan man who died near Broad Street Station?" It was a shot in the dark, but Abasi was the only man who'd made it into the U.S. that Vermeulen knew of. If Rosenbaum was involved, it stood to reason that he'd met him.

He wasn't prepared for what happened next. Rosenbaum pushed him backward toward the stairs. Vermeulen stumbled, grabbed Rosenbaum's arm, missed and got hold of the man's tie. That kept him from falling down the stairs, but it pulled Rosenbaum forward. The two men ended up standing cheek to jowl on the stoop.

A loud laugh came from the bottom of the stairs. Vermeulen let go of the tie, turned, and saw a blonde woman with a big grin on her face. She wore a well fitted down jacket, smart pants, and a scarf around her neck. Her short hair gave her a boyish look. If she wore any makeup at all, it was expertly applied.

"That was quite the recovery," she said to Vermeulen. "The old grab-the-tie trick. I love it. Good thing the doc had enough dead weight to keep you upright."

Rosenbaum snorted behind Vermeulen.

"Well," Vermeulen said. "I'll be off, then."

He extended his hand to the woman who was coming up the stairs.

"I'm Valentin Vermeulen. Nice to meet someone with a sense of humor."

The woman shook his hand. "It's the one thing that keeps you sane in this crazy world," she said.

What she didn't say was her name.

Chapter Seventeen

———— ♦ ————

Jackson couldn't make heads or tails of what he'd just seen. The man he'd pegged as the third party had gone up the stairs and rung the doorbell. After a while, another man, probably the doctor, had opened the door. That's when things got strange. The two men didn't know each other. Their body language was pretty clear. Which meant that the visitor wasn't the other party the doctor needed to consult before he could cut Jackson in on whatever scheme they had going.

The conversation didn't seem to go well. The doctor kept shaking his head. What was going on? The other man wasn't a patient either. Jackson was certain about that. Patients didn't show up after the office was closed, and the doctor wouldn't bother talking to one.

The visitor wasn't eager to leave. He leaned forward and kept talking. Rosenbaum only wanted to get rid of the man. Their argument seemed to get more intense. Right then a woman arrived. She stopped at the bottom of the stairs and just watched. Neither of the others had seen her. Who was she? The wife, a girlfriend?

Finally, the discussion got physical. The doctor pushed the man, who grabbed onto the doctor's tie to keep from falling down the stoop. The two ended up in a funny embrace. Jackson could see the woman at the bottom of the stairs laugh. The visitor turned and left, but not before shaking the woman's hand. It wasn't clear if they knew each other or not. The first man went back to his car and drove off.

Jackson had taken the time to write down the tag number of the car. It was a plain Ford Fusion, not the kind of car he expected some well connected hood to drive. And it was a rental. He'd seen the telltale barcodes on the windshield and the rear window. Not at all what he expected. Rental cars could easily be tracked. Nobody doing anything remotely illegal would rent a car, unless they had fake identities.

Since the barcodes were black on yellow, he assumed it was a Hertz rental. He'd written down the barcode too. His buddy Jamal worked at the Hertz rental office at the Newark airport.

JACKSON KNEW JAMAL WOULDN'T BE HAPPY to get his call. He was at work and wasn't supposed to get personal calls. They weren't really buddies anymore since Jamal went on the strait and narrow. He'd made it from counter rep to branch manager trainee.

"What's happening?" Jackson said.

"What do you want, Earle? You know I can't talk to you."

"What's bitten you? Can't I call my old friend?"

"We haven't been friends in a while."

"Ah, come on, man. That's harsh."

"I moved on. I'm trying to make something of myself. And you? You keep fleecing old folks."

"I ain't fleecing old folks. I guide them to my doctors."

"Who rip them off."

"They rip off the government. That's a big difference."

"Not to me it isn't. You could've made something of yourself."

"Well, that's why I'm calling you. I turned over a new leaf, just like you. And I need your help."

Silence.

Good, Jackson thought. *I got him thinking.*

"What do you want?" Jamal said.

"I got the barcode from a Hertz rental car. Can you find out who rented that car?"

"I knew it. No way."

"Come on, Jamal. This guy and I are partnering up for a new thing. Except I lost his business card, so I don't know how to contact him."

"Right. But you got the barcode from his rental? Gimme a break."

"Jamal. Don't be that way. I bet you can just look it up right there on your computers. I just need the man's address and phone number."

"Why? So you can steal from him, too?"

"No, I don't want to steal from him. I want to talk to him. He and I may have a common interest."

"What interest?"

This wasn't right. Jamal was quizzing him like he was a suspect or something.

"Come on, man. Just look it up."

"Earle, if you don't tell me why you need that information, I'll hang up right now."

"Wait, wait. Don't hang up."

And so Jackson told him the story about finding the Kenyan at Broad Street Station, about the man dying in his arms and about the paper in his pocket, about checking out the address and seeing another man argue with the doctor. He left out the bit about the twenty-five hundred dollars. He embellished the story, telling Jamal how having a man die in his arms had shaken him up. How the doctor had done wrong by Abasi. How he wouldn't have done that to a white patient.

"So you want to talk to the man in the rental because …?"

"You ain't listening, man. I think the doctor is responsible for the Kenyan brother's death and I think that the man who came around feels the same. I just want to talk with him and see what we can do to bring that doctor to justice. If I went to the police, nobody'd believe me. But if that man and I go together, maybe we can do something."

Jamal must have sensed the sincerity in Jackson, because his voice softened. "You know I could get in serious trouble for this. So, don't ever come back to me and ask for something like this again."

"I won't, Jamal."

"I'll call you back."

A HALF HOUR LATER, JAMAL CAME THROUGH for him. "That car wasn't rented at Newark," he said. "It was rented on the Upper West Side in Manhattan. It's already been returned. The renter is one Valentin Vermeulen. Here's his phone number."

Jackson wrote it down.

"What about his address?"

"I won't give that to you."

"What? Why not?"

"I checked and found the story about the dead man. So that's true. But I have no way of checking the rest. If you want to talk to the man, call him. That's all I'm gonna do for you."

Jackson knew better than to press his luck. "I really appreciate that, Jamal. You've been a true friend. I'll make it up to you."

"That's okay. Don't call me again unless you're *really* ready to turn over a new leaf."

"I am, man. I am."

Jackson ended the call and looked at the number. A man from Manhattan rents a car to drive to Newark and argue with Dr. Rosenbaum. Very strange.

Why didn't he take the train from Penn Station? Renting a car seemed over the top. Maybe he didn't like public transit. There was only one way to find out.

He dialed the number. The call connected.

"This is Vermeulen," a voice said.

"Yeah. You wanna talk about why you went to Dr. Rosenbaum today?"

CHAPTER EIGHTEEN

——◆——

VERMEULEN HAD JUST OPENED A BOTTLE of De Koninck when his phone rang. He had half a mind not to answer. His back was sore from sitting in the car all day. Add to that the bizarre experience in Newark, and all he wanted was a beer and a smoke. But the caller was Sunderland.

"Vermoolen, I have an update on Abasi. He died from blood loss caused by a knife wound. Somebody must've stabbed him and taken his things."

Vermeulen sucked in his breath. "In broad daylight? At a light rail station? That doesn't sound right."

"Give me a break. Life is cheap in Newark. If Abasi had anything of value on him, he'd be in danger, broad daylight or not."

Vermeulen put down his beer. Goosebumps crawled up his arm. Two illegal immigrants from Kenya. Both come to the U.S. using forged invitation letters from the UN. Both end up murdered, hours apart. It couldn't be a coincidence. But they weren't killed by the same person. The man who killed Odinga at the Elizabeth detention center couldn't have been at Broad Street Station to kill Abasi.

"I drove to York to speak with Luca, one of the other people you detained," he said. "Why do you hold him so far away?"

"It's all dependent on available spaces."

Vermeulen remembered Alma's point that moving detainees also made representation very difficult, but didn't pursue it.

"The man was scared out of his mind. Someone had offered him ten thousand dollars. He refused to say for what or give me a name. He as much as told me that his family would be harmed if he said anything. He asked me to write to them. Who or what could scare a man so much he wouldn't talk, even in prison?"

"Beats me," Sunderland said. "Not my concern. Let's hope Luca gets deported before something happens to him. You have no idea how much trouble Odinga's death is going to cause us. The pro-immigration nuts are probably already planning their march to the federal building in Newark."

Vermeulen opened his mouth but thought better of it. Sunderland's callousness was getting unbearable.

"Are you still there?" Sunderland said.

"Yes. I'm thinking. This thing is bigger than just a few fake letters."

"That's what I've been telling you. It's just the tip of the iceberg."

"No, it's not. You are talking about numbers. I'm talking about the fact that someone can threaten Luca's family in Moldova. What organization has such a global reach?"

"The Russian mob?" Sunderland said.

"In Moldova, maybe, but Kenya. That seems a stretch."

"Whatever, the real issue is that I want this flood of people with false UN invitations to stop. People in your outfit are issuing them. Find those people and stop them. That's my only concern."

"Listen to me, Sunderland. The issue isn't numbers. The issue is there's a network with international reach that smuggles people into the US. The UN invitations are just a small part of that. Don't you want to stop them?"

"Sorry, Vermoolen. I'm not Interpol, just Immigration and Customs Enforcement. All I need is you stopping those fake invitations that allow people to get visas. Are you going to do that?"

Vermeulen shook his head. "Yes. I'll be in touch."

He ended the call. He was glad he hadn't mentioned the meeting with Dr. Rosenbaum. He took a deep swallow from the bottle, lit a Gitane and sat down at the kitchen table. He didn't know what to do next. Here he was, working for the one organization that had the necessary global reach to deal with this network, except he had no authority to do so. But the people who had the power to act focused only on their little end. The irony would have been laughable, were it not for the fear that he'd seen in Luca's face, that Abasi and Odinga must have felt as they were being murdered. There would be more Abasis and Odingas, unless he did something.

Since moving back to New York, Vermeulen had quickly adopted the empty refrigerator habits of Manhattan residents. That wasn't a problem on most days, since there was so much prepared food available everywhere. But he didn't feel like going out again. Besides the beer, his fridge contained a jar of pickles, four eggs, some packets of soy sauce from the Chinese place down the street, and an old bagel. That limited his culinary options. He was in the middle of frying two eggs when his phone rang again.

Without thinking, he answered. "This is Vermeulen."

A male voice he'd never heard before said, "You wanna talk about why you visited Dr. Rosenbaum today?"

The spatula clattered on the stovetop, then to the floor. He stared out the window as if the mysterious caller were right outside, looking in at him. The eggs sizzled in the hot pan.

"Hold on," Vermeulen said and put the phone down. Who the hell was this? It obviously wasn't the woman with the short blonde hair. And it wasn't the doctor. He reached down to pick up the spatula. He turned down the burner. Nobody else knew he'd stopped by the doctor's office. He tried to remember faces he'd seen on the street. There was really only one candidate— the black man who'd followed him.

He picked up the phone again. "Who are you?"

"That's not important. What is important is you visiting the doctor. Why'd you go to him?"

"You're the black man who bumped into me and then followed me. So don't think for a moment I can't find out who you are."

The silence at the other end told him he was right.

"Okay, you saw me," the man said. "So did many people. That don't mean you're gonna find out anything. But I know you talked to the doctor who's got things to hide. So I'm thinking you've got things to hide, too. And that's what I want to talk about."

The eggs were done. Vermeulen managed to slip them onto the plate. He popped the bagel halves from the toaster, pulled over a stool, and sat down. This might take a while, and he wasn't going to let his eggs get cold.

"Sorry," he said, after forking a bite into his mouth. "You caught me in the middle of supper, and I hate cold eggs." He took a sip from the bottle. "Besides, you're operating on the wrong assumptions. I have nothing to hide. You, on the other hand, sound like an extortionist. Last I heard, that was still a crime in this country. I got your phone number on my display. It'll only be a matter of time before the police find you."

The last comment was pure bluster. He took a bite from the bagel and had another swig of beer.

"You're eating while I'm trying to have a conversation with you? Man, how 'bout a little respect?"

"You're the one who interrupted my supper. And why should I respect someone who's trying to blackmail me?"

"I thought you were somebody else. Just forget I called."

"No, I'm not going to do that. I'm also interested in what Rosenbaum has to hide. You seem to know something. How about telling me why *you're* after him?"

He finished the eggs and wiped the remaining yolk with a piece of bagel.

"Nah, let's just forget the whole thing, okay?" the caller said.

"No, not okay. How'd you like the Newark PD on your tail?" It was an easy guess. "Believe me, I can make that happen."

"I said forget about it."

"I won't, unless you tell me what you know. Right now."

"I'll only do it face to face."

"Fine with me. Be at the Azure Lounge in downtown Newark in an hour."

CHAPTER NINETEEN

---◆---

VERMEULEN HAD TO HUSTLE TO GET to Newark. With the rush hour over, train service was less frequent. He made it to Newark's Penn Station and got a cab to take him to the Azure Lounge near the Prudential Center on Broad Street. He could have chosen a place in Manhattan, but he figured meeting the man on his own turf would make him more talkative. One of his colleagues had spoken highly of the Azure Lounge and it was right in downtown Newark.

The bar wasn't as busy as he'd hoped. Three of the seven tables were occupied by couples. Two men sat at the bar. His man wasn't among them.

He chose a table against the wall, near the rear door. Always keep your back clear and your exit close. Not that he expected any trouble. He figured the black man was a hustler who'd found some dirt on Rosenbaum. Why else would he be surveilling the doctor's office?

He ordered a bottle of Brooklyn Sorachi Ace. It wasn't quite like De Koninck, but it came in a big bottle with a champagne cork, reminding him of the Belgian doubles and triples. His beer came and he poured the first glass.

A man entered, looked around, and slid onto one of the bar stools.

Vermeulen fingered his pack of Gitanes. The smoking ban in bars and restaurants was probably for the best. Still, nothing made him crave a cigarette as much as a nice glass of beer.

The next newcomer was the caller. There was nothing distinct about him. Short-cropped black hair, oval face without any distinguishing marks. His skin color was more toward the brown ales than the stouts. The clothes were a step above street casual, last year's designer stuff you'd find at outlets.

The man plopped himself into the chair opposite him.

"You buying?" he said.

Vermeulen had to smile. A hustler indeed.

"No."

"Suit yourself."

The man waved to the waiter and ordered a Hennessy.

"Okay," Vermeulen said. "Tell me how you found my phone number."

"I got my sources."

"And what sources might those be?"

"None of your business."

"Then let's start with your name? Since you know mine, it's only fair."

The man nodded. "I'm Earle. Earle Jackson."

The waiter brought a snifter of Hennessy for Jackson.

"Nice to meet you, Mr. Jackson. But I'm still curious how you found me."

Jackson shrugged. "Your rental car."

Vermeulen nodded and sipped more beer. "Nice. You have a creative side. Why are you keeping an eye on Dr. Rosenbaum?"

Jackson looked at him but remained silent.

"Listen," Vermeulen said. "You asked me what I wanted from Rosenbaum. I want to know the same about you."

Jackson tossed back his cognac. "The doctor is into something that isn't on the up and up," he said.

"So you want to cash in on that? Like you wanted to cash in on me?"

"I'm an entrepreneur. I'm always looking for opportunities. Why are you interested in him?"

A couple came into the lounge and took the next table over. The woman wore a wool beret over her hair and large sunglasses that covered her eyes.

"I came across his name during an investigation," Vermeulen said.

"You a cop?"

"No, I'm an investigator for the UN."

"I didn't know the UN had cops."

"I'm not a cop, although sometimes I wish I were. How do you know that the doctor is into something illegal?"

"Just like you. I came across his name."

"Was it on a piece of paper?" Vermeulen said.

Jackson looked at him, surprised. "What makes you say that?"

"That's how I found his name. Where did you find that paper?"

Jackson looked around the bar, then leaned forward. "On a dead man," he said.

"Was his name Abasi?"

Jackson jerked back. "How did you know that?"

"An educated guess. Rosenbaum's name and address seems to find its way into the pockets of foreigners. I heard that a Kenyan named Abasi was found dead at Broad Street Station. How did you find him?"

Jackson's face showed his suspicion. "He didn't look so good," he finally said. "I walked over to him to see if he needed any help. The man could barely talk. I was trying to get him to a doctor. He was bleeding like a stuck pig. Next thing I knew, he was dead. He died in my arms, man. Scared me bad, real bad."

"But not bad enough to keep you from going through his pockets."

"I don't know what you're talking about."

"Come on, Mr. Jackson. That's how you found the paper with the address. What else did you find?"

"Nothing. After Abasi died, I got out of there. Ain't no good for a black man to be found holding a dead body."

"So someone else took his things?"

"Must have," Jackson said.

"Then how did you know his name?"

Jackson looked at him, eyes narrow. "Okay, he might've had a passport."

"You took that. Anything else?"

Jackson shook his head.

"Was there money in his pocket?"

"Nope."

"You sure? The other man who had Rosenbaum's address had been promised ten thousand dollars."

"Abasi didn't have that much cash—"

"How much did he have?"

"I ain't saying anything else."

It was all the admission Vermeulen needed. "Did Abasi say anything to you?"

"Just 'JFK,' like he wanted to go to the airport," Jackson said. He got up. "I gotta be going now. Getting late."

"I don't know what Abasi had to do for the money, but I'm sure he did it to help his family. Think about that, Mr. Jackson. Think about it and do the right thing."

Jackson didn't strike Vermeulen as ruthless. He might do the right thing and return the money.

After Jackson left the bar, the man who'd come in with the woman left also. A moment later, the man on the barstool who'd come in after Vermeulen followed.

Vermeulen was pouring the last of his beer when he realized that Jackson hadn't paid for his cognac. He smiled. Just as he thought, a hustler to his core.

The woman with the beret got up from her table and turned toward him. She'd taken off her sunglasses. The moment of recognition lasted a couple of beats. It was the woman he'd met at the bottom of Rosenbaum's steps.

CHAPTER TWENTY

―――◆―――

"**W**E MEET AGAIN**,**" VERMEULEN SAID AS he rose from his seat. "A pleasant coincidence."

He was pretty sure it wasn't, although he couldn't imagine how the woman knew he'd be at this bar. He stuck out his hand.

"Indeed. Nice to see you again, Mr. Vermeulen," she said, shaking his hand.

"I'm afraid I forgot your name."

"You didn't. I didn't tell you. People refer to me as 'The Broker.' "

"The Broker? Even brokers have names."

"Yes, but it's immaterial."

"Why do I get the feeling our meeting isn't coincidental?"

"Because you are a smart man. The good doctor gave me your card. The rest was easy."

"What can I do for you?"

"You could start by telling me why in the world the United Nations is bothering with Dr. Rosenbaum."

"What are you? Rosenbaum's bodyguard?"

"My role is immaterial here; what matters is that you contacted the doctor. I want to know why."

"I'm afraid I can't tell you that. Besides, if you are here on the doctor's behalf, I'm sure he told you already."

He lifted his glass and finished the beer. Unlike that afternoon, the Broker was not smiling. But even her business expression was attractive. Her eyes were almond shaped and gazed at him with a wry scrutiny.

"He told me that you asked about a man from Moldova and a dead man from Kenya."

"That's correct." He had no reason to help her. But if he could string her along, he might find out what role she played in this scheme.

"Listen, Mr. Vermeulen, let's not waste each other's time. I want to know why you, a UN investigator, have a reason to contact Rosenbaum."

"There are many misconceptions about the UN. Such as, it only deals with international issues. As it turns out, we deal with a host of issues even at local levels. People in other countries are well aware of that. In the U.S., not so much."

She gave him a brilliant smile. "Nice deflection. But you won't get rid of me that easily."

"Why would I want to get rid of you? I enjoy the company of attractive women. May I ask what interest you have in my speaking with Rosenbaum?"

She signaled the waiter. "Would you like another one?" she said.

"No, I'd rather have a mineral water."

"Good." She turned to the waiter. "Two Evian, please."

"With lemon?" the waiter asked.

She looked at Vermeulen with a raised eyebrow. He nodded.

"Yes, please," she said.

When the waiter had left the table, the smile was gone.

"Here's what I'm prepared to tell you. Dr. Rosenbaum is a busy surgeon with varied interests related to his profession. I take care of the business end of his endeavors. So when the doctor gets a visit from a UN investigator, it's my job to be interested. The poor man can't be expected to worry about such details, so I do it for him."

Vermeulen nodded. The Broker was the exact opposite of Rosenbaum. She was in complete control of herself.

"What are these interests? Surgery? What else?" he said.

She smiled again. "That is public information. You should take a look at the hospital website. Dr. Rosenbaum is a world-famous surgeon."

The waiter brought two glasses of sparkling water. The lemon twists were lodged on the rims like yellow glass ornaments. Vermeulen took a sip.

"I'm sure the website presents glowing accounts of his lifesaving work. Are there pictures of grateful patients?"

"Look it up yourself," she said. "Why does the UN have an interest in Rosenbaum?"

"I'm curious why poor people from less-developed countries show up in the U.S. with fraudulent visas and the doctor's address in their pocket."

"And how does that affect the UN?"

"Ms. Whateveryournameis, now you're wasting our time. You know as well as I do that Mr. Luca and Mr. Abasi had obtained their visas using fraudulent invitation letters from UN offices."

A flicker of annoyance flashed across her face.

"Abasi died, apparently on his way home," he said. "And Luca is sitting in detention after having been promised ten thousand dollars. They are collateral damage, but for what?"

There was a new fire in her eyes. "Don't stick your nose into business that isn't yours, Mr. Vermeulen. I will put an end to the use of the UN invitations. That should terminate your involvement in this matter. Do not bother Dr. Rosenbaum any further or I will bring my own resources to bear."

"The kind of resources that killed Joseph Odinga in Elizabeth?"

It was the impossible header into the upper left corner of the goal. Her face turned into a mask, her lips into thin threads. He'd scored.

"That's all I needed to know," he said. "The next time we see each other, it'll be when someone puts handcuffs on you."

The Broker put on a brave smile. It was a mere shadow of the radiance with which she'd almost charmed him.

"That won't happen, so you can stop fantasizing," she said. "We will see each other again, but you'll regret the circumstances of that meeting."

He shrugged.

"Just like your friend will regret this evening," she said.

"Who? You mean Jackson?"

"Oh, is that his name? He also harassed the doctor. A bit more crudely, to be sure, but he's a bother nevertheless."

"What are you doing to Jackson? He's just a little hustler."

"Well, he got in over his head. Should have thought about that before he picked up the phone."

"You're having him killed just because he called Rosenbaum?"

His blood was pulsing in his temples now. This woman was evil.

She glanced at her watch. "Not yet. He's probably at the regret stage right now. And spilling his guts telling my associates everything he knows. Because he thinks it'll keep him alive."

"But it won't."

"Of course not. Just like you won't survive our next meeting."

Chapter Twenty-One

———◆———

Jackson didn't know what to make of Vermeulen. The man obviously knew that he'd taken the money from Abasi, but he didn't push it. "Do the right thing," was all he said. *Man, just like Grandma*, Jackson thought. *Do the right thing, Earle, and you never have to worry.* Yeah, right. As if that was gonna work. You live in Newark, you're gonna worry, no matter what you do.

Vermeulen wouldn't turn him in. His threats were just for show. Vermeulen also knew the doctor was up to no good, but rather than squeeze him, he wanted to bust him. *Do the right thing.* Man, what a waste. Between the two of them, they could've milked the doctor for a pretty penny.

Jackson was walking along Edison Place toward the Newark Penn Station to catch a bus home. *Do the right thing.* He couldn't get that out of his head. The envelope with the money—now down a couple of C-notes—felt heavy in his pocket. The Kenyan brother came all that way to make money for his family. Damn, that was a bad spot to be in.

Edison Place was deserted. At that time of night, those who ventured into downtown Newark took cabs. Earle wasn't worried, though. He'd grown up here and knew how to navigate the streets. Which was why he didn't pay much attention to the footfalls behind him.

When he reached Mulberry Street, the steps were still following him. He turned around. In the glow of the streetlights, he saw a white man maybe fifty paces behind him. He hadn't seen a white man walking a Newark street at night in a long time. The man slowed down when Jackson looked at him. Then he started to run.

Jackson didn't think twice. Ninety-nine times out of a hundred, the white man running after you was a cop. He sprinted diagonally across the intersection to a parking lot. Weaving through a few parked cars, he headed straight for the Edison parking garage. No better place to lose the guy than in the concrete maze of a six-story structure. He leaped over the boom that controlled access to the ramp.

He wasn't particularly athletic. It'd been a while since he last shot hoops with his buddies. His side started aching with a stitch, and his lungs were burning. Running uphill to the second level didn't help.

Except for a smattering of parked cars, the deck was empty. Not really the best place to hide. He turned left, ducked behind a concrete pillar and crouched next to a Chrysler 300. The car offered plenty of cover, but Jackson knew he had to keep moving. The man had been too close. He crawled between the car and the wall toward the next car. There, he got stuck. The idiot had pulled so close, there was no way to squeeze past. Good thing it was dark. He tried to keep his breathing quiet and crawled back next to the Chrysler.

The steps had slowed at the top of the ramp. There was a moment of quiet. Then the scratching of shoes on concrete came closer.

Running away was always better than picking a fight. Jackson knew that. He'd never let some false idea of manhood goad him into a confrontation. He'd known too many brothers who'd taken a bullet because they didn't run. But there were times when running wasn't possible. That's when it was much better to attack. He crawled toward the center of the aisle and knelt next to the trunk of the Chrysler.

The steps kept coming, haltingly and cautious, but the man was not going to give up. Jackson put his left knee on the ground and tensed his right leg like a sprinter in the starting blocks.

The steps stopped. Even though his eyes had adjusted to the dark, he couldn't see the man. The temptation to rise and glance through the car windows grew. He resisted. He had the advantage. He knew where the man was. No sense in giving that up.

A step. More silence. Another step. Jackson could make out a leg. *Wait*, he told himself. *Let him come to you.* One more step. The leg was now in full view. Not yet. The next step put the man right in front of him. He lunged forward and slammed his shoulder against the man's knees. In the NFL, that would have been an illegal block. And for a good reason. The man went down. His scream echoed through the garage. Something metallic clattered on the concrete. A gun? A knife? Jackson didn't hang around to find out. He raced toward the end of the aisle, turned toward the down ramp, and almost skidded into another man who was pointing a gun at him.

"End of the road for you, asshole," the man said. "Amateur night's over." The man waved his pistol. "On your knees, hands behind your head."

Jackson lowered himself onto his knees and put his hands up. *Amateur night? Dumb prick.* But wounded pride wasn't going to help him now. He needed to get away, and he couldn't see how. His reliance on anticipation had a built-in flaw. If you couldn't anticipate something, you couldn't prepare for it. And this, Jackson didn't anticipate. He stared into the gloom. In front of him, the ramp descended to the ground level. No cover anywhere.

The man moved past him to look down the aisle. The gun didn't waver.

"Where you at, Andrej?" he shouted.

"Over here," Andrej moaned. "I can't walk. The bastard musta broke my leg."

"Shit," the man said. He turned and kicked Jackson in his side. "You gonna be sorry." Then to Andrej, "Can you make it over here?"

"I told you I can't walk. Get the car. I gotta go to a doctor."

Jackson noticed the hand holding the gun drop down.

"What about this asshole?"

"Just shoot him."

"I can't shoot him here. The cops'd be here in no time. We're supposed to take him to the mudflats."

"I ain't going to the mudflats, Gergi. My leg's busted."

The gun wasn't pointed at Jackson anymore. This would have been a good moment to tackle Gergi. Except he stood next to Jackson. The time it'd take for Jackson to turn would be enough for Gergi to raise his hand again and fire.

"The Broker isn't gonna be happy about this," Gergi said.

"Her leg ain't busted."

"She's gonna have a fit, just sayin'."

Jackson examined the down ramp again. On one side, the ramp was bordered by a concrete wall that went all the way up to the next level. But the other side was open. A two-foot curb was the only barrier. He couldn't tell what was below. It was a risk he had to take.

"The bitch ain't happy on a good day," Andrej was saying. "How much worse could it be?"

"I don't want to find out. We need to deal with this clown first."

"Just knock 'im out, then get the car."

Jackson decided not to wait any longer. He jumped to his feet, raced to the curb, and vaulted over it. A shot rang out. The bullet ricocheted through the garage with a high whine. The drop wasn't very deep. A car was parked right below. Jackson hit its hood much sooner than he'd expected. He didn't manage to roll away, like they did in the movies. He just slammed sideways into the sheet metal. The car's alarm began wailing, something he wanted to do in response to the pain that flashed through his body.

He rolled off the car and hobbled away from the flashing lights as fast as he could. Mounted to the next column he found a fire extinguisher. He yanked it from its bracket and ducked behind the concrete.

Gergi came racing down the ramp. The wailing and flashing car was like a homing beacon. Jackson counted on that. He pulled the safety pin from the handle and pointed the nozzle. The moment Gergi appeared against the flashing lights, Jackson squeezed the handle. A thick cloud of foam hit the man in his face. He screamed, let go of the gun, and rubbed his eyes. Jackson slammed the extinguisher against Gergi's head. He dropped like a stone.

JACKSON DRAGGED HIMSELF TO HIS STUDIO apartment above the storefront church off Hawthorne Avenue. He felt like he'd been hit by a Mack Truck. On the way, he stopped at Hawthorne Liquors and got himself a fifth of Hennessy. Maurice, the owner, was half asleep behind the counter.

At home, he didn't bother with a glass. He took a big gulp of cognac. The burn in his throat made him forget the pulsing bruise on his side. He had half a mind to finish that bottle.

What the fuck had happened? It still didn't make sense. He calls Vermeulen to figure out how he was involved. The man turns out to be kinda snooty, first jerking him around with empty threats, then laying a guilt trip on him. Next thing, he's held up by guys with guns. Did they work for Vermeulen? Nobody else knew he was gonna be at that lounge. But why would Vermeulen tell him to do the right thing and then send two goons after him?

He tried to remember who else had been in that lounge. There were four men at the bar. Nothing stuck out there. Three tables with pretty ordinary folks not doing much of anything special, just talking and drinking. And Vermeulen. He had to be the one who sicced those men on him.

After the third gulp, just before the point of no return, he put the bottle down. Gergi in the garage had mentioned a broker, and Andrej with the busted knee had called her a bitch. So there was a woman involved. There was a woman who'd come into the lounge with a man. With his back to them, he hadn't seen what she looked like. How would she be connected? He thought about the woman at the doctor's earlier, the one with the short blonde hair. She could have been the third party the doctor had to consult. The comfortable buzz in his head cleared with a flash. The woman in the bar and woman at the doctor's house were the same.

He should've been happy with the twenty-five hundred dollars.

Chapter Twenty-Two

T HE CALL CHANGED EVERYTHING. THERE WAS a long pause when he answered, as if someone were wondering if they'd called the wrong number. He was about to push the End button when a Flemish voice he hadn't heard in nine years said, "*Is dat u*, Valentin?"

He couldn't speak. A picture of her appeared in his mind's eye. They'd just met at a rally in Antwerp. She was willowy, with long, strawberry blonde hair, the very image of a 1970s cover girl for a hippie magazine. He'd forgotten all about the cruise missile deployment they were protesting.

"*Bent dar u*, Valentin?"

"Yes," he said hoarsely. "I'm here." He sank into his chair. There were more pictures, now streaming like a newsreel montage: the walks, the courtship, the wedding, bringing their daughter Gaby home from the hospital.

"I have some bad news," she said.

"It's Gaby." He knew it. Ever since he reconciled with his daughter two years ago, he'd been haunted by the fact that he'd wasted eight years before speaking with her. "Tell me she's alive, Marieke." He hadn't spoken his ex-wife's name since the divorce.

"She's alive."

"What happened?"

"She was in an accident, a skiing accident. She's in a coma."

"Where is she?"

"A hospital in Vienna."

"Are you with her?" he said, and knew it was a stupid question.

"Yes."

"How long has she been this way?"

"Three days."

And you're only calling me now? He wanted to say. But he stopped himself. It probably took that much time for the hospital to find the next of kin. "What's the prognosis?"

"I don't know. The doctors say that she's stable and that it's only a matter of time before she wakes up. She's got some cracked ribs, but the real problem is her head trauma. I'm worried. Part of her head is wrapped in bandages; it's all so scary."

"Do you know how it happened?" he said.

"What difference does that make? Our daughter is in intensive care. It doesn't matter how she got there. It wasn't her fault, if that's what you're asking."

There was that familiar anger again. It used to drive him crazy. He'd done his share of damage to their relationship, he knew that now. But Marieke's sudden and unpredictable outbursts of anger had been right up there when it came to why their marriage failed.

"It's not what I was asking," he said. "That was uncalled for."

"You're right. I'm sorry. I took the train here as soon as I got the call yesterday. Since then I've been in her room. The hospital was kind enough to put a cot next to her bed."

"I'll come right away. We can take turns keeping her company."

"I was hoping you'd say that," she said. "When can you get here?"

"I have to make a few calls before I can take off. I'll probably arrive early the day after tomorrow. Sooner if there's a morning flight."

"I'm glad you are coming. You've got my number now. Call me when you come in. I'll text you the hospital address."

She hung up. His body was pinned to the chair by the weight of words said and left unsaid, of missed opportunities to make amends, of love slowly being buried under layers of the irrelevant detritus of everyday life; and worse still, by the weight of the knowledge that he hadn't done anything to stop it. Tears flowed down his face.

WELL PAST MIDNIGHT, HE ROUSED HIMSELF. *Self-pity is just another form of selfishness*, he thought. It had gotten him to that spot in the first place. And longing for a different past was a waste of time. Instead, he could make the present and the future better by being there for Marieke and Gaby when they needed him. He opened his laptop and searched for the first available ticket to Vienna. Five minutes later he booked a flight, leaving at five fifty that evening. The price was ludicrous.

There was no question of sleeping, so he started a load of laundry, got his suitcase from the storage locker in the basement, and sorted what he needed to bring.

At six in the morning, he dialed Suarez's home number.

"This'd better be good, Vermeulen," Suarez said.

"Sorry for the early call, but I've had some bad news. My daughter was in an accident and is in a coma."

"I'm sorry to hear that. I didn't know you had a daughter."

"She lives in Düsseldorf, but the accident was in Austria and she's in a hospital there. I'm going to Vienna to be with her. So I need some time off."

"Oh."

"I think I still have three personal days and all of my sick days. So that shouldn't be a problem."

"But you aren't sick."

"If you'd read the human resources manual, you'd know that I can use those days to care for a sick relative."

"How long will you be gone?"

"A week, probably more. It all depends on when she comes out of her coma and what care is needed then."

"What about your investigation? Are you done with it?"

The investigation. The shock of hearing Marieke's voice and her devastating news had pushed all other thoughts away. Odinga, Abasi, Luca, the woman, and Dr. Rosenbaum—none of them mattered at the moment.

"Not quite. I received more information at the prison in Pennsylvania that is pertinent. I might have a chance to speak with Dufaux while I'm in Vienna. The rest will have to wait."

"Well, I didn't think it was worth your time anyway. What about Sunderland? Will he follow through on his threat to hold up UN visitors?"

"I'll call him before I leave. I'll tell him I'm making sure that Vienna doesn't issue any more fake invitations."

"Call me if it's going to be more than a week. Safe travels. I hope your daughter will be okay."

The call to Sunderland rolled over to voicemail, which was what he'd intended. He left a brief message explaining that he'd be going to Austria to get to the bottom of the fake invitation letters and put a stop to the scam. It had to be enough.

In the middle of folding laundry, the phone rang. It was too early for Sunderland. He checked the display. The number was unfamiliar. He didn't want to answer, but his finger tapped the button anyway.

"Vermeulen here."

"Yeah, Mr. Do-The-Right-Thing. You almost got me killed last night."

CHAPTER TWENTY-THREE

---◆---

JACKSON! VERMEULEN HAD FORGOTTEN ALL ABOUT him, too.

"Hey, Jackson. Are you okay?"

"Yeah, barely. They tried to kill me and dump me in the mudflats."

"Who?"

"Two guys. They musta followed me from the lounge."

"I was worried about you. The woman, she called herself 'The Broker,' said her associates were coming after you."

"Why didn't you warn me?"

"By the time she told me, you were long gone."

"I got a phone. And you got the number."

"Where did they get you?"

"Tried to corner me in the garage off Edison. But they hadn't met someone like Earle Jackson before. The first one didn't even get to me. I decked him before he saw me. The second one was trickier. He had a gun. Had to jump down to the next level. Got me a bruise the size of Delaware. But I showed him, too. Good thing they got fire extinguishers."

So Jackson got away. Vermeulen couldn't figure out what that meant. It was irrelevant.

"Listen, Jackson, I just got some bad news about my daughter. I'm leaving tonight to see her."

"What? You leaving me alone here? You were the one who got me into this. You can't just leave town. Where you going, anyway?"

"I'm going to Vienna. My daughter is in a coma."

"Sorry, man, but that doesn't change the fact that I'm in hot water because of you."

"What? You better get your facts straight. First you stole money from a dying man, then you tried to blackmail Dr. Rosenbaum, and now you want to blame me?"

"Yeah, but they never woulda found out about me if you hadn't told me to come to that bar. The woman followed you, not me."

"I'm sorry," Vermeulen said, "but I have to go to Vienna. It's my daughter."

"What am I going to do about that woman and her muscle?"

"Lay low. They don't know where you live. As long as you stay away from the doctor and his office, you should be okay. Maybe you could leave town. I also think you should send the money, or what's left of it, to Abasi's family. There's got to be an address in his passport."

"If I send the money back, I got nothing to leave town with."

"I don't know how much you took, but I'm sure you can do both," Vermeulen said.

"Come on, man. I know you want to bust the doctor and that woman working for him. Okay, I made a mistake. I tried to get in on the action. That was wrong. We gotta work together on this."

"Right now, the only thing on my mind is my daughter. I'll be in touch once I know she's okay. Until then, remember, do the right thing."

Vermeulen ended the call.

* * *

GODDAMN IT, VERMEULEN HUNG UP ON him. Jackson was angry. Leaving town just when the heat had been turned up. Sure, the man had sounded genuine about his daughter and the accident. So that was probably true. Still, they could've made a plan or something.

All these years, nobody had ever been after him. Not that he was scared. Hell, he'd shown those clowns in the parking garage. But the idea that somebody wanted him dead, wanted to throw his body into the mudflats, spooked him. He'd always thought that only happened to the brothers who didn't plan right.

What had gone wrong?

Jackson mulled over each step he'd taken since Abasi died in his arms. *Nah.* He'd been smart. He'd been cautious. Maybe he shouldn't have called Vermeulen. But he needed to know how he fit into the picture. And the meeting? He should have cased the lounge for a while. Maybe he'd have recognized the blonde woman. Yeah, he should've done that. But otherwise, he'd been doing okay.

All that thinking brought him back to Vermeulen. It was his fault. He'd drawn that woman to them. And now he was skipping town.

Well, as Satchel Paige said, don't look back, somebody might be gaining on you. He needed a new plan, one that kept his ass out of trouble. Those two hoods were going to be after him. He'd played them, and they were guaranteed to be pissed off. Even without the Broker, they'd be wanting payback. For all he knew, they were pounding the pavement calling in whatever chits they had to find out who the black dude was that made them look like pussies. Good thing Vermeulen had picked that fancy bar to meet. Nobody there had ever laid eyes on him. So he was clear there.

Where he wasn't clear was the burner phone he'd used to call the doctor. Jackson wasn't up on the technology, but he figured that, somehow, that phone could be traced back to the bodega where he bought it. Did that place have a camera? He didn't remember, but he wouldn't be surprised. These days, especially the little places had those systems, what with all the hold-ups going down. So, worst case, they'd have him on video buying the phone.

Even that didn't amount to much. All they'd have was a picture of a black man wearing run-of-the-mill clothes. It'd be a vague picture of his face. Just like Abasi's passport picture. It could be any one of a hundred thousand black men in Newark.

He poured a shot of cognac into a water glass. This time, he sipped. Tried to appreciate the liquor.

Thinking of Abasi's passport brought up a whole different train of thought. He could skip town for a while. He could probably pass for Abasi and go to Kenya. Nobody'd even know he'd gone abroad. He pulled the passport from his pocket and paged through the booklet. The last page listed a residence. Kibera, Nairobi. No number or anything. Maybe they didn't have house numbers in Kenya.

The e-ticket receipt showed that Abasi was scheduled to fly back to Kenya in a day. *Do the right thing.* Man, that line had really got under his skin. He could give some of the money to Abasi's family.

Jackson stopped himself. Was he going soft in the head? He wasn't gonna run away. He was gonna stay right here in Newark and bust that doctor. The Broker and her hoods probably were thinking he'd be hiding. They'd be wrong. Attack was the best defense.

CHAPTER TWENTY-FOUR

———◆———

CAMILLE DELANO SIPPED THE VODKA IN her usual slow fashion. It didn't produce the desired effect. The liquor burned her throat instead of warming her. Drinking booze wasn't a good idea when you were upset. And she was upset.

First, her men managed to lose that black guy and get beaten up in the process. And then Vermeulen disappeared without a trace. The watcher posted outside his apartment reported him getting into a cab. He followed him to JFK and lost him there. Bad news all around.

She knew Jackson would disappear. Newark was a large city. If he didn't want to be found, he wouldn't be. Her crew, made up of Bulgarian and Romanian freelancers who'd come over after the collapse of the Soviet Union, harbored that casual racism still common in Eastern Europe. Which made them the worst possible candidates for tapping into Newark's black criminal networks. She had the number from the phone he used to call the doctor. It was a long shot. If Jackson had any sense at all, it'd be a burner with no personal information attached to the number. For what it was worth, she'd asked one of her crew who had a relative at one of the cellphone carriers to check into it. The good news was that Jackson was a crook. He wasn't going to the police.

Vermeulen was an entirely different story. She took his card, which the doctor had given her, from her purse. United Nations Office of Internal Oversight Services. What an odd name. It had an Orwellian ring to it.

The UN connection had puzzled her. Yes, her business involved smuggling foreigners into the U.S., and human trafficking was high on the UN's agenda. Every year, some agency or other published a report on it, everybody wrung their hands, and then they went back to writing the next report to be published a year later. What they didn't do was investigate.

She pushed the vodka aside and signaled the waiter.

"I'd like a coffee, please. And a slice of chocolate cake."

That's why it didn't make sense that some UN investigator would show up at Rosenbaum's door. But then, Vermeulen as much as told her that the visa scam was the tip-off. Immigration officers must have noticed that some of the people using the letters didn't look like UN conference attendees. It was one of the downsides of recruiting only the poorest. But they were the ones who were most easily tempted by the money.

It also didn't help that the good doctor had lost it completely when Vermeulen showed up at his door. It only made the man more suspicious.

The waiter brought the coffee and the cake. She poured cream into the cup, added sugar, and stirred. The coffee was nice and hot. It did what the vodka didn't do. She picked up the fork and carved a piece of cake. But then she put the fork down again. Instead, she took her phone from her purse and dialed the number on the card. Maybe his office would tell her where Vermeulen had disappeared to.

A female voice answered, "Good afternoon. Office of Internal Oversight Services."

"Good afternoon. Mr. Vermeulen, please," the Broker said.

"I'm afraid he's not available at the moment."

"Hmm, that's too bad. Is there a number where I could reach him? He asked me to call back with some information he was looking for."

"Uh, I'm sorry, he didn't leave one."

"He said it was important. Maybe you have his cell number?"

"I'm sorry, I can't give that out."

"Do you know when he'll be back?"

"It's hard to say. There's been an accident in his family. He had to go to Vienna on short notice."

"Oh. I'm so sorry to hear this. I'll try again later."

She took another sip of coffee and ate a forkful of cake. It wasn't as good as what she'd had in Europe. Too sweet and not chocolaty enough.

It had to be Vienna, Austria. He wouldn't go to JFK to fly to Vienna, Virginia—or any of the other Viennas in the U.S.

She dialed another number, this one much longer. She knew it by heart. A man answered after the second ring.

"Yes?"

"I want to return an item. It doesn't fit."

"What's the order number?"

"HTL83974002."

"One moment, please, while I connect you."

She listened to several clicks. Her call was being routed through a series of exchanges in at least three countries. That made tracing it impossible. Muzak played for several seconds. Another click, then another male voice came on the line.

"Talk to me."

She knew this voice well.

"I need international assistance. One of my prospects has gone to Vienna, Austria."

"Particulars?"

"Vermeulen, Valentin, male. Try hospitals. A relative has had an accident."

"Desired outcome?"

The Broker hesitated. It would be best to eliminate Vermeulen. Even better if that happened outside the country. But she wasn't sure how much he'd shared with his colleagues. Killing him only made sense if he'd kept things to himself. Otherwise those who also knew would be warned by his death.

"Surveillance for now," she said. "Find out who he talks to."

"Covert?"

"No. Let him know someone is watching. It'll force his hand."

"Electronic means, too?"

"If you can."

"Consider it done."

The Broker put her phone back into her purse and concentrated on the cake. It wasn't very good. In Vienna, there'd be Sachertorte. That alone was reason enough to go to Vienna herself. But such a trip would require approval from the higher-ups. The operation was strictly compartmentalized. Besides, she didn't need extra attention at the moment. She had a mess to clean up. Afterward, there could be a trip. If it was still necessary.

She sipped her coffee. It was getting cold. She put the cup down and got up, leaving half the cake. It just wasn't worth the calories. Her phone rang. She answered.

"We have a picture of Jackson. Video footage from a bodega where he bought his phone."

"Good work. Find him. Highest priority," she said.

Once Jackson was dispatched, she'd go to Vienna.

CHAPTER TWENTY-FIVE

———— ◆ ————

THE MORNING SKY OVER VIENNA WAS leaden. The few pink fringes in the east didn't stand a chance against the gunmetal clouds racing across the sky from the west. The Airbus A330 yawed in the crosswinds, and a sudden drop jammed the meager breakfast offered to Vermeulen by the cabin staff back into his throat. Since his booking had been last-minute, he ended up wedged into Seat 41D between a hyperactive toddler and an overweight priest, complete with black suit and clerical collar. The flight took almost nine hours. The movies were mediocre and the jumpy boy kept him from sleeping most of the flight. His iPod and the Clash were his salvation.

Waiting in line for the passport control, he thought about how Odinga must have felt, standing in a similar line at JFK. Vermeulen had never fully appreciated the privilege of being able to go anywhere in the world. With his Belgian passport and his UN authorizations, there was no place he couldn't visit and only a few that required him to obtain a visa beforehand. How easy it was to forget what privilege felt like. The thought of the Odingas of the world queuing at ports of entry, always in fear, always just a suspicious glance away from arrest and deportation, filled him with anger. It was profoundly unjust. But then he remembered the deep-seated suspicion against foreigners he'd seen in West and Central Africa, mostly aimed at fellow Africans, and he wondered if his musings were just another manifestation of his privilege.

"*Wie lange bleiben Sie in Österreich?*" the officer asked.

German wasn't Vermeulen's forte, so he replied in English. "A week, maybe two, I don't know. My daughter was in a skiing accident and is in a coma."

"I'm sorry to hear of her misfortune. As a Belgian national you may stay here for ninety days. If you need to stay longer, you can apply for a residence permit. It's not a problem."

Vermeulen took his passport and walked through the customs area toward a large sliding-glass door. Those ahead of him activated the door, and he could see throngs of people waiting. Marieke would be among them.

His legs slowed as he neared the sliding door. It wasn't a conscious action. To the contrary, he was eager to get out into fresh air after spending the last nine hours breathing recirculated oxygen. But another part of his body remembered the pain from nine years ago and was reluctant to encounter it again. He stopped in the middle of the walkway and wondered if his body was wiser than his mind. Another passenger bumped into him and propelled him toward the door. The man apologized and rushed past. Vermeulen smiled. When your body and your mind are at odds, a push from a stranger could be the best way forward.

MARIEKE WAS WAITING FOR HIM. HE recognized her despite the fact that she'd changed her hair. The long 1970s mane was gone, replaced by a short bob. Her face was more drawn, her cheekbones more pronounced, her lips tighter. A profound sadness radiated from her pale blue eyes. Was it Gaby's accident? Or was her life so difficult? He knew that she worked in a social service agency, a job that could wear out even the most contented person.

She saw him, and her smile wiped the sadness from her face. It was the smile he'd fallen in love with, the smile that used to speed up his heartbeat and make him behave like an idiot. Now it just reminded him of the day nine years ago when he'd packed his bag and left for New York, of the emptiness inside he'd felt for so long. How could they have screwed things up so badly?

She stepped forward and reached out to give him a hug. Dropping his bag, he put his arms around her. Unsure of what to do, he held her lightly, the kind of embrace one reserves for distant relatives. But Marieke pulled him close and he let go of all the stupid hang-ups that clogged his mind. They hugged like a couple who hadn't seen each other in nine years, desperate to squeeze away the wall between them. No words were necessary.

"How is Gaby?" he said after an eternity.

"She's stable. Her body is functioning well. It's just her brain that hasn't recovered from the impact."

"Let's go and see her."

As he said these words, he glanced over her shoulder and saw a face that shouldn't have been there, that couldn't have been there. A face that should've been far away. Somewhere in Africa. It had to be someone else. But it wasn't. The cinnamon skin, the titanium glasses, the thin braids held together by a rubber band—there couldn't be another woman like her. His arms dropped to his sides. He looked at Marieke and then back at the familiar face. There was no doubt. It was Tessa Bishonga.

Instant panic made his forehead damp. He pushed away an errant lock of hair. Did Marieke know of Tessa? His daughter did; he'd introduced them a year ago when he was recovering from an injury he'd suffered at his assignment in Darfur. Tessa, a Zambian freelance journalist, was there covering the conflict. They'd become lovers, and had maintained a long-distance relationship ever since. They'd last been together three months ago when Tessa came to Manhattan on an assignment for Al Jazeera.

He shook his head. Why was he getting hot under the collar? He hadn't done anything wrong. He opened his mouth to launch into an explanation, but Marieke put her index finger on his mouth.

"No need to explain. I met Tessa yesterday. She showed up at the hospital. She told me she knew Gaby. I told her what happened and we started talking. It's okay."

As quickly as his body had tensed, it relaxed again. The air suddenly felt cool on his forehead. He shivered involuntarily.

Tessa planted a kiss on his cheek. "Sorry that the circumstances are so sad, but I'm glad to see you," she said.

"And I you." He kissed her back.

"Let's go. We've got a taxi waiting," Marieke said.

They squeezed into the back of the Mercedes, Vermeulen sitting between his ex-wife and his on-again-off-again lover. The cab wound its way past the glass fronts of the airport. The tower, which stood apart from the departure/arrival structure, looked like a twisted piece of white licorice, keeping watch over a parking lot. The foliage was surprisingly green for the time of year. Did spring come earlier in Austria? Maybe the Danube mellowed the climate.

The cab merged onto an expressway that led through a surprisingly rural area. Freshly plowed fields extended on both sides of the road. The bucolic idyll didn't last long. A huge refinery took its place, and soon the road wove through the suburbs of Vienna. The expressway ended near a river, and the cab took the road along the southern bank.

"Is that the Danube?" Vermeulen said.

"No. It's the Danube Canal. The river is larger and farther north," Tessa said.

They passed another industrial area and a large cloverleaf interchange. Then the city of Vienna swallowed them. Five- and six-story buildings lined the motorway, many with red tile roofs. Most seemed to be residential. The occasional office structure, often modern with glass façades, interrupted the nineteenth-century feel of the city. They crossed the canal, passed a large light rail station, and came to a stop in front of a concrete structure the size of a city block.

"That's the hospital," Marieke said. "They specialize in accidents and they have a famous trauma unit."

"That's great. Gaby is lucky to be here. No, what I mean is that I'm glad they know what they're doing."

Marieke just looked at him and shook her head.

Vermeulen gazed up at the façade. It was modern and rational, promising competent care. He hoped that the promise held true when it came to his girl.

CHAPTER TWENTY-SIX

———◆———

G ABY'S FACE WAS PALE. SHE LAY in the hospital bed, motionless. Someone had raised the top section so that her upper body was elevated. An LCD screen attached to a stand beeped monotonously. Several lines in white, green, and red told the story of her condition. The chopped-off sine curve presumably represented her heartbeat; the rest was a mystery to Vermeulen. A drip bag containing a clear liquid was attached to her arm. Her chest rose slightly with each breath. Seeing her like that, Vermeulen slumped. His stomach turned into an empty hole, filled with fear. Tears ran down his face. He bent down and kissed her cheek, which felt soft and warm.

"There was nothing she could have done," Marieke said. "Some idiot cut her off and she hit a tree. The ski patrol caught the guy and the police are talking to him."

That news made him stand up again. Anger replaced fear.

"Are they going to lock him up?"

"I don't think so."

"What? Isn't he liable? If she dies, that's manslaughter. "

"Calm down. She isn't dying. The prognosis is that she'll wake up soon. The coma is just the body's way of shutting down all unnecessary systems to let the brain heal. Her insurance will take care of it."

"Who is he? He should come here and see what he did."

Marieke sighed. "I don't know his name, and I don't want him here. What good will it do? Let's focus on Gaby."

He swallowed hard. She was right, of course. And he knew better than to fly into a rage. He wiped the tears from his eyes.

"Sorry, it's just so sad to see her lying there. I can't bear the thought of her not waking up."

"Do you think I could? But that's not the prognosis. She will wake up. Let's focus on that."

He swallowed again. They assumed their old roles too easily. Only an hour after meeting again, they were at each other like in the old days.

"Listen, Marieke, you've been here for days. I'm happy to take over so you can take a break. Go out, get a change of clothes."

"I don't have any place to go. I just camped out here on the cot."

"You can use my room," Tessa said. "I'm staying at the Hotel Amadeus. There's an easy subway connection. Take the U6 to Spittelau, then change to the U4 to Friedensbrücke. I'll write down the directions."

Tessa took a piece of paper from her notebook and drew a map. She handed the sheet to Marieke with her key.

"Rest a little, take a bath, make yourself at home. You have our numbers?"

"Yes, thanks so much. This is very nice."

Tessa gave her a radiant smile.

Marieke took her bag. "It'll be just a little while. I'll be back after lunch," she said.

"Take your time," Tessa said.

"I'll call you if anything changes," Vermeulen said.

How did you end up here with Gaby and my ex?" Vermeulen said.

"Gaby and I have stayed in touch since last April. We text each other, so I knew she was going on a skiing vacation."

"You're in touch with my daughter?"

"Sure, why not? We enjoyed each other's company in Düsseldorf."

"How come I don't know about this?"

The idea of his lover and his daughter texting felt weird. He didn't know why.

"Probably because you didn't ask. Besides, why does it matter?"

"I don't know. It just seems odd."

"Why?"

"I don't know. Not sure I like you talking about me."

"Give me a break, Valentin. Don't you think we have other things to talk about? You're not that important."

The verbal jab hit home. He winced.

"Sorry, I didn't mean it that way," she said. "I don't talk about our relationship, or what passes for one."

Another jab.

"What do you mean?"

"We don't see each other very much anymore."

"I know. Between your work and mine, there's little time."

He didn't like the direction the conversation was taking. She had asked him to visit more often, but he never could get away. Or so he thought.

"We could make time. There are plenty of occasions when we're close enough that a quick flight wouldn't be out of the question."

"Hmm."

"Is that all? Hmm?"

"What do you want me to say?"

Tessa looked at him, fixing her eyes on his. He looked back. They held each other's gaze for a minute.

Tessa relaxed. "I'm sorry. I do love you, and I wish we could be together more. That's all. Seeing each other twice in a year isn't enough for me."

Vermeulen couldn't quite sort out if she blamed him or was just stating a fact. He decided to opt for the latter. He pulled her close and held her without saying anything. It turned out to be the right choice.

"Anyway," she said, "I'm working on a piece about organized crime, and the UN Office on Drugs and Crime is headquartered here. It took me a while to organize an interview with the director. When I finally got an appointment, I told Gaby. She was coming to ski in Semmering, an hour south of here. When I got in, I called at her guesthouse. Imagine my shock when they told me she'd been brought to the Trauma Center in Vienna. I came here and ran into Marieke. It was a little odd at first, but we both cared about Gaby, so that worked out okay. Although I did have to contain myself when I found out you were coming."

He shook his head. "I don't know what to think. Is she going to be okay?"

"According to the doctors, yes. Marieke isn't just saying that. They have experience here with skiing accidents. It's just a question of time. I don't know if she knows we're here, but it can't hurt. If we take turns, someone can be here all the time."

He liked that plan. "I need a place to stay."

"You can share my room. Al Jazeera's paying for it."

"If Marieke is going to use it, too, it's not a good idea."

Tessa frowned. "You're probably right. I don't think she's eager to pay for a hotel in Vienna."

"I'll get a room. Later."

They settled in the chairs and looked at Gaby. Nothing had changed. Her face was blank; her eyes remained closed. Not even a flutter of the lids. The only thing moving was her chest rising and sinking with every breath.

"What are you working on at the moment?" Tessa said.

"The strangest case. It started with a man from Kenya who'd gotten a visa with a fake UN letter."

He filled her in on the details of Odinga—the death of Abasi, the sad face of Luca in the York County Prison, the unhinged surgeon Rosenbaum, and Jackson, the small-time crook. He reserved the end for the Broker, whatever her name was.

"It sounds like human trafficking to me. Part of the project I'm working on," she said.

"You think so? I don't understand what the doctor is doing in this. Women are trafficked for sex, and they constitute the majority of victims. Then there are people trafficked for sweatshops. The men I saw could have fit into that category. But they had the address for Rosenbaum in their pockets. I can't think of a sweatshop that requires a surgeon."

She paused to consider, tapping her chin. "I wonder if it's something like the pharma trials they did in poor countries. But there they brought the pills to Africa, not Africans to the pills. And it got a lot of bad publicity, like that case in Nigeria, where the control group was given an inferior medicine against meningitis."

Vermeulen hesitated. "I guess it could be drug testing," he said. "Maybe the bad publicity has brought testing back to the U.S."

"It seems a far costlier approach."

"And why would the contact person be a surgeon rather than an internist? Or a specialist for infectious diseases?"

"You've got a point," Tessa said. "But if isn't drug testing, what else could it be? It's definitely human trafficking. But what for?"

A rustling came from the bed. They stopped. Vermeulen looked at Gaby. Had she moved? Nothing seemed different.

"I'd better pay attention to her," he said. "I'm not here to solve that case."

CHAPTER TWENTY-SEVEN

———◆———

THE FIRST CRACK IN VERMEULEN'S RESOLVE to put the case aside appeared the next morning. Tessa had reserved a room for him at her hotel, where he'd crashed the evening before. He woke up from a sleep that hadn't really refreshed him. The time change and the lack of rest the night before had left him disoriented, his head aching. He luxuriated in the shower, letting the jets massage his neck and shoulders. The soft-boiled egg with croissant and coffee almost restored his balance. He'd forgotten the pleasure of eating a perfectly done five-minute egg.

The pleasant feeling didn't last long. His phone informed him that he had a voicemail. He tapped in his code. It was Jackson. The headache rebounded.

Jackson's voice was tentative. "Yeah, Vermoolen. Earle here." Pause. "You enjoying your trip? Is your daughter okay?" Another pause. "Listen, man, I done some diggin' on the Broker. Since I work in the medical field, I figured I'd talk to one of my doctors. Asked him if he'd ever heard of a woman called the Broker. At first, he's like I don't know what you're talking about. Then I mention Rosenbaum and he goes crazy on me. What d'you know about the Broker and Rosenbaum? Nuthin', I say. Just curious. He looks at me, kinda angry and scared at the same time. You lookin' for other work? I just shrug. He pokes his finger at my chest. You get involved with that woman, he says, you will never get away from her. It's not just her, there're others. They're like the mob, except much worse. He said that twice. So, that's what I found out. Call me."

Vermeulen listened to the message again. Jackson's news wasn't surprising. He'd assumed the Broker was part of an organization. She took the time to meet with him. That told him she wasn't at the head of the organization, but up high enough in the hierarchy to make decisions on her own. There had to be others above her who didn't get their hands dirty by threatening to kill him.

Did she know he'd gone to Vienna? All it would take was a call to his office under some pretext. Jenna, the administrative assistant, would know better than to give out his whereabouts. But there were others. They might blab. He should have thought of that and asked Suarez to keep his trip quiet.

A more disturbing thought struck him. The Broker's organization had to have operatives in Vienna. How else would they've been able to bribe a UN employee here to have these letters signed? That meant they'd be able to get to him here, too.

The next thought made his stomach clench and his breath turn shallow. The terrifying truth was that they were able to get to Gaby, Tessa, and Marieke, too.

The switch to survival mode was instantaneous. This thing had to be contained before it got out of hand. His first call was to Tessa. He filled her in on the new developments.

"Damn," she said. "You're right. What do we do?"

"First, there must always be someone with Gaby. We must keep the door closed and check before letting anyone in."

"Right. I'll go over now. Marieke is there."

"Good, I'll be there soon. I have to make a call first."

"Should I tell Marieke?" Tessa said.

"Better wait. I'll try to explain it when I come. Just find a reason to keep her there until I arrive."

"Good. Who are you going to call?"

"A colleague of mine here in Vienna. He's working this end of the case. But he doesn't know all that's involved."

"I'm on my way. See you soon."

The call to Dufaux took some planning. As far as the man knew, it was a simple case of fraud. A few unauthorized invitation letters. No big deal in the overall scheme of things. Vermeulen wasn't sure if he should tell him everything. It was bound to get back to Suarez, and that meant trouble. He dialed Dufaux's mobile number.

"Dufaux here," a voice answered.

"Pierre. It's Valentin Vermeulen."

"Oh, hello. Any news on this visa thing? I called your office yesterday and left a message."

"I'm in Vienna—"

"You are? How come?"

"My daughter was in a ski accident and is in the hospital here. I took some time off to be with her."

"Oh no. I hope it's not serious."

"It is. She's in a coma."

"I'm so sorry, Valentin. We can never stop worrying about our children, can we?"

"No, we can't. Listen, I'm calling to see if you've made any headway in finding out who secured the fake invitations?"

"Still on the job, eh? Just like what I heard about you. The short answer is 'maybe.' We're going on the assumption that someone slipped those letters into a pile of correspondence that needed Wilmot's signature. There are only two individuals who could have done that. One of them is on extended sick leave, which leaves the other the most likely culprit. Of course, if the signatures were forged, then we are nowhere. But I'm pretty sure they weren't."

"Why?" Vermeulen said.

"The signatures on the letters weren't quite identical. That tells us they were actually signed by the right person."

"How so?"

"Think of the letters you sign. There are always variations, you may be hurried and one of the loops isn't quite as round as if you took your time. When forgers get a signature right, they write them without such variations. That's why I'm pretty certain the letters were slipped in for Wilmot's signature."

"I need to speak to the person who did that."

"We can't do that yet. There are staff rules and regulations. She is entitled to representation. Besides, we won't get anywhere if we come down hard on her."

"Time has run out for such niceties. The forged letters are just a small part of a large conspiracy involving human trafficking. I've confronted one of the principals in the U.S. and she has threatened me. I'm sure the organization has a presence in Vienna as well. Finding out who they are is crucial. I don't want my daughter dragged into this."

There was a long silence on the other end. "The other thing I've heard about you is that I'm better off not listening to you, because it will get me into trouble," Dufaux said.

"Is that true? Well, I don't give a damn. I must speak to the person, and soon."

"Relax, Valentin. I'm just telling you what I've heard. It doesn't mean that I believe it. I'll call you as soon as I've secured a place where we can speak to her."

Chapter Twenty-Eight

Marieke looked confused when Vermeulen finished his explanation.

"Why would someone be after Gaby? Or me?" she said.

"They aren't. They're after me. Possibly. I'm worried that they'll go after Gaby or you to get to me."

"So let me get this straight. You are involved in some investigation in New York and the bad guys are coming after you. And they might come after us, too. Or maybe they won't? What the hell is this? I asked you to come and be with Gaby. I didn't ask you to bring your shit with you. How dare you put Gaby in danger?"

Vermeulen looked out the window. *There she goes again.* It was as if the last nine years had never happened. He was back in Antwerp, desperately looking for Gaby, who'd run away during their acrimonious divorce. Of course, it had all been his fault. Marieke took every opportunity to point that out. He'd forgotten how bad things had been. He swallowed hard and brushed his hair from his forehead. This wasn't the time to take the bait.

"I'm sorry, Marieke. I was in the middle of an investigation when you called. I had just confronted one of the principals of a criminal ring. I dropped everything and came here. This morning I received a voicemail that reminded me that this ring operates internationally. I don't even know if they're aware I'm here. So this is just a precaution. I hope you know that I would never do anything to put Gaby in danger."

Marieke looked at him and shook her head. "How much do you know about this?" she said to Tessa.

Tessa shrugged. She obviously didn't want to be drawn into the fight.

"I'm just as surprised as you are. But I think Valentin's precaution is a good idea."

Marieke took her bag and stormed from the room.

Vermeulen stared out the window. "What does she want?" he said after a moment.

"I can see why she's upset."

"You think I can't? Hell, I'm upset, too. I didn't want any of this. But why does she always have to blame me? As if I personally conspired to put Gaby in danger."

"You know she didn't mean it that way. She's under a lot of stress. We all resort to familiar behavior patterns when we're under stress."

"I guess. Except her familiar pattern is to make me the shit heel. I haven't seen her in nine years and I'm already tired of it."

Tessa pulled him toward her and held him. "She'll come around. Don't let it distract you."

He brushed his lips against hers. "Thanks."

All the ruckus hadn't affected Gaby one bit. Her face had the same blank expression as the day before. Her eyes were closed, her lips slightly open. The only movement was her chest rising and falling with her breath. He took her hand and stroked it gently.

"Come back to us, Gaby. Please," he said.

AT THREE O'CLOCK, VERMEULEN PHONED HIS New York office assistant at home. It was six in the morning on the East Coast. She was an early riser, and he wanted to catch her before she went to the office.

"Hi, Jenna, this is Valentin. Sorry to call so early. Did anyone call and ask for me yesterday?"

Jenna was the public face and voice of the OIOS. For the past decade, she'd screened visitors and callers before they were allowed to meet or talk to whoever they were looking for. She took her responsibilities very seriously.

"Let me think," she said. "There were only two calls for you. One was from Pierre Dufaux in Vienna. I sent that to your voicemail. Bridget took another call for you. A woman having information you requested. She didn't want to leave a voicemail. But Bridget noted it and I put the slip in your mailbox."

Bridget was the other front office person. She was new and being groomed to take Jenna's place after her retirement.

"Did she tell the caller that I went to Vienna?"

"It wouldn't surprise me. I'll have to ask her. Call me back in five minutes."

Bridget hadn't yet learned the stoic façade Jenna deployed to dispatch callers without being unfriendly, but also without revealing anything that wasn't the caller's business. Her chattiness on the phone was a constant thorn in Jenna's side.

"That girl is impossible," Jenna said when he called back. "She thinks she said that you were abroad. She can't remember if she said where. She might have said Vienna. Why do you need to know?"

"It's a long story. From now on, please keep my location under wraps."

"I'll tell her. How's your daughter? Any improvement?"

"Not yet. But they expect her to wake up soon. All we can do is wait."

"I hope you won't have to wait long."

"Thanks."

He ended the call still not knowing if he had to worry about the Broker or not. There was no other option but to assume that some gangsters would show up sooner rather than later. Which made interviewing whoever had obtained the signatures all the more urgent. But Dufaux was taking his time.

"Anything new?" Tessa asked, looking up from her book.

"No. A woman called my office. The assistant doesn't remember if she told her where I was. So nothing has changed. We still need to be alert. And I need to go for a smoke, okay?"

"Sure."

"Don't let anybody in."

She grimaced.

He followed a long corridor to an interior courtyard. Despite the cheery off-white paint and the red and green highlights, the ambiance couldn't change the fact that behind these doors lay sick people who'd much rather be well and elsewhere.

A male nurse walked past him, pushing a small cart with a box. As soon as they passed each other, Vermeulen slowed and looked back. Was that a real nurse? Or someone pretending to be one? Or was he being paranoid?

The nurse entered a room. Vermeulen took a deep breath and continued. Once outside, he lit his Gitane and inhaled deeply. He didn't know how he'd cope with stress if he didn't have a cigarette. The courtyard was a surprisingly green oasis in the middle of this concrete structure. A large tree that almost covered the sky provided pleasant shade for the benches along an oval path that enclosed a grassy area. A few patients ambled along, one of them pulling along a wheeled IV pole holding a sac of clear liquid.

Vermeulen had just taken a seat on a bench when his phone vibrated. It was a text from Tessa: *Come quick!*

CHAPTER TWENTY-NINE

———— ◆ ————

VERMEULEN RAN THROUGH THE CORRIDORS. HE bumped into visitors, nurses, staff without taking time to apologize. His mind was busy laying blame. He shouldn't have left for a smoke. He should've known they were on his heels. He shouldn't have come in the first place and put Gaby at risk. He shouldn't have ….

A looming collision with a doctor jerked him out of the stream of incriminations. The doctor stepped to one side and shouted at him in German. Something about not running and not putting the patients in danger. Vermeulen didn't have time to respond. He kept running. The maze of hallways was confusing. At one intersection he hesitated before recognizing the colorful stickers someone had plastered on a door that probably led to some kid with a broken arm. He turned and hurried onward.

After the next turn, he saw Gaby's room near the end of the corridor. Two nurses pushed carts with plastic cups and medications. A nurse left a room, noting something on a clipboard. A man in a blue and green tracksuit walked toward him. He was in his forties, had a pronounced widow's peak and a five o'clock shadow. He seemed in no particular hurry. As Vermeulen ran past him, the man nodded to Vermeulen with the sort of expression that said, *I hate hospitals, don't you?* Vermeulen didn't have time to nod back.

From the distance, Vermeulen could tell that the door to Gaby's room stood open. Tessa was supposed to have closed it. He searched his pockets for a suitable weapon. The key to his apartment in Manhattan was the only useful object. Another key would have been great, but the hotel used keycards. He wedged the blade between his index and middle fingers and closed his fist around the bow. Just in case. Worse than brass knuckles, but better than nothing.

The room was quiet. Through the door, he could see Gaby, eyes closed, the monitor beeping softly.

"Tessa?" he said.

No answer.

"Tessa?" Louder.

Still no answer.

He inched into the room, holding the fist with the key ready to strike at a moment's notice. The room was empty. He looked again. No Tessa. He opened the closet. Empty. He went into the bathroom. Nobody. Where was Tessa? She shouldn't have left Gaby alone.

Hasty steps came from the corridor. He stuck his head out. Tessa came jogging toward him.

"What happened?" he said.

"Something strange." She stopped at the door and caught her breath. "I don't know what to make of it."

"Where did you go? Gaby isn't supposed to be alone."

Tessa pulled him inside the room and closed the door. "First, I thought I heard a knock on the door. Nothing unusual. The orderlies do that before they come into a room. But then nobody entered. There was a second knock. I went to the door and looked through the little window and saw what looked like an orderly. When I opened the door, he said that I should come to the nurses' station. There was a phone call for me. He knew my name. I asked who was calling, and I think he said it was my office. It didn't make any sense. My office has my mobile number. But my German isn't very good, so I wasn't sure I understood him. He kept telling me to come."

"And you went?"

"I texted you and waited. But he became agitated, saying it was urgent. I figured I'd take the call, tell them to call my mobile, and come back. We left and went to the end of the hallway."

"Which end?"

"This one." Tessa pointed in the opposite direction than the one he'd come from.

"What did he look like? Did he wear a blue and green tracksuit?" Vermeulen said.

"No, why? He wore what orderlies wear, that weird light-green smock and pants. He also wore one of those funny caps."

"So you followed him?"

"Yes. I know I was supposed to stay here, but it could have been important. When we turned the corner, he started walking faster. I had to hurry to keep up. The nurses' station is in the middle of that corridor. The guy just pointed to it and kept going. I stopped one of the nurses and asked where the phone was. She told me that it wasn't for private calls. I told her that an orderly had just fetched me because there was a call for me. But she just looked at me as if I were loony. I asked if she'd sent an orderly to get someone from Room 412. She shook her head and went back to work. I came back as fast as I could."

Vermeulen was breathing hard. "I saw a man in a tracksuit in the hallway. He didn't look in a hurry, more like a visitor who was glad to get out of the hospital. You didn't see him?"

"No. There was nobody else in the hallway."

He looked at Gaby. She lay there, motionless, like before, her chest moving in the rhythm of her breathing. Nothing had changed.

"This is very odd," he said.

The room looked unchanged, too. The vase with flowers, the chairs, nothing had been moved. He blinked. "A vase with flowers?

"These flowers weren't here before, were they?"

Tessa looked at them, then at him.

"No, they weren't."

He checked Gaby one more time. That's when he noticed that her left hand lay on her belly, not beside her, where it had been when he left. Had she moved it? His heart leaped. She moved her arm. She was coming out of the coma. Then he saw the piece of paper under the hand.

It was an embossed note card, the kind one would enclose in an envelope with a Thank You note. Except this card didn't have any expressions of gratitude written on it. Just one sentence: "*We know where you are.*"

CHAPTER THIRTY

———◆———

J ACKSON SAW THE TWO MEN NEAR Hawthorne Liquors. They weren't going
anywhere, just standing there as if waiting for the bus. His mind switched
to instant alert, because they were white. White people didn't hang out on
Hawthorne Street. Especially not in the morning. The alert turned into a
flashing red light when he recognized the thugs from the garage, Gergi and
Andrej. He turned back into his side street and ducked behind a ramshackle
storefront belonging to a clothing store that had been out of business for as
long as he'd lived in the neighborhood.

Ever since Dr. Patel told him how dangerous the Broker was, Jackson had
gotten a lot less eager to bust Rosenbaum. He'd run out of ideas. No matter
how he turned it, he'd have to contact Rosenbaum again. The moment he did
that, the Broker would be involved. That was bad news. Maybe there was a
way to make a deal with the doctor to frame the Broker. Or make a deal with
the Broker to frame the doctor. None of it looked promising, so he'd decided
to just lay low and let the whole thing blow over.

Until he saw Gergi and Andrej standing by the liquor store. They must've
traced the phone to him. But that still didn't explain how the two found him.
Could they have followed him from the Edison parking garage? He thought
he'd hit them good, but maybe not. Beating people wasn't his strong suit. He
preferred persuasion.

Two against one were odds he didn't like. He could maybe take one of
them, but not both. Especially since they had guns. He could follow them,
see where they led him. Find out where the Broker hid out, then get the cops
involved. Nah. That didn't work either. The cops'd be asking questions about

how he knew anything about them. Before long, they'd be asking about the twenty-five hundred dollars.

The longer he carried that cash in his pocket, the more he wished he hadn't taken it. Actually, he wished he hadn't called Rosenbaum. He'd been greedy. If he'd just taken the cash, he'd be sitting pretty now. Just like his grandma used to say, *Greed destroys everything*. That made him remember Vermeulen's advice. *Do the right thing*. Easy for Vermeulen to say. He didn't have to hustle every day to make a living. Still, that phrase kept niggling him. Abasi coming all the way over here to get money for his family. Man, they were waiting over there in Kenya. Waiting for the guy to come back with the cash. They'd be waiting a long time.

He took his phone and called the liquor store.

"Yeah, Maurice, this is Earle. Listen, there's two white guys standing outside your store. They're bad dudes who are after me. Do me a favor and call me when they leave, okay?"

"Which white guys?"

"The ones outside your store."

"There's no one outside my store, white, black, or purple."

"You sure? Check again."

"I got eyes, don't I?"

Jackson ended the call and went back to the corner. He peered around the edge of the house there and saw that Maurice was right. The two men were gone. About to step onto Hawthorne, he heard steps behind him, turned, and saw Gergi and Andrej running toward him. Andrej couldn't keep up because he was still limping from the hit against his knee. But Gergi was closing in, and he looked pissed off.

Jackson sprinted across Hawthorne to the liquor store. He yanked the door open and stormed into the store. Maurice looked up, surprised.

"Hey, Jackson. Still lookin' for those dudes?"

"Nah, they're right behind me. You still got that shotgun behind the counter?"

Maurice raised his eyebrows, but nodded.

"Do me a favor. Keep these guys pinned down here for fifteen minutes. I'll run out the back and call the police."

"Man, it's way too early for that kind of grief."

"Come on, Maurice. I gotta get away from them."

"Okay, just this once. I ain't savin' your ass again."

Jackson ran into the back room just as the buzzer from the front door sounded.

"Freeze, suckers!" he heard Maurice say. That man loved the movies.

Jackson opened the rear door while dialing 911.

"Yeah, there's an armed robbery going on at Hawthorne Liquors." He hung up before they could ask more questions. By the time he reached his room, he could hear the sirens approaching.

This whole thing was out of control. It had to stop. And the only way to stop it was to leave town. He stuffed some clean clothes into a bag, added the e-ticket receipt, Abasi's passport, his own passport, and ran.

Jackson had never been to JFK. The only time he'd ever been on an airplane was a trip to the Virgin Islands with doctors Patel and Mulberry. It was the reason he even had a passport. They'd departed from Newark. JFK was in an entirely different league. Taking the AirTrain from the Jamaica E train station, he saw that the terminals all looked different. Terminal 8 was a glass structure that jutted out at odd angles. Inside, it had a light, airy feel. White steel beams spanned across an impossible distance. After entering the terminal, he just stood and gaped for a moment.

It was still too early for Abasi's flight. During the train ride to midtown and the subway ride to Jamaica Station, he had to remind himself that his name was now Okeyo Abasi. He didn't think he'd have any problems at JFK. He was leaving the U.S. Leaving was always easier than arriving. Getting into Kenya was another story. He'd worry about that when the time came.

He meandered past the long row of airline counters. The mural of the Manhattan silhouette was pretty cool. People hurried around him, trying to make a flight. The PA system provided a regular stream of announcements. He drank some coffee but didn't buy any food. There'd better be some on the plane. Since he'd decided to go to Kenya, he felt a strange urge to preserve as much of the money as he could.

When the Qatar counter opened for the check-in of Flight 702 to Doha, he waited for the first ten or so passengers to be served before he joined the line. He felt the blood coursing through his temples, could hear his heartbeat in his ears. Why was he so nervous? Abasi's picture wasn't very clear. He could easily pass for him. He mumbled "Good afternoon" before giving the woman in the maroon outfit the e-ticket receipt and Abasi's passport.

"Do you have any luggage, Mr. Abasi?"

He shook his head. The woman raised her eyebrows.

"The bags were stolen," he said.

"I'm terribly sorry. I hope you didn't lose anything valuable."

He shook his head. He didn't know what Kenyans sounded like, so he didn't want to speak too much.

The woman nodded.

"I have you checked in to Doha and then onward to Nairobi. Here are your boarding passes. Have a pleasant flight."

"Thank you."

He made his way through security, found his gate, and settled down to wait. It was all too crazy. Running from the Broker all the way to Kenya. Was that the smart thing to do? He could go south. Visit his auntie in Atlanta who he hadn't seen in ages. Wait for things to settle down. The money would last him a while. But the idea of traveling to Kenya trumped those thoughts. There was a tingle of anticipation in his belly. He'd gotten this far. No reason not to go all the way.

An hour into the wait, he dialed Vermeulen again. No answer. He left another message, telling the man that he was going to Kenya. Why hadn't he called back after the first message? Sure, his daughter was having a bad time, but still, he could've called. Just to say thanks for the information on the Broker. But Vermeulen was one stuck-up guy.

Two hours later, Earle Jackson took his seat in the Airbus A340.

CHAPTER THIRTY-ONE

———◆———

FOR THE SECOND TIME THAT DAY, Vermeulen raced along the hospital corridor, slowing only to inspect alcoves and sitting areas where the man in the tracksuit might have taken cover. Startled faces looked back at him. He stopped at a different nurses' station, but nobody there could remember a middle-aged man in a tracksuit. The elevator took forever on its way down. In the lobby, he ran to the reception desk.

"Did you see a man in a blue and green tracksuit come in or go out?"

The first woman frowned, then shook her head. "Sorry, sir. I don't remember anyone like that."

Her colleague had a better memory. "A tracksuit with green stripes down the arms?"

Vermeulen nodded.

"Yes, he came and asked for a patient. He carried a bouquet of flowers. They were very nice."

"Did you see him leave just now?" he said.

"No, sorry, it's pretty busy here."

"Did he give a name when he asked for the patient?"

"Yes, he said it was Vermöhlen or something like that."

Vermeulen nodded his thanks and scanned the lobby. The receptionist was right—it was a busy place, people coming and going. He ran outside.

There was a fair amount of traffic outside the hospital. Pedestrians on the sidewalk all seemed dressed in grays and browns. No blue and green tracksuit anywhere. Vermeulen sprinted across the street. A silver Fiat honked at him, its driver wagging her index finger. He jumped on the edge of a large concrete planter with a bush. From that perch, he saw a flash of blue just near the next intersection to the left.

Crossing the street again earned him more honks. Apparently, the Viennese didn't like jaywalkers. He raced to the intersection. Halfway there, he collided with a man in a brown coat.

"*Passen Sie doch auf!*" he said, shaking his head.

Vermeulen shouted "Sorry" over his shoulder and continued. The cross street was bounded by the hospital on one side and a light rail track on the other. Between the track and the street stood a multi-story parking garage partially hidden behind trees. Had the man parked there? He wouldn't have come alone. Which meant there'd be a car waiting for him close by. Vermeulen ran along the side of the hospital. The sidewalk widened halfway down the block to accommodate a dozen trees, evenly spaced in cast-iron grates.

At the first tree, he caught a second glimpse of something blue. A gray Audi was parked in a long row of cars down the street. The man in the tracksuit was just getting into the passenger side. The car backed out leisurely and drove toward him. Vermeulen ran into the street. The car sped up. He jumped into its path. The car accelerated. Vermeulen stared at the two men through the windshield. They smiled. But they didn't slow down. At the last moment, he jumped out of the way. The passenger side mirror hit his right forearm. The car turned right at the intersection and was gone. But not before Vermeulen got a good look at the license plate. He swallowed his anger. He rubbed his arm. It was bruised, but nothing was broken.

BACK IN THE HOSPITAL ROOM, TESSA eyed him with raised eyebrows and shook her head. He caught himself just before letting out a stream of invective.

"He got away," was all he said.

"I see."

"I did get the license plate."

"Good."

"It started with white letters WD followed by a dash and the numbers 99530."

"Hmm."

"Why so monosyllabic?"

"Because we don't need you playing the lone avenger. Gaby is in danger. If this organization is as far reaching as you said, chasing after one of its gofers and leaving your daughter exposed is not smart."

"I thought I'd catch him and find out who sent him."

She shook her head in that pitying manner that drove him up the wall.

"What do you want me to do?" he said, ready to let her have it.

"Figure out where to move Gaby so that these people can't find her. She's the only one who can't look out for herself."

He took a deep breath and let it out slowly. She was right, of course. And fighting made no sense.

"Okay, I'll talk to someone. There's got to be a private clinic that protects the identity of their patients."

At the nurses' station, he asked for the doctor.

"The doctor will come in three hours," the nurse said in accented English.

"I need to speak to her now. It is urgent."

The nurse studied a monitor for a moment.

"I see nothing changed in Room 412," she said. "Why is it urgent?"

Vermeulen pulled out his UN ID. "I can discuss this only with the doctor. But it is an emergency. Could you please call the doctor?"

The nurse shrugged, picked up the telephone receiver, dialed a short number, and said something in German. Her tone was exasperated.

Ten minutes later, the doctor showed up. She was petite, about as tall as Tessa, who was a head shorter than Vermeulen. But Tessa had a well-trained body that signaled its strength through even the most stylish clothes. The doctor seemed fragile in her pink and blue smock.

"I'm Dr. Mueller," she said. Her voice belied her stature. This was a woman in charge. "What's the emergency that couldn't wait a couple of hours and required waving around diplomatic IDs?"

"Can we speak in private?" Vermeulen said.

She pointed to a door. Vermeulen opened it. It was a supply closet barely large enough to accommodate them both. She closed the door behind her.

"Here's the issue. I'm an investigator for the UN in New York. I was involved in a dangerous investigation there when I found out that my daughter had an accident and was in a coma. Room 412."

The woman's arms were folded defensively across her chest. "I know who you're talking about."

"I left New York in a hurry. Somehow, the people I confronted there found out I came here. They left a threatening note with my daughter."

He pulled the note from his jacket. The doctor examined it and nodded.

"Is there a private clinic where Gaby could disappear for a while until this blows over?" he said.

"Of course. But this is the best place for your daughter. We specialize in head trauma. A private clinic doesn't have the resources we have here."

"I'm aware of that, but the circumstances make her stay here too dangerous. At the moment, it seems we are waiting for her to come out of her coma. I'm sure she can do that elsewhere."

"Oh, so you are a medical expert, too." She raised her eyebrows. "Let me tell you, the crucial part is when she comes out of the coma. Only then can we really determine what damage has occurred and what the best course of therapy is."

Vermeulen raised his hands in apology.

"I'm sorry ... that was presumptuous of me. Of course, you know what is best. But she's not safe here. The best care in the world won't do any good if the gangsters get to her."

"You have a point. There are two suitable institutions. I'll make some calls."

"Thank you, Doctor. I know this is uncommon. I appreciate your help."

"This is only a temporary fix. You'd better sort out what you are involved in. Your daughter can't stay in hiding forever."

"I know."

Dr. Mueller turned and left. Vermeulen went back to Gaby's room.

"It's a UN car," Tessa said when he came back.

"What?"

"The license plate you got. It's a UN car. The WD stands for *Wien Diplomatisches Korps* and the first two digits, 99, are reserved for UN cars. Talk to Dufaux; he should be able to tell you who the car's driver was."

BY EIGHT THAT EVENING, GABY HAD been moved to the *Privatklinik Alsergrund*. Vermeulen was surprised by the quiet efficiency. Two orderlies and a nurse wearing a starched white outfit appeared. They rolled Gaby's bed to an elevator in the back. At the emergency take-in, the two orderlies shifted Gaby to a gurney. An unmarked white van waited at the ambulance ramp. Inside, the van was equipped with a plethora of medical apparatuses, their purposes beyond Vermeulen's comprehension.

The two orderlies loaded the gurney into the van. Vermeulen wanted to climb into the back, but the nurse shook her head. She and one of the orderlies were the only ones allowed. Tessa and Vermeulen could take a taxi and follow the van. Dr. Mueller had arranged for the paperwork to be transferred electronically. Whatever bills Gaby owed the hospital would be sent directly to her insurance. It all seemed too easy.

Vermeulen called Marieke to tell her about the move. Her icy response left no doubt that she was still upset.

The private clinic put Gaby into a lovely room that could have been mistaken for a comfortable studio apartment, had it not been for the medical equipment. The ceiling was at least ten feet high, and tall windows faced a pocket park planted with trees. The entire building radiated calm and healing. The only person unaffected by that atmosphere was Marieke. She stared at Vermeulen with barely contained fury when Gaby was brought in. Since she had decided to take the night shift, Vermeulen and Tessa let her be. He was happy about that. There were more important things to do than fight. He needed to get to the bottom of the Vienna connection.

On his way out, he turned his phone back on. The display told him he'd gotten another voicemail from Jackson. He ignored it.

CHAPTER THIRTY-TWO

———◆———

THE NEXT MORNING, VERMEULEN TOOK THE subway to Dufaux's office. Like the other UN offices, it was located in the Vienna International Centre, a modernist edifice built in the 1970s, when massive concrete and glass structures were still considered the epitome of good architectural taste. Situated on the large island between the Old and New Danube arms, it consisted of a jumble of skyscrapers grouped around a vast circular wading pool surrounded by the almost two hundred flags of the UN member states. The buildings varied in height but had the same shape—curved façades butting into concrete shafts. Fortunately, Dufaux had given Vermeulen instructions on how to get to his office. Otherwise, he would have lost his way in the maze of forty-five hundred offices housed in the complex.

He finally made it to the twenty-fifth floor of the right building. Dufaux waited for him at the elevator. He was a bit shorter than Vermeulen and had a clean-shaven, open face and well-coiffed gray hair. A tailored gray suit and tie gave him that confident yet patient appearance that was the hallmark of successful diplomats. Vermeulen could imagine him negotiating with an odious dictator without ever losing his cool.

"Welcome to UN City," Dufaux said. "Once you are inside, you don't have to look at it. Instead, you have a nice vista of the rest of the city."

He was right. From the twenty-fifth floor, Vermeulen saw Vienna spread out in the sunlight, reaching to the horizon. The city had a squat quality to it. Except for the soaring tower of St. Stephen's Cathedral and a handful of other tall structures, it looked solid and close to the ground. The world around it might be in upheaval, but Vienna wouldn't budge.

"Yup, that's Vienna," Dufaux said, noticing Vermeulen's gaze. "As Fritz

Molden once quipped, nothing has changed in a century, except that the emperor doesn't come anymore."

"Who's Fritz Molden?"

"A resistance fighter and diplomat of the early years after World War Two. He's still alive and known for his *bons mots.*"

"Where are we meeting the assistant?"

"There's a little café near the entrance. It won't be busy yet."

"A café?" Vermeulen was expecting an interrogation room.

"Yes. Let me remind you again that what we are doing is in total violation of the rules. So we have to play nice. The moment she suspects she's in trouble, she'll clamp shut like a bad mussel. And she has every right to do that. So let's be diplomatic."

"Okay, I promise to be on my best behavior. Could you check something else for me? The man who left the threatening note with Gaby drove away in a car with the license WD-99530. I understand that's a UN plate. I need to know who is driving that car."

"Sure, no problem."

Frau Waldmüller, the executive assistant to Frank Wilmot, the deputy director of the UN Environment Programme, was the consummate office manager. She radiated efficiency. In her late forties, she was well dressed, a bit overweight, and sported a no-nonsense, short haircut. She seemed at a loss as to why the head of the OIOS had asked her to the café. Dufaux offered her one of the three cups of coffee he'd brought to the table.

"Good morning, Frau Waldmüller. This is my colleague Vermeulen from New York. He's investigating a case and thinks you might be able to help him."

Vermeulen was a little surprised that Dufaux wasn't taking the lead. It was his jurisdiction, after all. Maybe he wanted to deflect responsibility if this interview didn't work out. Vermeulen had wondered if the best approach was to ask general questions and then slowly move to the fake letters or confront her right away. He was leaning toward the latter, if only because he had so little time. But that tactic could backfire quickly. And Dufaux didn't seem to want to get involved.

"Good morning," Vermeulen said. "Thanks for coming to meet with us. I have a bit of a problem. I'm investigating a case that involves the use of forged UN documents."

He watched her face, but didn't see any reaction.

"I don't see how I could help with that," she said. "I work in Vienna, not New York."

"Let me be more specific. The documents were invitation letters that were used to obtain visas to the U.S. fraudulently. The U.S. authorities are quite upset and blame the UN."

She looked at him with a blank expression, but didn't say anything.

"Some of those letters are on the letterhead of the UN Environment Office in Vienna and signed by your boss, Wilmot."

He saw a quick flash in her eyes.

"I can't believe that Mr. Wilmot would do something like that. It must be a forgery."

"We are certain it is his signature. He has seen the letters and attested to that. But he doesn't remember signing them."

"He signs so much correspondence. He wouldn't remember a single letter," she said.

"That's what we assumed. Don't you usually bring him the letters to sign?"

She put her cup down. Her face vacillated between anger and puzzlement. "What are you saying?"

"We have reason to believe that you helped with the forged documents."

Waldmüller's anger took over. "I have worked here for fifteen years. Three different departments. All my reviews have been positive. I won't sit here and have you accuse me of violating my duties."

This was the moment Vermeulen had feared. The woman looked genuinely angry. If he pushed any further, Dufaux's warning would come true. She'd simply get up and file a complaint.

"Nobody is accusing you of anything," Dufaux said. "If this were an official investigation, we'd be meeting in my office, not in a café. We're hoping you could help us find the people behind the scheme."

Vermeulen shot him a grateful look. Dufaux had set the right tone.

"I don't know anything about letters and I want to leave now. If you wish to speak to me further, I'd like a representative from the ombudsman's office here."

"We had hoped we could avoid those formalities," Dufaux said.

"Those 'formalities,' as you call them, are there for the protection of employees. I have a spotless record and I won't have it sullied by an investigator from New York. If you are accusing me, I want a record of anything that is said."

This woman was tough. Undoubtedly, she had to be to manage her job in such a busy office. Bullying her wouldn't do. She knew her rights and would stonewall until it was too late.

"We're not interested in you, Frau Waldmüller," Vermeulen said. "We only want the people behind the scheme."

"Well, that may be reassuring, but I don't know what you are talking about. Are we done?"

She rose to leave. Vermeulen made one last attempt. "Do you have children, Frau Waldmüller?"

She hesitated a moment.

"Yes, a son."

"How old is he?"

"Twenty-seven."

"Just a year older than my daughter. Let me tell you about my daughter." Frau Waldmüller sat down again.

"I was in the middle of the investigation that involved the forged letters. Just after I confronted one of the gangsters, I found out that my daughter had a skiing accident. She is in a coma, in a hospital right here in Vienna."

"Oh, I'm so sorry." Her expression changed from ambivalence to concern.

"The doctors expect her to recover. But in the meantime, the gangsters have found out I came to Vienna. They have located my daughter and have threatened her."

Frau Waldmüller sucked in her breath. "That's awful." She took a sip of coffee.

"Tell me about your son, Frau Waldmüller."

"Please leave my son out of this. He's none of your business."

"I'm sure you care about your son as much as I care about my daughter. If he were in danger, wouldn't you do what you could to protect him?"

Her eyes were the tell. He'd hit on something, but he didn't know what.

"I'm not here to accuse you or cause you trouble," he continued. "I just want to protect my daughter. To do that, I need your help."

"I'd like to help you," she said, "but I haven't forged any letters and I don't know anything about the people who threaten your daughter. Can I go now?"

"If your son were in the same situation, wouldn't you move heaven and earth to help him? That's all I'm doing."

There was that expression again. Something was going on with her son. An idea formed in his head. It was worth a try.

"Frau Waldmüller. Has your son asked you to get Mr. Wilmot's signature on those letters?"

She shook her head, but didn't say anything. Her face twitched. She was fighting with herself.

"Let me rephrase that question. Has your son introduced you to someone who asked you to get those letters signed?"

She didn't say anything.

"Please, I need to know who that man is. My daughter's life is at stake. I promise you, nothing will happen to you. Right, Pierre?" He looked at Dufaux.

"Of course," Dufaux said. "You'll have to tell us everything, but I think we can keep this quiet."

"What about Mr. Wilmot?" she said.

"I can't promise I won't tell him, but if it's just a couple of letters, I think we can leave him out of the loop."

"I've never worked for anyone as nice and considerate as Mr. Wilmot," she said. "I would die of shame if he found out."

"Why don't you tell us what happened?" Vermeulen said.

"My son isn't a bad person, but he's always running around with a bad crowd. He was a good boy. Good in school, playing soccer afterward. Then my husband up and left. Just disappeared. Didn't even bother to file for a divorce. I had to do that after I hadn't heard from him in five years. I tried so hard."

She took a tissue from her purse and blew her nose.

"I couldn't do it all. A boy needs a good man in his life. He got bad grades. University was out of the question. Then he sold hashish, got caught, put on probation. I thought that would scare him, but it didn't. He got in deeper and deeper."

She drank from her cup and looked out the window. The tears flowed again.

"I hadn't seen him in weeks. Then one day he came home with this man. He said that he was in trouble and the only way out was for me to get those letters signed. I told him I couldn't do it. That I liked my job, that I'd be fired if anyone ever found out. He told me nobody would find out and that it was just a few letters."

"Did he tell you what these letters were for?" Vermeulen said.

She shook her head.

"How many of them did you get Wilmot to sign?"

"I don't know, maybe thirty. It wasn't a regular matter. Sometimes I wouldn't hear from the man for a few weeks. Other times, he'd come with three or four letters at once."

"What's his name?"

"He never gave me a name. He always meets me on my way to work, on the subway. He sits next to me and leaves a bag with a brown envelope containing the letters when he gets up. He picks them up the same way when I go home."

"When did you last see him?"

"This morning."

CHAPTER THIRTY-THREE

———— ♦ ————

Dr. Rosenbaum went over his schedule of surgery. It was a light day. Two regular ones in the morning and one of the brokered transactions in the afternoon. There was always aftercare, but that wasn't too taxing. The news that the pesky UN investigator had left the country had put him in a better mood than he'd been in for a long time. Even the buzzing of the intercom didn't dampen that feeling.

"Doctor, there is a Mr. Woodleigh waiting for you."

"I don't recognize the name. Is he a patient? He's not on my calendar for today."

"I know. He says he needs a transplant."

Rosenbaum sighed. "He's not the only one. Send him in."

The man who appeared in his office was of medium height, very tan, with a shaven head that gleamed. Despite the tan, Rosenbaum could tell he wasn't well. His cheeks were hollow and his eyes had a yellow tinge.

"How can I help you, Mr. Woodleigh?"

"I need a kidney."

"Please, have a seat. You've come to the right surgeon, Mr. Woodleigh. Kidneys are my specialty. I assume you've had the necessary consultations to ensure that a transplantation is right for you. Are you on a waiting list?"

Settling in the chair across from Rosenbaum's desk, the man said, "Yes, I've already gone through one kidney and the current one is failing. I'm not going back on dialysis."

"Where have those transplantations been performed?"

The man shifted uncomfortably in the chair. "One in Switzerland and the other in Los Angeles."

"Have your doctors determined the reason for the failures?"

"Yes, AMR something, something."

Rosenbaum made a steeple with his fingers and looked up at the ceiling. "Antibody-mediated rejection, how unfortunate. It is a big hurdle we face in our profession."

"Spare me the medical talk. I know what I need, a perfect match."

Rosenbaum raised his hand. "Can you tell me how long the first kidney lasted?"

"A little over a year."

"Hmm," Rosenbaum said with a smile of encouragement. "That's actually a bit of good news. Yours seems to be a case of chronic AMR. That gives us some wiggle room. How long since you received your current kidney?"

"Nine months."

"That's to be expected. The failure of the transplants is directly related to your immune system. Your body produces these antibodies to combat what it considers an invasion of human leukocyte antigens, most likely class one and class two of the major histocompatibility complex. Each subsequent transplantation faces an even larger army of antibodies."

The man drummed his fingers on the arm of his chair. "You don't have to repeat what my doctors have told me already."

"I'm trying to tell you that with a proper desensitization therapy before your next transplant, you may see much better results."

"Ha," Woodleigh snorted. "You think you're the only kidney pro in the country. It's too late for that therapy. My current kidney isn't going to last long enough. I need a kidney from a donor who's both ABO blood type and HLA matched. That's why I'm contacting you."

"That's flattering, but you know that even with paired exchanges, there will be an unknown wait time for such a specific match. As you are on a waiting list, you must know that."

Woodleigh leaned forward. "I'm willing to pay to make that time as short as possible."

"That doesn't change anything. No country in the world permits the buying or selling of organs. No country, that is, except Iran."

"I'm not going to the mullahs for a transplant. Forget that. I'm asking you. I know you can help."

Rosenbaum stood, as if the appointment were over. "I can help only when there is a kidney. Without it, my skills are of no use."

"A good friend of mine tells me that you have ways to make such a kidney appear."

Sitting again, Rosenbaum asked, "And who might that friend be?"

"Samir Rashad, the network king."

"Ah, I do remember Mr. Rashad. Are you in the same line of business?"

"Yes. I do the software side; he does the hardware side. We are competitors, but also friends. He spoke highly of you. He told me that for the right sum, you could make the waiting time disappear."

"And what sum did you have in mind?"

AT A GUT LEVEL, THE BROKER scared the hell out of Rosenbaum. She was everything he was not—tough, determined, ruthless. He knew she'd have him killed if he ever got in her way. She might even do it herself. But there were moments when that very quality attracted him. She was so different from Mitzi and her charities, her shopping, her craving to be seen in the company of the rich. There was a raw beauty about the Broker that was far more pleasant to look at than Mitzi's carefully maintained face that always needed buffing and still looked like it might crack if she ever laughed spontaneously. This evening meeting was such a moment. His good mood and the good news that came out of the afternoon appointment with Mr. Woodleigh were definitely responsible for that. The excellent Pinot Grigio and her pleasant demeanor were icing on the cake.

"So the man just walked into your office and offered you a million dollars for a matching kidney?" she said.

"He did."

"And you weren't concerned that it was a setup? How did he know you could get a matching kidney outside the normal channels?"

"I was concerned, of course. But he was referred by Rashad. He's a software billionaire in Silicon Valley. He's regularly in the headlines. There's no way he's playing informer for the police."

"Your caution is very much appreciated. We need to avoid any attention, particularly after the earlier mishaps. What do you need from me?"

"I need a perfect match, and it has to come from a living donor." He handed her a printout. "Here's the pertinent information, blood group, HLA and MHC data. I need it fast. But for five hundred thousand, you can make it happen, right?"

"I'll send out the request immediately. Our associate in Nairobi is just tapping into a new pool of candidates. It's a medical testing station in one of the slums. They collect meticulous data on each person tested, and our associate has access to that. It shouldn't take more than a week to find a suitable candidate. Without bureaucratic mishaps, you could have that kidney here in ten to fourteen days."

"Good. Mr. Woodleigh is understandably anxious. His kidney is deteriorating quickly and he's not eager to subject himself to the troubles of dialysis again."

He raised his glass to toast with her. She responded in kind, but he had no sense that she considered this occasion as anything other than a business meeting. He wondered who shared a bed with her. She had to have a lover. She was too good looking. Was it someone who knew about her work? He couldn't imagine that. Who would put up with what had to be a crazy schedule?

"Would you like to have dinner with me?" he said.

She smiled that Sphinx smile of hers, then shook her head. "Thanks, Doctor, but no. Better not mix business with pleasure. I'll be in touch as soon as I know more."

She picked up her bag and left. He could have sworn her hips swayed just a little more than usual. He wasn't surprised that she'd left him the bill.

CHAPTER THIRTY-FOUR

———— ◆ ————

VERMEULEN STOOD ON THE PLATFORM OF the Kaisermühlen subway station, waiting for the Vienna-bound train. Frau Waldmüller sat on a bench not too far away. A white plastic bag with the red logo of Steffl, the Vienna department store, lay next to her. After her confession, she'd cried a lot—more from relief than anything else. It was clear to Vermeulen that she had participated in this scheme only because she feared for her son. It was also clear to him that her son was a crook rather than the victim of circumstances, as Frau Waldmüller had claimed. Could she really be so blind? But Vermeulen knew what children could make their parents do.

After she'd admitted the whole thing, she wanted nothing more to do with it. But Vermeulen convinced her otherwise. She was to deliver the signed letters as usual, one last time. Once Frau Waldmüller turned over the letters to the man, Vermeulen would follow him. The letters would be passed on to someone higher up in the gang. Vermeulen would identify the people and turn over that information to Dufaux, who, in turn, would hand it to the police. Dufaux had assured him that he had good relations with the Bundeskriminalamt, the Austrian Federal Criminal Police.

The Kaisermühlen station was above ground. The weather had improved from the day before, but the setting sun didn't do much to warm Vermeulen. He wished he'd brought a warmer coat. Maybe there'd be a chance to buy one when this whole thing was over.

The platform was busy. The end of the regular workday meant that many of the three-thousand-odd UN employees were on their way home.

He called Tessa to check if things were okay at the clinic. She assured him that all was well, given the circumstances. Gaby was still not responsive.

The train pulled into the station. It was painted a sleek gray with a bright red stripe about a third of the way up from the platform. Frau Waldmüller entered the second car. He stepped into the third and inched his way through the standing passengers to the rear of the second one. The interior was gray, too, but the red seats and bright lights made it a pleasant space. The seats were facing each other in rows of two on both sides of the aisle. They had filled quickly. Vermeulen squeezed past Frau Waldmüller. Near the other end of the car, he grabbed the plastic strap hanging from the ceiling and waited.

The train stopped once more and then plunged beneath the Danube, toward the city center. There was so much he didn't know about Vienna, and he knew he wouldn't have time to find out. He hadn't even visited one of the famous coffee shops. The place at the UN City wasn't really what one could call a Viennese café.

A lot of passengers got off at the next station. The rider next to Frau Waldmüller was one of them. She placed the Steffl bag on the empty seat. The car became more crowded as others squeezed in. A few threw angry stares at Frau Waldmüller, but no one asked her to free up the seat. A man carrying an identical bag pushed his way forward. She took hers from the seat and put it on the floor. He sat down and put his next to hers. He wore faded jeans and a black leather jacket. Vermeulen recognized the face and the widow's peak. It was the man who'd worn the tracksuit at the hospital. Turning away, he hoped the man hadn't recognized him.

A few moments later, he glanced back, but nothing seemed amiss. The man looked straight ahead, uninterested in his surroundings.

The next stop was Praterstern. According to the map on the wall, it was a major station with many transfer opportunities. It was also the gateway to the Prater amusement park. If the man got out there, Vermeulen would have a hard time keeping him in sight. The train slowed. People began crowding toward the exit. The man remained seated. The train came to a stop. The crowd pressed against the doors, which opened with a hiss. The surging mass pushed against Vermeulen. Was the man leaving or not? Vermeulen craned his neck to keep an eye on the suspect. Sure enough, the man got up at the last moment, grabbing Frau Waldmüller's plastic bag.

Vermeulen pushed against the passengers blocking his way. A ding sounded and a voice announced in German that the doors were closing. He was still a yard from the doors. With a hiss, the doors began sliding together.

"Hold the door!" he shouted in English. People looked at him curiously, but at least one of them understood and put his arm between the doors. With a sigh, the doors opened again. Vermeulen stumbled out of the train.

He scanned the platform in both directions. There were people everywhere, and black seemed to be the favorite jacket color. Finally, he saw the man approaching the escalator at the end of the platform. He hustled through the crowd. The escalator was too busy and too narrow to get ahead any farther.

Most of the crowd hurried to connect to the other subway line or the light rail lines that stopped at the station above street level. Which made Vermeulen's search at the subway exit a bit easier. In the waning light of the day, he could make out the man, approaching one of the entrances to the Prater.

Vermeulen was pretty sure the man didn't know he was being followed. Frau Waldmüller had been as circumspect as he could have hoped. And the man didn't double back or stop suddenly—maneuvers a well-trained operative would have employed as a matter of course. The gang was feeling secure. They had done as they were told and put a scare into Vermeulen. It hadn't occurred to them that he might follow them.

The amusement park was all lit up. Above the carousels, tilt-a-whirls, and assorted rides rose one of Vienna's landmarks, the giant Ferris wheel. It was no longer the tallest structure in the park. A tower carousel at the far end of the park stood even taller. But with its illuminated red cars suspended between dual gray steel girders, the wheel was certainly the most impressive ride.

The man walked into the park.

It was still early in the year. Tourists were visiting the ski resorts in the Austrian Alps rather than Vienna. The Prater was still the domain of locals, and mostly teenagers at that. The man stopped under the large blue marquee with white neon lettering that spelled 'Wiener Riesenrad.' He bought a ticket and disappeared through the doors. Vermeulen couldn't figure this out. He'd just picked up a bag with fake letters. Why was he taking them for a ride on the Ferris wheel?

Vermeulen saw another man wearing a trench coat and a gray fedora buy a ticket and walk through the door. He also carried a Steffl bag. Before Vermeulen could sort out what he'd just seen, a couple stepped up to the ticket counter. Vermeulen stopped waiting. He ran to the ticket booth, bought his ticket, and followed the other passengers through the door.

Inside, the flexible barriers guided a smattering of riders to stairs that provided access to the cars. The wheel stopped each time one of them approached the nadir of its journey. Its occupants left by one side while the new riders entered from the other. Four people entered. The two men were next. Vermeulen could see one of them hand the attendant money. The man nodded and locked the door after them.

The next car arrived. The process repeated itself. The two men entered. When the couple ahead of Vermeulen wanted to follow, the attendant stopped them.

"*Bitte warten Sie auf den nächsten Waggon*," he said. The two shrugged and stepped back to wait for the next car.

Vermeulen pushed past the couple.

"*Ich bin mit Denen*," he ad libbed in bad German. I'm with them. The attendant looked confused, but then opened the door and let him inside. The two men stared at him with astonishment. The one in the leather jacket who'd been at the hospital recognized Vermeulen. His mouth fell open.

"*Was soll das?*" the one with the fedora said. He had a clean-shaven face, a hawkish nose, and dark eyes under bushy eyebrows. With his hat and coat, he looked like a Hungarian aristocrat.

The first one recovered his speech. "*Das ist er!*" He shook his head. *It's him.*

"Yes, it's me," Vermeulen said. "You threatened my daughter. That will stop here and now!"

CHAPTER THIRTY-FIVE

———◆———

THE MAN WITH THE FEDORA EXAMINED Vermeulen head to toe. The car shook slightly as the Ferris wheel began its rotation.

"Mr. Vermeulen, is it?" He spoke accent-free English and pronounced the name correctly. "What a surprise. I did not think I would have the pleasure of meeting you."

"Spare me your pleasantries, Mister …."

"Mr. Schmidt will do. Well, let us talk, then."

"I'm not here to talk. I'm here to blow your operation sky high."

The wheel stopped to let the couple board the next car.

"My, my. You have only just arrived, but you have already become Viennese."

Vermeulen's face must have shown his confusion, because Schmidt continued, "One of Vienna's literary figures once said that Vienna has many landmarks and every Viennese thinks he's one. But let me caution you, Mr. Vermeulen, your brashness will not serve you well here. You ought to go careful in Vienna. Everybody ought to go careful in a city like this."

The saccharine smile on the man's face so invited a punch, Vermeulen had to muster all his willpower to restrain himself. The Ferris wheel began its rotation again. This time it kept moving. Apparently there was nobody waiting to board below. The car rose above the trees and all of Vienna appeared spread out in a panorama that was stunning even under the darkening sky.

"Don't bother threatening me. I know about your operation. All it takes is a few calls and it will end."

"You forget your daughter."

"I took care of that. You won't find her again."

Schmidt raised his eyebrows and looked at the man in the leather jacket.

"*Ist sie nicht mehr im Unfallkrankenhaus*, Popescu?"

Popescu looked surprised. Which was good news to Vermeulen.

"What am I saying?" Schmidt said. "Please forgive me for resorting to threats. I am sure we can arrive at an arrangement that is mutually beneficial and would leave your daughter out of things."

In the distance, Vermeulen saw the illuminated spire of St. Stephen's Cathedral, marking the center of the old city of Vienna.

"I have no interest in making a deal with you."

"Please, hear me out. Did you ever see *The Third Man*?"

Vermeulen nodded.

"A spectacular film, don't you agree, Mr. Vermeulen? The line about going careful in Vienna came from it. Do you remember the conversation between Holly Martins and Harry Lime right here on the Ferris wheel?"

Vermeulen shook his head. All he remembered were the dark black-and-white scenes of a bombed-out Vienna. So different from what he saw now. The car had reached the apex of the journey. Spread out to one side was the old city, full of churches, museums, and sights. On the other side stood the Millennium Tower and the high-rises of the Vienna International Centre, where he'd met with Dufaux. The wheel stopped again to let new passengers board.

Schmidt opened the window of the car. A gust of wind blew inside, sending a chill down Vermeulen's back.

"In the film, Harry opens the door and tells his friend, 'Look down there. Would you really feel any pity if one of those dots stopped moving forever? If I offered you twenty thousand pounds for every dot that stopped, would you really, old man, tell me to keep my money, or would you calculate how many dots you could afford to spend? Free of income tax.'

"You see, Mr. Vermeulen, today, we can't open the door anymore. But we wouldn't want to, because we are the opposite of Harry Lime. Harry Lime was willing to kill people with bad penicillin for profit. We don't want any of those dots to stop moving. We want them to thrive. That's why all our clients volunteer in exchange for generous compensation. Compared to Harry Lime, we are angels. It's just that the law doesn't quite understand that yet. Hence the subterfuge. Of course, I won't be able to offer you twenty thousand pounds for each of our volunteers, but you won't be disappointed by our offer. Won't you reconsider your refusal?"

Vermeulen held on to the rod attached to the ceiling of the car. Despite Schmidt's smile, he had no doubt the man would've pushed him out of the car if he could have opened the door. Good thing safety locks had been installed. The Ferris wheel continued its rotation and the car began its descent.

"I'm not going to be bribed by you, Schmidt. And I will stop this operation, Viennese adages notwithstanding. I know you are connected to the UN office, because Popescu here drove away in a car with a diplomatic license issued to the UN. Your gig will be over sooner than you think."

The smile disappeared from Schmidt's face when he heard about the license plate, but he recovered quickly.

"You are an enterprising investigator, Mr. Vermeulen. But your threats do not faze me. Since you work for the UN, you know its byzantine structure and rules. Even if you were to identify me, it would take a lot more than accusations from a rogue investigator to stop me."

The word 'rogue' startled Vermeulen.

"You see, Mr. Vermeulen, we've done our own little investigation. I know of your complicated career at the UN. I also know that OIOS isn't the best-liked bureau in the secretariat. Finally, I know you are on sick leave to attend to your daughter. You have no authority to investigate here."

The car passed the tree line again. The ride was almost over.

"But Pierre Dufaux has," Vermeulen said. "I'm only assisting him."

"Dufaux won't follow up. He likes his job too much. Which is not what people say about you. And harassing a ranking UN employee won't sit well with your superiors. Remember what happened to you during the Iraqi oil-for-food investigation. How would you like to go back to doing audits in places like Sierra Leone?"

"You're just blowing smoke, Schmidt. The UN can't afford to have an employee involved in human trafficking."

"Well, there are always other options. As another famous Viennese once said, 'In Vienna you'll have to die first before people remember you. But then you'll live on forever.' "

CHAPTER THIRTY-SIX

———◆———

Jackson stood at the edge of a dirt square. An odor of charred meat and rot hung in the air. Although the Nairobi sky was overcast, the temperature felt like Newark in August. Behind him lay the train tracks that cut through Kibera. Rusty corrugated tin shacks crowded the tracks, sometimes leaving only inches between their roofs and where the train would go.

The square was the only open space he could see. In one corner, a few kids played soccer, leaving clouds of ochre dust in their wake. To his right, a carpentry shop had set out several rows of bed frames made from solid wood, some with padded headboards, their posts expertly turned. They were much nicer looking than what he'd seen at the cheap furniture places in Newark. No particleboard here. Their quality stood in sharp contrast to the ramshackle hovels that surrounded the square.

It was total insanity that he should be here. What had seemed like a smart decision when Gergi and Andrej were running after him with their guns drawn now felt like little more than acting on impulse. He'd run without thinking. And the whole damn world had played along. Nobody stopped him, not at JFK, not at Jomo Kenyatta International Airport. *Have a nice flight, Mr. Abasi. Welcome home, Mr. Abasi.* He'd needed someone to say, 'Wait up, bro, don't do anything stupid.' Like flying one-way to Kenya on a dead man's passport.

The first person to express any doubts about his plan was the hot-looking woman at the Tourist and Travelers Aid desk at the Nairobi airport. He'd asked her how he could find the Abasi family in Kibera and she'd stared at him like he'd asked her for the shortest way to Mars. She told him there were a half-million people living in Kibera—and yet no addresses or phonebooks.

Seeing his face, she took pity on him and suggested that he check with the churches and mosques in Kibera. They'd be his best bet. "Take a *matatu*," she said. Seeing his confusion, she added, "taxi."

Those taxis were no yellow cabs. *That's for damn sure!* Even the worst gypsy cabs in Newark were luxury rides compared to the minivans driven by maniacs with fifteen people occupying nine seats. The only reassuring part was being squeezed on all sides by other passengers, like the airbag had already inflated.

He ended up standing at the edge of Kibera, wondering what the hell to do next. If he returned the money to Abasi's widow—always assuming she could be found—he'd be stuck in Kibera until he hustled up enough cash to get a ticket back home. If he didn't return the money, then why the hell had he come here in the first place? The flight home would probably take all the money he had.

Across the square, a sign advertised the African Brotherhood Church and Pre-School. Someone had worked hard to create a professional look. The letters were hand-painted, baby blue against a white background, and spaced nicely, the caps painted in the right proportion. The sign evoked care and order, exactly what was missing from his life. He crossed the square and went into the church. A young man was sweeping the sanctuary. Despite having misgivings about his last snap decision, Jackson made another one.

"Excuse me," he said. "I'm looking for a family. Can you help me?"

The man stared at him, befuddled. He shook his head and left the room without saying a word. That seemed kinda rude, Jackson thought. Not like the people he'd met so far. He was keenly aware that his American accent instantly set him apart from the people he encountered. He heard steps approaching. A middle-aged, portly man in a gray suit and white shirt entered, his round, fleshy face shiny with sweat.

"I'm the minister," he said. "You need help?"

"Yes, I'm Earle Jackson from America, and I'm looking for the family of Okeyo Abasi."

The minister looked him up and down, then stroked his nonexistent beard.

"Hmm, Okeyo Abasi. Sorry, I don't know that name. Not a member of this church. Don't you have more information?"

"No, all I have is Kibera, Nairobi."

"You will be looking for a long time. There are so many people here. Sorry, I can't help you."

That response became the refrain for the rest of the day. He checked the YMCA, the Church of God, Christ the King, Turning Point Church, Changing Times Church, the World Fellowship Church, the Laini Saba Mosque, and another mosque whose name he never found out. It was a tiring job, what with his jet lag and all. The stink of the open sewers everywhere didn't help. He had to choose his steps carefully. There were plenty of little shops that sold soft drinks and food. He had no clue what to eat, so he got a few bags of peanuts and chips.

Corrugated metal sheets were the preferred construction material, giving Kibera a rusty color. He couldn't figure out if it was the dust or if the metal was really rusting.

Around six, the sun began to set. He found his way back to the YMCA and asked for a room. They didn't have rooms, but they did have a public toilet and ablution shed that was well kept. He paid a few shillings to use the facilities before finding his way to a guesthouse the Y clerk had recommended.

The guesthouse was a combination of repurposed shipping containers and more corrugated iron. It looked like a heap about to collapse. The hand-painted sign under a single light bulb promised first-class rooms. Jackson was too tired to laugh about that. It was run by a tall woman who had the darkest skin he'd ever seen. It had a bluish hue.

"Welcome, you need a bed?"

"Yes, please."

"You're not from Kenya?"

"No, America."

"Nice. We sometimes have guests from America. Are you a student?"

"No, I'm looking for someone."

"You come all the way from America to look for someone?"

"Yes." Jackson knew how crazy it sounded.

"I have a good bed for you. Seventeen hundred shilling."

Jackson thought that was expensive, almost twenty bucks. But then, he was probably paying the tourist rate. He expected other lodgers, but he seemed to be the only one. The inside of the guesthouse was as clean as one could get a place with rammed dirt floors. The woman obviously took care of her establishment. She led him to an alcove, its entrance covered by a curtain. He looked inside and found a clean bed that looked comfortable.

"Would you like food or a drink?" the woman said.

"Yes to both. What do you have?"

"*Nyama choma* and *changáa*."

"I don't know what that is."

"Goat stew and moonshine. I make everything myself. Slaughtered the goat just yesterday, and my *changáa* is the best. Traditional recipe from my grandmother. Not the terrible stuff they make elsewhere and bring in. I only use good ingredients—no chemicals or jet fuel."

He couldn't even imagine why people would drink booze with jet fuel.

"What does *changáa* mean?"

The woman smiled.

" 'Kill me quick.' But it's good. I have a business; I don't want my customers to die."

It wasn't what he'd call a ringing endorsement, but he put his bag on the bed and followed the woman to another room at the end of the compound, a combination bar and restaurant. Five older men sat at two tables and drank a clear liquid from water glasses. She stepped behind a counter made of scrap pallet wood and took another glass from a shelf. On the counter stood a large bottle. She filled the glass halfway. He smelled it. The harsh fumes of alcohol burned in his nostrils. He hesitated a moment, but then thought, *What the hell?* and poured the drink down his throat.

This was no Hennessy. It took his breath away. He coughed, sputtered, his eyes watered. A line of fire cauterized his gullet all the way to his stomach.

The woman laughed. So did the men. It broke the silence his entry had provoked.

"It's strong, yes?" she said.

Tears running down his cheeks, he nodded. "Yes, it's strong."

"How about the *nyama choma*?" she said.

"Okay. It can't be worse than the liquor."

The men liked his comeback and laughed again. The owner left to get the food. Jackson sat down at the counter. He was beat. Searching for a needle in a haystack, that's what he'd been doing. And he was tired of it. He'd given it a shot. It hadn't worked out. Time to think about going home. He turned to look at the other patrons. Okay, one last try.

"Evenin' folks," he said. "I'm looking for the family of Okeyo Abasi. Do any of you know him?"

"Okeyo who went to America?" a man at the far table said.

CHAPTER THIRTY-SEVEN

———————— ◆ ————————

CAMILLE DELANO'S PHONE RANG. THE DISPLAY said 'Private.' That could only mean two things. Someone misdialed, or it was a call from the top. The chances for the former were slim, so she'd better not ignore the call.

The familiar male voice came straight to the point. "The Vienna operation backfired."

"How so?" She breathed a little easier. Someone else was responsible for that mess.

"The subject, Vermeulen, confronted Kurtz."

"How did he manage that?"

"We assume he found our source at the UN, saw Popescu, and followed him to his rendezvous with Kurtz."

"That sounds like him." She had to admit to a grudging admiration. Vermeulen turned out to be far more effective than she had assumed.

"We need to eliminate him. He knows too much," the voice said.

"I agree."

"The question is where. In Vienna it will cause too much attention. Can you deal with him when he comes back?"

She didn't like that suggestion at all. "We can't afford to wait that long. He's dangerous right now. We don't even know when he'll come back."

"That's correct. But there are other issues at stake. As you know, Kurtz is a public figure in Vienna. Vermeulen has met him. If the man turns up dead, the police will ask questions. Someone's bound to have seen the two together. Kurtz can't afford that kind of scrutiny."

"And I can?" *Dump the dirty work on me*, she thought. *Typical.*

"You aren't nearly as exposed as Kurtz is. You don't have to maintain that kind of public persona. So, yes, you could stand more scrutiny."

"What about the time factor? What if he stays in Vienna and investigates more? Besides, I have Jackson to deal with here. He's disappeared again."

"We know that Vermeulen's only got a week's leave. If his daughter recovers, he'll be coming back shortly. If not, we'll deal with it then."

"Any progress on the special order?" she said.

"It's been relayed to Nairobi. Vienna doesn't have such detailed data on candidates. Keep your phone nearby."

"Good," she said. Although it was far from good. The reason her operation functioned so smoothly was that everybody involved got something out of it. That kept them from rocking the boat. Then management started to push for higher numbers, and things went south. Like that UN visa scam. Yes, it was easier than forging papers to get people into the U.S., but the likelihood of discovery also increased. Usually, the ones who got caught were deported. Abasi's death had been a real disaster.

Disposing of Vermeulen would only cause more attention. Her crew wasn't good enough to deal with that. They were good at bullying people who didn't know better, but they didn't know how to deal with people who stood up to them. The way Gergi and Andrej had underestimated Jackson was exhibit A of their record of incompetence. She couldn't send these jokers after Vermeulen. And they were the most reliable. No, she'd have to take on Vermeulen herself. And the more she knew about him, the more that prospect worried her.

* * *

VERMEULEN WAS BACK IN GABY'S ROOM. He'd taken the necessary steps to make sure he wasn't followed, including switching subways at the last minute, diving into the massive Gerngross department store, leaving via the employee exit, and taking two cabs back to the clinic. Since Marieke had insisted on covering the night shift, Tessa was still sitting with Gaby.

She beamed when he came in. "Gaby moved. On her own account. About three hours ago. She turned and mumbled something."

"Why didn't you call me?" Vermeulen said.

"I didn't know where you were; it might have caused problems."

He knew she was right. Still, it irked him.

"What does the doctor say?"

"She says it's a very good sign. The longer someone stays in a coma, the greater the chance of brain damage. It's been six days, and that's still within the realm of full recovery. Of course, nobody knows if any vital parts got injured."

He stepped to the bed and took Gaby's hand. It felt soft and warm. Her face remained still. There was no sign she felt his touch. Just the slow rise and fall of her chest as she breathed in and out.

"Did you tell Marieke?" he said.

"I've decided to wait. She's asleep right now. She needs the rest."

"You're treading on dangerous ground. She won't forget that you didn't tell her."

"Oh, come on. You're exaggerating."

"Trust me. I know her."

Tessa just shook her head. "What did you find out?" she said.

"Just as I thought. The executive assistant of the head of the UNEP here was pressured by her no-good son into getting these letters signed. The good news is that she was to deliver a batch today. I followed her contact, who was the same man I saw at the hospital, and met the boss."

Tessa sat up with a start. "You *what*?"

"I met the local boss. A dapper gentleman in a trench coat and fedora. He calls himself Schmidt."

"What did you talk about?"

"We took a ride on the Ferris wheel. He told me that they were helping people. Even invoked the movie *The Third Man* to show how much good they were doing."

"Did he explain what their operation was all about?"

"No, he didn't. But he did offer me a bribe."

"And you didn't accept?" Tessa smiled.

"Of course not. And then, just like the Broker, he threatened to kill me."

"You seem remarkably calm for someone who's got a penchant for bringing out the worst in crooks."

"I do have to take precautions. It took me almost two hours to get back here. But I'm not too worried. They can't attract too much attention. Their network depends on the silence of everyone involved."

"That doesn't mean they won't try to get rid of you."

"I'll just have to get to them first."

She frowned. "And how are you going to do that? Schmidt is about as common a name as you can find here."

"There was a photographer by the Ferris wheel. He takes photos of everyone exiting the cars and then harasses them until they buy a picture. They told him to bug off in no uncertain terms. I doubled back after I lost them and paid him way too much money. He insisted that I should come back for the framed print, but emailed me the digital version." He pulled his phone from his pocket. "Here is your Mr. Schmidt."

"You're right, he does look dapper."

CHAPTER THIRTY-EIGHT

———— ◆ ————

Getting from Mr. Schmidt's photograph to his real name and address turned out to be easier than they thought. Tessa uploaded the photo and did a reverse image search on her laptop. A few seconds later, they saw many images of the same man and the search engine's best guess that the photograph depicted a Mr. Kurtz. More searching revealed that Mr. Kurtz was well connected in Vienna and served as director of some kind of outreach program of the UN Office in Vienna that brought in students for internships. More importantly, the two located his home in the Währing district.

"I should go there," Vermeulen said.

"And do what?"

"I don't know, keep tabs on him. Know where he goes?"

"You'll need a car for that. And it's dark."

"I can rent a car, and dark means I won't stick out sitting outside his house."

"And just sit there?" She shook her head.

"I've interrupted their routine. They've got to be nervous, running around and tying up loose ends. Look at Kurtz. He seems pretty prominent. Which means he's got a lot to hide."

"Yes, but will he do it at his house? I don't think so. You'll end up sitting outside until the police get wise to you and ask what you're doing there."

"That's a chance I'll have to take. If they really are into human trafficking, they've got to stash the people somewhere. Now that I rattled their cage, they'll have to do something with them."

"Good point, but I don't see how sitting outside his house will help you find them."

"You could come with me and we could catch up."

Tessa grinned. "You are crazy, you know that? I need some rest. Sitting here all day is tiring. The last thing I need is sitting in a car all night."

He gave her a playful punch in the shoulder. "Oh, come on. At least we'll be together. It's the only thing I can think of doing. And I've got to do something. Can you find me a car rental close by?"

Tessa tapped some more on her laptop. "Here's one that brings the car to you."

Vermeulen dialed the number. Ten minutes later, after reciting driver's license and passport numbers, he hung up.

"All set. Once Marieke starts her night shift, we'll go for a ride."

There was a rustling from the bed. Both of their heads spun toward Gaby. Her left arm moved. Her hand reached for her head. Her eyelids fluttered. She opened her mouth. Some incomprehensible sounds emerged. Spittle ran from a corner. Then the hand fell back on the bed.

"Gaby, can you hear me?" Vermeulen shouted.

He ran to her side.

"Gaby, are you awake?"

Her eyelids fluttered again, then stayed open. Her eyes looked vacant, unfocused. She breathed heavily, almost like a sigh.

"Gaby," Tessa said from the other side of the bed. "Are you coming back to us?"

Gaby uttered more sounds. They didn't amount to words. She turned her head toward Tessa and her eyes focused on her. A bare hint of a smile appeared on her face. Vermeulen felt a momentary twinge of jealousy but banished it immediately. He reached for her hand and stroked it. Gaby reacted by turning toward him. She still looked confused. She closed her eyes again. Vermeulen reached for a tissue and dabbed the spittle from her chin. Gaby didn't react. Her breathing calmed again.

Tessa had pushed the call button, and a nurse appeared at the door.

"I think she's coming to," Tessa said.

"Yes," Vermeulen added. "She opened her eyes, looked at us, and mumbled something."

"Good," the nurse said. "Very good. The time frame is about right. But don't get your hopes up yet. It will still be a while."

"A while until what?" Marieke's voice came from the door.

"A while until she is fully awake," the nurse said. "Recovery from a coma takes time. Nobody just pops up and is back to normal. It could take a week, even a month."

"Let's hope it doesn't take that long," Vermeulen said.

"Why?" Marieke said from the door. "You got some place to be?"

Much to Vermeulen's relief, the nurse answered, "The sooner she recovers, the better are her chances of not having lasting problems."

THEY PARKED HALF A BLOCK AWAY from Kurtz's address on a quiet street. Währing was definitely an upscale district. No five-story buildings here. Generous villas lined the streets. There were tall trees everywhere. The district exuded a quiet gentility. Before they approached Kurtz's house, Tessa again pointed out that sitting in a car surveilling a house would attract attention. But it turned out there were enough cars parked on the street that one more wasn't noteworthy.

They'd barely settled in for what could have been a boring, long night when a white Audi A6 drove up to the Kurtz house. A man got out. In the bright cone of the streetlight, Vermeulen recognized him right away.

"That's Popescu. He left the note in Gaby's hand and took the letters from Frau Waldmüller."

Popescu turned up the collar of his black leather jacket and walked to the door. He rang a bell and disappeared inside moments later. Whatever message he had to convey was short. He came out again and got into the car. But he didn't drive away. The Audi just sat there, condensation from the exhaust wafting up to the night sky.

Ten minutes later, Kurtz emerged from the house. He'd switched from the trench coat to a woolen one and wore his fedora. Kurtz got into the rear of the Audi and they drove away.

Vermeulen started the car and eased into the street. Only when Popescu had turned onto a busier street did Vermeulen switch on his headlights. He followed the Audi, keeping far back so as not to arouse suspicion. Fortunately their rental, a Fiat, was a common enough car on the street.

Popescu wove his way through the quiet streets until he reached the beltway that separated the suburbs from the interior districts that make up old Vienna. True to its name, the beltway consisted of a four-lane boulevard divided by light rail tracks and a wide greenbelt. Everything was well lit, so Vermeulen dropped back.

The farther south they drove, the busier the road became. The traffic lights were synchronized, which meant Vermeulen couldn't afford to fall too far behind, or he'd get stuck at an intersection and lose the Audi. He pulled up closer. Despite his best efforts, they were caught by red lights just as they passed the Westbahnhof, one of the two major railway stations of Vienna. With cabs darting in and out of traffic, it was impossible to keep up.

The synchronized traffic lights turned out to benefit him, because Popescu had been forced to stop at the next one. Vermeulen got a green sooner and caught up. Popescu followed the beltway until it divided near the Vienna

River. He continued along the southern lanes, leaving old Vienna behind.

They passed a massive rail marshaling yard. Under the tall sodium halogen lights, stubby locomotives pushed railcars onto different tracks. Shortly afterward, they passed Vienna's main railroad station. There, the beltway turned south and became a freeway. Popescu exited, continued east, and then took Simmeringer Hauptstraße south. They entered a low-rent district. The stately buildings of the inner districts gave way to workers' housing, long blocks built without much adornment or beauty and interspersed with warehouses and light industrial buildings.

They passed a vast cemetery that seemed to go on forever. An elaborate a sign at the entrance identified it as the Zentralfriedhof. That was followed by a large repair shop for the light rail system. A street sign indicated that they had left Vienna and entered one of the suburbs. Tucked between the repair shop, another light rail station, and a brewery lay several apartment buildings. Popescu parked in front of the second one. Vermeulen continued straight ahead, took the next right, and parked near a small hotel that had never seen better days.

"What do you want to do now?" Tessa said, and yawned.

"I want to find out what's happening in that building."

CHAPTER THIRTY-NINE

—◆—

THE APARTMENT BUILDING WAS A FOUR-STORY stucco edifice. The plaster had broken off in many places, revealing scarred cement blocks. The front door led to a vestibule lit by a dim bulb.

He tried the door. It opened. Inside, there were rows of mailboxes on the right wall. Above them were ringer buttons and dull aluminum grates covering communication devices that looked like they hadn't worked in a long time. The cracked tiles on the floor were missing many pieces, making the ground uneven and easy to trip on. A gray steel door with cloudy safety glass led to the interior.

"Look at all these names. There's got to be whole clans living in each apartment," Tessa said.

Some of the names were unreadable. The others sounded Eastern European, but that was just a guess. It looked like the kind of place where poor immigrants lived, fifteen or more packed into subdivided apartments.

"Apartments 1A and 1B don't have any names," he said.

"What do we do next?"

"I wonder if Kurtz is a slum landlord. This place sure looks like it."

"But why would he come here after you confronted him?"

"Maybe this is where he keeps his victims until the paperwork is arranged."

"That's a lot of apartments."

"Most are probably rented to immigrants. That makes it easy for him to put two or three units aside for his trafficking victims. Few would notice new faces and nobody would ask any questions."

He heard sounds from behind the interior door.

"We'd better get out of here," he said.

It was too late. The door opened and two women came out. They were young, very young. Their hair was teased, their faces made up, and they wore impossibly high stiletto heels and skirts that barely covered their buttocks. Everything about them spoke of a night out clubbing, except their faces. Both looked glum. They brushed past Vermeulen and Tessa without a look or a nod.

"Those girls are going to get a urinary tract infection in this weather," Tessa said.

Vermeulen could tell she was only half joking.

"They didn't look too happy, either," he said.

"I know. I think I'll follow them. I have a suspicion."

"What kind of suspicion?"

"I told you I'm working on a series on organized crime. That's why I'm in Vienna in the first place. One aspect is sex trafficking. I just want to see where those girls are going."

"Want me to come along?"

"Aren't you busy here?"

"This neighborhood looks like the kind of place where a few neo-Nazis would be cruising the streets hoping to beat up some immigrants."

She frowned. "You think so?"

"Looks like plenty of immigrants here. That often brings out the vermin, too. This isn't the well-to-do, worldly Vienna."

"Don't worry, I'll be fine."

She turned and left. He wondered what to do next. The sight of the two women had startled him enough that he'd forgotten to catch the door. He rang the bell of a top floor apartment in the hope that someone would buzz the door open. Nothing happened. He rang the next apartment. The speaker above the button crackled with some incomprehensible sounds.

"*Ist* Miroslav *zu Hause*?" he said, hoping an inquiry about a made-up name might do the trick. More sounds followed. He wondered if his voice was any clearer than what he heard.

"Miroslav, *bitte*."

The door buzzed and he pulled it open.

Inside, he smelled stale food and urine. To the left was a staircase that wound its way to the top floor. He heard a door open somewhere upstairs. With a loud thump, the hall light came on. Someone shouted something. He walked to the first step and glanced up. A man was leaning over the topmost banister three floors up.

"*Was wollen Sie*?" he shouted.

Vermeulen didn't want to be shouting back since he didn't know if Kurtz could hear him. He gave the man a thumbs up and turned back from the stairs toward apartment 1A and 1B. The man shouted another question. This time someone else responded. As far as Vermeulen could make out, he was telling the first man to stop shouting. The rejoinder had the opposite effect. Others joined the fray.

Happy that he'd managed to divert their attention, Vermeulen followed the hallway into the building. The first two doors, across from each other, were labeled 1A and 1B. There were no name plates at either door. Another thump sounded and the hall light went out again. The shouting stopped. Vermeulen remembered these timed hall lights from the tenements in Antwerp where he had questioned suspects. He found a switch and turned the light back on.

Stepping close to 1A, he put his ear to the door. No sound. None of the usual background noise that indicates an inhabited place. Not even a refrigerator humming. That apartment was empty. He went to door 1B and listened again. This apartment was noisier. He could hear a faint, monotone voice, like a radio or TV turned very low. And there were the other sounds of an occupied living space.

He was tempted to knock, but he held back. What would he do when someone opened the door? Kurtz and Popescu might be inside. He was in no position to challenge them. If anything, this was the perfect place to make him disappear.

There were two more apartments on this floor. Vermeulen inched down the hallway. When he passed doors 1C and 1D, he heard loud music coming from one door and the drone of a TV from the other. The janitor had left a bucket and mop near apartment 1C. With another thump, the light went out again. There was nothing else to discover back there. He was about to go back to the entrance when the door of 1B opened.

Kurtz stepped into the slant of light that fell into the dark corridor.

CHAPTER FORTY

---◆---

VERMEULEN INCHED BACKWARD, DEEPER INTO THE dark. Popescu followed Kurtz into the corridor. They turned and spoke to someone in the apartment. Vermeulen couldn't make out the words. He crossed to the other wall, which seemed darker, and stumbled over something in his way. The bucket. The mop clattered to the ground. Spinning around to run deeper into the gloom, he slipped in the puddle of water that had run from the bucket and landed on the hard tile floor.

That turned out to be the least of his worries. With a loud thud, the hall light came back on. The men looked startled to see Vermeulen getting back to his feet. Popescu pulled a pistol from his jacket.

"Mr. Vermeulen," Kurtz said. "I don't know how you found this place, but I'm glad you are here. It will make our next task so much easier." He turned to Popescu. "Fetch him."

Popescu raised his gun and advanced toward Vermeulen. Vermeulen looked back. There was no place else to go. His only hope was the timed hallway light. He walked toward Popescu, hands in the air. Just as he reached him, the light went out again.

He lunged at Popescu, whose figure was outlined against the sliver of light coming from apartment 1B.

"*Licht! Mach das Licht an!*" Popescu shouted and dodged Vermeulen. Vermeulen's momentum carried him past the man. Popescu regained his footing and raised the gun again. This time, Vermeulen stood outlined against the slant. He dropped to his knees just as Popescu fired. The shot's report echoed like thunder through the narrow hallway. Vermeulen launched himself at the feet of Popescu, who reacted too late. The two crashed to the floor. The gun slid from Popescu's hand. Vermeulen's head hit something hard, maybe Popescu's knee. A shower of shiny stars crossed his retina. He squeezed his eyes together to stop the fireworks.

Popescu recovered faster. Pushing Vermeulen down, he grabbed his throat with both hands. Having gotten his eyesight under control, Vermeulen found he couldn't breathe. The guy may not have been tall, but he had hands like clamps. Vermeulen heard the blood roaring in his ears. He opened his mouth and gulped like a fish out of water. Having Popescu sit on his chest only made matters worse. With another thud, the hall light came on again.

Popescu had held the gun with his right hand, so Vermeulen assumed that his left arm was comparatively weaker. He grabbed the man's left wrist and dug his fingernails into the assortment of veins that crossed into the hand. Popesu screamed. The clamp around Vermeulen's throat loosened. He sucked in air as fast as he could. Then he twisted Popescu's left wrist slowly but inexorably clockwise. The motion forced it from his neck. Popescu must have realized that he couldn't strangle Vermeulen with one hand. He let go of his neck and punched him in the face. A lightning bolt of pain shot from Vermeulen's nose through the nociceptors straight to his spinal cord. It was way past the threshold his body considered acceptable. Tears began streaming from his eyes.

The pain ignited a rage Vermeulen hadn't felt in a long time. The surge of adrenaline gave him new strength. He pushed Popescu off, raised himself, and delivered a vicious kick to the man's groin. He tasted blood at the corner of his mouth. The gun, a dull black Glock, lay against the wall. He picked it up. The light went off.

Kurtz had run back into the apartment and slammed the door shut. Vermeulen stood in the dark. He inched his way along the wall until he felt the button. He pressed it and the light came back on.

Popescu was struggling to his knees. Vermeulen helped by yanking him to his feet. With the muzzle of the Glock pressed against Popescu's head, he pushed the man to the door of apartment 1B. He gave the door a hard kick right next to the lock. The old wood splintered like kindling.

Inside were four men and Kurtz. Three men cowered in the right corner. The fourth one, the biggest, stood in front of Kurtz. Vermeulen only saw a sliver of the hand that held the pistol against the man's head.

"Drop the gun, Vermeulen, and let Popescu go. I will have no compunction about killing Milosh here if you don't."

"Then you'll go down for murder."

"That's very unlikely. I'm not worried."

"I'll make it my mission to make you worry about it."

"And do what? Kill Popescu and sacrifice Milosh here in the pursuit of your mission? I know you won't do that."

Vermeulen swallowed. His father had always told him, never draw a gun unless you're willing to use it. He hadn't thought about that advice for a long time. Now it was too late. Kurtz had called his bluff.

"But can you live with murdering Milosh? He hasn't done anything," he said, stretching out the conversation while his mind raced. He had to use the gun; it was the only option.

"He's just one of the dots we saw from the Ferris wheel. For me, he's the cost of doing business. What is it the Americans call it? Collateral damage."

"And Popescu?"

Kurtz shrugged. "He knew what he got into. But you aren't going to shoot him. We've established that already."

"I'm not sure Popescu is quite as sanguine about this proposition," Vermeulen said. "Your boss is ready to sacrifice you."

As long as he kept talking, there was a chance that he could find an opening. And he needed an opening. As it stood, the situation favored Kurtz. Big time. The three men in the corner were useless. He saw the fear in their eyes. Milosh, Kurtz's human shield, didn't look like he had any intention of fighting back.

"Do you really think you could rile Popescu? Use him against me?" Kurtz said. His mouth formed into a sneer. "He knows, just like I do, that you will never pull that trigger. You're not that kind of man. We established that at the Ferris wheel. So give the gun to Popescu and accept your failure."

Vermeulen needed an ally. Of the four men, Milosh seemed the only one who might hold his own in a fight. But the gun against his head canceled that. That left the other three. He pushed Popescu to the left. Kurtz followed suit by moving right, always keeping Milosh in front of him. That put Kurtz right between Vermeulen and the three other men.

Vermeulen stared at the three men, moving his head almost imperceptibly to signal them to make a move. One of them nodded.

Popescu saw the nod, too. "*Vorsicht, hinter Ihnen, Herr Kurtz,*" he said, warning him of the men behind him.

"Oh, those three? They aren't going to do anything. The only one with a shred of initiative is standing right in front of me."

Whether it was Kurtz's taunt or the fight stimulus finally kicking in, Vermeulen would never know. In any case, the one who'd nodded took a step forward. Popescu saw it.

"*Er kommt wirklich,*" he said, telling Kurtz of the approaching man.

Kurtz couldn't resist. He turned back. His hand with the gun turned with him. Vermeulen kicked Popescu in the back of his knee. Popescu screamed with pain. His knee gave out and he sank to the floor.

Milosh saw his chance, spun around, and tried to grab Kurtz's gun. Kurtz reacted too fast. He pistol-whipped Milosh. Blood poured from Milosh's nose. He buried his face in his hands and dropped to his knees. That gave Vermeulen the opportunity he needed. He took a big step right, grabbed the Glock with both hands, aimed, and fired at Kurtz's arm. Remembering his army training, he fired again, the insurance shot. Good thing he did. The first bullet missed, but the second struck the hand holding the pistol.

Kurtz stood frozen as his Glock smashed against the wall. He stared at his bleeding hand, then at Vermeulen, then back at his hand. Blood poured onto the floor. It was a mess. That reality must have sunk in, because he let out a howl. It sounded more like frustration and surprise than pain.

"Popescu, get a towel and wrap it around his hand," Vermeulen said.

Popescu roused himself.

"Kill him!" Kurtz shouted. "I want him dead, destroyed. Do you hear me, Popescu?"

Popescu limped from the kitchen with a dishtowel and reached for Kurtz's wounded hand.

"Get away from me with that filthy rag!" Kurtz was ranting now. "I want you to kill him, Popescu. I *order* you to kill him."

Popescu just slapped Kurtz. The look on Kurtz's face was an ugly mixture of hatred and surprise. Popescu ignored it and wrapped the bleeding hand in the towel. He looked like he'd wanted to slap Kurtz for a long time.

CHAPTER FORTY-ONE

———————◆———————

JACKSON HADN'T SLEPT WELL. DESPITE THE jet lag and the long flight without real rest, he couldn't get to sleep. There were the strange smells, the new sounds. There was the stagnant air inside the tin building. Most of all, there was the worry about what to do next. Now that he had a lead on Abasi's family, the real question loomed large. Was he going to give money to them? If so, how much? Maybe he should forget the whole thing. Skip out early, find a travel agency, get a ticket, and go home. He'd have enough cash left to hole up someplace until the Broker and her goons forgot about him.

That he was going back home soon was not a question. In just one day, he'd seen enough of Nairobi to know that he preferred Newark. This wasn't even a short-term solution. Even if he kept all the money, he'd run out eventually. The only steady job he'd ever had was being a tout for doctors Patel and Mulberry. He was pretty sure there was no demand for those skills in Kibera. Which meant he had to hustle. But here, everyone hustled. He was competing with a half a million hustlers, and they knew their way around. He didn't.

He got up and looked for the bathroom. The woman was already up. She anticipated his needs and pointed him to a latrine behind her compound. There was no water. He realized why people here smelled. There were no places to wash. A trip to the Y was in order.

The woman handed him a cup of tea and a plate with two slices of white bread covered with some strange brown paste. Jackson didn't care. He was hungry. The spread was unlike anything he'd ever eaten. Like a mixture of bouillon and molasses. He couldn't imagine any circumstances under which he'd get used to that taste. But it calmed his stomach, and the hot tea got his circulation going.

In the middle of the breakfast, the man from the night before who knew Abasi came back. He'd decided to bring Jackson to the family. Jackson sighed. He went back to his alcove, closed the curtain, and counted the cash. Two thousand dollars and change.

Decision time.

He put a thousand dollars in one pile. That was the minimum he figured he needed to get back home. He put another hundred on the pile. Food, drink, and accommodation until he got his flight. Another hundred. That left eight hundred for the family. He took another C note. Who knew what problems he'd still have to face? Seven hundred. It was more than they'd ever had.

He put the thirteen hundred in his shoe and stuffed the rest in his pocket.

The man took him deeper and deeper into the slum. As on the day before, Jackson saw how busy people were. Only the children lingered to steal glances at the stranger in good clothes. There was a feeling of tension in the air. The flow of people made it hard to sort out where that sensation came from. His guide acknowledged some passersby but actively avoided looking at others. Jackson started examining those the guide didn't look at. He couldn't tell how they were different. Some seemed to have darker skin. Was that it?

As they walked farther from the road where the taxi had let him off, a new worry crept into his head. What if the man was just leading him to some spot to steal his money? There were few legal ways to make a living, and what easier way than to hit a rich American upside the head and clean out his pockets? He hadn't said that he carried any money, but if Abasi had gone to America to make money, chances were good that Jackson was bringing some of that back.

His worries were unnecessary. They rounded yet another corner in the maze that was Kibera and the man stopped and greeted a woman wearing worn but clean clothes. Her hair was short and brushed back. Her eyes were red. She had cried. She knew why he was there.

"Good morning. Mrs. Abasi?" he said.

She nodded. Tears began flowing again.

"I have some sad news, Mrs. Abasi. Your husband Okeyo died in America."

The woman broke into a wail that made Jackson take a step back. He'd seen his mother and her sisters mourn at his grandma's funeral, but it was nothing compared to Mrs. Abasi.

"I'm very sorry," he said.

The woman held her head with both hands as if to keep it from blowing apart. Anguish and pain contorted her body, pressing, pushing to be let out in the open for everyone to hear. There was nothing he could do, or should do, until it had come out. She stomped on the ground. She arched her back and hollered at the sky. Neighbors came out. The women joined the wailing.

They held her. There was no harmony to the crying. It wasn't melodic in some *National Geographic* documentary sort of way. It was pain bursting out and it was ugly.

He felt tears coming to his own eyes and was about to join in, but he noticed that the men stayed back and didn't participate in the mourning. The raw energy of it struck him like a knife in the gut. It peeled away the layers and layers of cynical calculations that had accumulated during his adult life. There was no angle to exploit here. Or rather, he didn't want to look for an angle. It was an entirely new feeling, and it was unsettling.

The woman's crying had ebbed to irregular sobs. All strength had left her body. If it hadn't been for the neighbor women holding her up, she would have crumpled to the ground. Another ten minutes later, Mrs. Abasi stepped toward him and took his hand.

"Thank you," she said.

"You're welcome," he said. "It's the least I could do."

She frowned and Jackson realized that she didn't understand English. He looked at the man who'd led him here. He said something and the woman nodded. She motioned to her shack, pulled a creaky sheet of iron away, and went inside. He followed, as did the man who'd brought him. The rest remained outside, but they peered through the open door.

The inside was dark and sparsely furnished. Two mats, neatly rolled up in one corner. A low table, a kerosene cooker, a small shelf with two bowls, two cups, and two plates. He figured the large plastic bag served as a wardrobe, since clothes were spilling from it. She sat on the ground and invited him to sit. He tried to sit down but didn't know where to put his legs. So he just knelt on them.

He took the envelope he'd used to hold Okeyo's passport and the money he'd allocated to the family and gave them to her. She opened the passport and looked at Okeyo's picture. Tears swelled up again. Her breasts heaved, but she sighed loudly and closed the passport. She looked at the money, folded it, and stuck it into her bra. That made him feel better. The wailing almost got him to add a few hundred to the envelope.

"Thank you," she said again.

Jackson nodded and took her hand in his. He squeezed it gently.

"I'm so sorry."

She said something. The man translated, "She says, you no sorry. You no kill him."

Jackson's ears pricked up. He hadn't told anyone that Abasi had been killed. But he didn't pursue it. No need to get more involved. He'd done the right thing, just as bloody Vermeulen and his grandma had told him. Now he wanted to get out of here as fast as possible.

The woman and the man followed him outside. The crowd still stood there. Looking at the benefactor who'd come all the way from America. The woman blinked in the light, her eyes still red and swollen. Jackson heard her suck in her breath. He turned and saw her stare at someone in the crowd.

She shouted something. The people standing there turned to a young man who stood out because he wore better clothes than anyone except Jackson. His skin was as dark as that of his hostess at the guesthouse. The young man turned to leave, but the people around him wouldn't let him. The woman shouted louder. Hands grabbed the young man.

Jackson looked at his guide. "Who is that?"

"The man who promised Okeyo the money in America."

CHAPTER FORTY-TWO

---◆---

THE NEIGHBORS DIDN'T HESITATE. THEY WENT after the man who'd lured Abasi to America. Abasi's wife joined them.

"Stop!" Jackson said. "Don't beat him."

Looking at the man on the ground with blood running down his face, he couldn't help but see himself. A tout, who solicited clients for someone higher up. That guy didn't have the wherewithal to get tickets, visas, and whatever else was needed to send someone to the U.S. Someone more powerful was above him. Someone Jackson wanted to meet.

The beating stopped. The guy got up. His natty clothes were soiled and torn.

"This man is not responsible for Okeyo's death," Jackson said. "Somebody in America is. There are people above him, people who only want to exploit poor people like yourselves. Let's ask him who they are."

It was a new role for him, standing there, talking folks into something. He'd never done that, never been a leader. Doing his own thing was his usual mode of operation. But the people were listening to him, looking at him, waiting for his next command. Too weird.

"What's his name?" he said to his guide.

"Wycliff."

"Do you speak English, Wycliff?" he said to the young man.

Wycliff nodded.

"I want to know who hired you to find people like Okeyo."

Wycliff looked at the people crowding him, saw the anger in their eyes. "A European."

"Man or woman?"

"Man."

"What's his name?"

"Renko."

"Where do you meet this Renko?"

Wycliff didn't answer.

"Listen, Wycliff, these folks here are ready to beat you bad. If you tell me all you know, I'll try to persuade them to let you go. It's your choice."

Wycliff wiped his face and straightened his clothes. Jackson saw fear in his eyes—something else, too. Something that told Jackson to be careful with this man.

"I will tell you," Wycliff said. "Renko calls me and I meet him at AIDS Clinic in Lindi. They test people at the clinic. But people don't want to go. Why? You got AIDS, you gonna die. They don't give medicine. People don't want to know they gonna die. When they get sick is soon enough."

Jackson saw the logic in that. He'd seen that kind of fatalism in Newark, too. Without AIDS drugs, knowing you were sick didn't make any difference.

"So you bring him people?"

"Yes, the clinic want to test people. I bring people there and they pay me a little. Renko is there. He sees all the tests. He finds someone healthy, he calls me to bring them back. I bring the person. He tells them they are going to America or Europe and get much money. Then he pays me."

"Do you know what happens to the people he picks?"

He shook his head.

"You really don't know?"

Jackson wasn't sure. He knew a hustler when he saw one, and Wycliff was a much poorer version of himself. It didn't matter. He'd said enough. This Renko was piggybacking on some legit operation. That gave him access to data about patients, and he used that to select certain patients to send to the U.S. Those folks must have felt like they won the lottery. They got to go to America, and if the twenty-five hundred in Abasi's pocket were any indication, come back with more cash than they'd ever had. Of course, Renko made a lot more than that. Another indication of how much money was involved in whatever this racket was.

"Can you bring me to Renko?"

Wycliff's eyes grew wide again. He shook his head.

"No, I no bring you to Renko. He's very bad. Only sees me when he calls first."

Jackson felt the familiar buzz of discovering a new opportunity. Renko was like the Broker in Newark. Middle management, pulling strings locally. He'd blown it in Newark, didn't get to speak to the Broker. Mostly because Vermeulen got to her first. This was another chance. Renko might be willing to talk business. But it was crucial that he do proper recon. Anticipation. This time he wasn't going to walk into a trap.

"Okay," he said. "No meeting, but you show me where the clinic is. Bring me there."

Again, Wycliff shook his head.

"No, no. I don't do that. Renko kills me."

"He won't know. Just show me the clinic. He won't see you."

Wycliff looked genuinely scared. "He said to me, you tell anyone, I kill you."

"You already told me, Wycliff. He doesn't have to know. Just show me who the man is. I'll take it from there."

"No, Renko knows I told you. Who else tells you?"

"Well, it's your problem. Either you show me, or I let these people have at it."

Wycliff looked around. "You no understand. They nothing like Renko. He's an animal."

"I'll worry about that. You come tomorrow morning and show me Renko." Wycliff looked dejected, but he nodded.

"And don't think you can skip out of this. These folks will find you. All they need is a word from me."

Wycliff nodded again.

"Okay, folks," Jackson said, turning to the neighbors. "Wycliff will bring me to the man who sent Okeyo to America. I'll speak to that man and see what he can do for Okeyo's widow."

The guide translated and the crowd nodded. They were satisfied.

As was Jackson. It was the break he'd been looking for. If he played his cards right, he might get back to the U.S. without having to use his own cash.

CHAPTER FORTY-THREE

———————◆———————

V ERMEULEN HAD A LOT TO ANSWER for. The Federal Police had taken over
the case and were focusing on him first. He had seriously upset Austrian
sensibilities by having a gun without a permit, firing it and wounding Kurtz,
investigating without a license, and altogether playing the lone ranger. He
was handcuffed and locked in an interrogation room at police headquarters.
Popescu was elsewhere in the building, as were the four men who had been
held in the apartment. Kurtz had been brought to a hospital to have his
wounded hand treated. When Kurtz's lawyer showed up, he more than made
up for Kurtz's absence. He made sure everybody at the police headquarters
knew how prominent his client was. In the middle of the night, things looked
bleak for Vermeulen.

At three in the morning, Vermeulen finally had the opportunity to tell his
story. Outside he could hear Kurtz's lawyer shouting. Once Vermeulen told
the police what happened, the tide turned in his favor. The captive men, and
particularly an extremely grateful Milosh, eagerly testified that they'd been
held in apartment 1B by Kurtz and Popescu for nearly two weeks while they
waited for their visas to the U.S. When they were asked about that, all they
said was that they'd been offered money to test a revolutionary new drug in
America. It sounded farfetched, but it corroborated Vermeulen's version of
events.

Then Tessa showed up. She'd followed the girls to the sleazy hotel and
found out they were indeed prostitutes. She talked to them and found out that
Kurtz held their passports and threatened to have them arrested if they didn't
play along. The accusation that Kurtz was involved in sex trafficking changed
the direction of the investigation. Kurtz's lawyer alternated between calling

the claims an outrageous slander and invoking the stellar reputation of his client as an important member of the community. The louder he shouted, the less the police believed him.

The final bit of evidence came from a sleepy Dufaux, who'd been yanked from his bed and urgently called to headquarters to confirm Vermeulen's account of his investigation. He also verified that the license plate Vermeulen had seen at the hospital was indeed assigned to the office that Kurtz administered.

It was seven the next morning when the Federal Police commander of Vienna finally let Vermeulen go. They gave him back his things. He was told not to leave the city and to remain available for further questions.

VERMEULEN AND TESSA HURRIED TO THE clinic to relieve Marieke and see if Gaby had made more progress. Marieke had the drawn look of someone who hadn't slept all night.

"Where have you been?" she said. After looking at them, she added, "You look like you've spent the night in your clothes."

"We did," Vermeulen said. "At police headquarters."

Marieke sighed and rolled her eyes. "Don't tell me you are in trouble again."

"I wasn't looking for it. How is Gaby?"

"She slept through the night. What happened to you?"

"We cornered the people who threatened Gaby. There was a little altercation, the police got involved, but I'm cleared, for now."

"For now?"

"For good. The important thing is that Gaby is safe again. Those people are behind bars."

Marieke looked at Tessa, her eyebrows raised, looking for confirmation.

Tessa nodded. "Things happened very quickly. I wasn't present at the shooting because I was following up on a different lead, but Valentin's been cleared and the bad guys are in custody."

"There was a shooting?" Marieke said. "Who shot whom?"

Vermeulen hesitated. "I shot Kurtz in the hand. He was threatening to kill someone."

"And Kurtz was the one who threatened our daughter?"

"Yes."

"Good. I'm going to get some sleep now. Gaby hasn't said anything or moved since last night. Call me if that changes."

She left.

It wasn't the reaction Vermeulen had expected. But he preferred it to another confrontation.

"I'll go and find some breakfast," he said. "What would you like?"

"Why don't I go? I'm not sure what I'm in the mood for, but I know what you want."

"Am I that predictable?"

"When it comes to breakfast, yes. Coffee and croissants."

"You got it. Thanks for making the run."

After Tessa left, he settled in a chair, put his feet up, and closed his eyes. What a night. He wasn't sure if he was happy about how it went down. He needed more evidence to make a solid case against Kurtz. If Tessa was right, Kurtz could have been using the cover of the internship program to lure young women to Vienna on the pretense of working for the UN. Once they got there, he coerced them into prostitution. But the police had to get the women to testify, and that was the problem. Testifying would only be a prelude to deportation, so the women likely had disappeared already.

The visa scam was still a puzzle. They had the letters that Frau Waldmüller gave to Popescu, who turned them over to Kurtz. The four men in the apartment were probably the intended recipients of the visas, but what for? He didn't believe the drug testing claim anymore. Tessa was right. It seemed too expensive to fly people to the U.S. Pharma corporations didn't need to do that. And they certainly wouldn't use illegal means to obtain visas. Unless the recruitment of the volunteers was subcontracted to some crook like Kurtz. *Nah.* It didn't make sense.

Worse, the letters hadn't been used yet. So there was no evidence of fraud. The only person in trouble was Frau Waldmüller, who least deserved it. Not a good night. Not knowing the purpose of the visa scam left him restless. There had to be more to it. He'd put a stop to the Vienna operation. Suarez and Sunderland in New York would be happy about that.

There was still Nairobi. How did Abasi and Odinga fit into this scheme? Was there somebody like Kurtz in Nairobi, doing the same thing? He took out his phone to call Bengtsson. The display reminded him that he still hadn't listened to Jackson's message. He had just tapped the keys to connect to his voicemail when the bed linens started rustling.

Gaby's eyelids fluttered, then popped open. She turned her head, looking around the room. When she saw him, she appeared puzzled for a moment, then smiled. Vermeulen stuck the phone back in his pocket and went to her side.

"Good morning, sweetie," he said. "How are you feeling?"

"Hi, Dad," she mumbled. "Where am I? What are you doing here?"

"You're in a clinic in Vienna. You had a skiing accident and were in a coma for over a week. I came as soon as I heard."

She frowned, her brain visibly searching through the recesses of her memory, trying to reconstruct the past week.

"Is Mummy here?" she said.

"Yes, she just left. We're taking turns sitting with you. Tessa is here, too."

Gaby closed her eyes again. Her breathing was more ragged now. The conversation must have exhausted her. The sight made his stomach tense. He'd come to think of her as a twenty-something bundle of energy who could manage a big division in her company and go hiking and skiing. What if the accident had put an end to that? What if …. He forced a stop to that train of thought. She'd opened her eyes and recognized him. She'd be well again. That was all that mattered.

As if to disabuse him of that notion, his phone rang. He checked the display. Unknown caller. Against his better judgment, he tapped the Reply button.

"Vermeulen here."

"This is Igor Oserov."

Vermeulen waited for more, but apparently, Mr. Oserov thought his name alone was enough of an introduction.

"I'm sorry, Mr. Oserov, but I don't know who you are."

"I'm the Director-General of the United Nations Office in Vienna."

"Oh, of course. Good morning, Mr. Oserov. What can I do for you?"

"For starters, you can stop sullying the good name of the UN in Vienna. Then you can stop dragging a valued UN representative into disrepute with unfounded accusations. Finally, you can present yourself at my office in one hour and explain to me what in the world possessed you to start investigating someone under my authority without notifying me."

CHAPTER FORTY-FOUR

———— ◆ ————

Vᴇʀᴍᴇᴜʟᴇɴ ᴇɴᴛᴇʀᴇᴅ Iɢᴏʀ Oꜱᴇʀᴏᴠ's ᴏꜰꜰɪᴄᴇ ᴛᴡᴏ and a half hours late. It hadn't taken him that long to deal with his anger. In fact, he'd calmed down quickly. His tardiness was calculated. Ordinary lines of authority didn't apply to OIOS investigators. How else could they investigate people who occupied a higher rank at the UN? So he'd talked more with Gaby, had breakfast with Tessa—sharing part of his croissant with Gaby, who was ravenous—and gone back to the hotel for a shower and fresh clothes.

Oserov waited for him in his spacious corner office on the top floor of the central building in UN City. The windows on each side showed off Vienna at its best. The office was furnished with a seating area, modern paintings on the wall, and a large mahogany desk. The lack of any sign of work on the desk—he saw only a telephone—told him all he needed to know about Oserov. The man was punctilious to the extreme. And he was furious. Which was okay, because Vermeulen was calm.

"Your blatant insubordination will be noted in your file," Oserov said for an opening volley. His voice was strained. The man could barely keep himself from screaming.

Vermeulen smiled. "My direct superior is Mr. Suarez in New York," he said. "His superior is the Under-Secretary-General for Internal Oversight Services. Her superior is the Secretary General. I don't see you anywhere in that line of command."

Oserov looked at him, dumbfounded. He swallowed several times. He was obviously not used to having someone talk back to him.

"You …" Oserov rushed from behind his desk and stabbed his finger at Vermeulen, "don't talk to me that way. Nobody talks to me that way, especially not some rogue investigator from New York." When Vermeulen raised his eyebrows, Oserov continued, "Yes, I know about you and your checkered history with the organization. It will be my crowning achievement to see you fired in humiliation."

"First off, you can't fire me, Mr. Oserov. Second, to get my superiors to fire me, you have to present cause, which you don't have. So, I don't see any need for threats. Can we discuss the real issues instead?"

"Oh, I have cause. I have plenty of cause. Do you want to hear the charges before I forward them to the Secretary General?"

Vermeulen shrugged.

"First, you undertook an investigation in Vienna without notifying me. Second, you have no authorization from your superiors to investigate in Vienna. Third, you questioned a long-time employee without providing her with the necessary representation, which is in violation of the UN staff agreement. Fourth, you discharged a firearm in Vienna without having the necessary permits and authorizations, violating the host agreement with Austria and the city. Fifth, you assaulted a valued UN manager with that firearm, in violation of more rules and regulations than I can list here. That man has permanently lost the use of his hand. I'm sure he will sue the UN for damages. Is this enough, or should I continue?"

Vermeulen sat in one of the chairs and crossed his legs. "You've been busy this morning, haven't you? Trouble is, you haven't got your facts straight. If you'd be so kind as to listen to what I have to say, you might change your mind. But I think you are more worried about protecting your image than actually dealing with the cancer that exists right under your nose at UNO City. I will file my own report. It will have a special section on the Director-General of the UN Office in Vienna shielding a sex trafficker. I'm sure it will do wonders for your career at the UN."

Oserov stepped back behind his desk. "Those are totally unsubstantiated allegations. I've known Mr. Kurtz for almost a decade. Under his leadership the internship office has grown dramatically and has offered young people a direct chance to work with the UN. I won't stand by as you besmirch his name."

"Maybe you got a cut from his business. Or maybe free use of the women who didn't quite make it into an internship. I should raise that possibility in my report."

"Your impertinence is outrageous. Don't you dare drag me into your dirty business."

"*My* dirty business? I came here to visit my daughter, who is sick in the hospital. Merely a day after I arrive, the gangsters in the U.S. contacted Kurtz, who threatened my daughter."

"That's laughable," Oserov said, sounding less angry.

"The car used by Popescu was registered to Kurtz's UN office."

"I don't know this Popescu. He probably took the car without permission."

"Forget it. Kurtz and Popescu are working together. They drove to the apartment building where I confronted them. I know because I followed them. My associate interviewed two of the trafficking victims, who said that Kurtz kept their passports and threatened them with deportation. I also spoke to four men in the apartment who had been lured to Vienna by Kurtz. Do you want me to continue?"

Oserov mopped his forehead with his handkerchief. "You are putting unrelated events together," he said. "Kurtz had only just found out that some of the people he had invited to Vienna had been hoodwinked by gangsters. Popescu and his consorts are the culprits here. Kurtz is simply a victim of circumstantial evidence that Popescu created to shield his illegal activities. Had you paid any attention and had you informed my office of your activities, we could have told you."

"So now you *do* know Popescu? Then you must know that a prostitution ring was operating from the offices of the UN."

Oserov must have realized he'd said too much. "No, no. I have no knowledge of that. I'm saying that Kurtz was doing his own investigation of Popescu."

"That's ludicrous. I saw them together. I saw Popescu give forged letters to Kurtz. There was no investigation. They were in it together."

"It can't be true. You are making these things up to make me look bad, to denigrate the UN."

Vemeulen finally ran out of patience. He rose from the chair, put his palms on the mahogany desk and leaned forward. "I'm not worried about your image or that of the UN. I'm not in public relations. I bring perpetrators to justice. That's my job. In the end, it comes down to one simple fact. Kurtz threatened to kill an innocent man to protect his racket. I prevented that by wounding him. That's all. The image of the UN suffers more from cover-ups like the one you are trying to engineer than from my exposing a crook. As to your image, if lies are the only way you can maintain your good name, you haven't got one. Good day!"

CHAPTER FORTY-FIVE

———◆———

CAMILLE DELANO'S PHONE RANG. ANOTHER CALL from "Private." Unscheduled calls from management usually meant trouble. They had no reason to call if things were going smoothly. Her guys still hadn't found Jackson. He was a loose end, and management didn't like loose ends.

Jackson had left town; she was certain of that. After the stunt he pulled—getting the liquor store owner to hold Gergi and Andrej with a shotgun until the police showed up—he'd better make himself scarce. Gergi and Andrej wanted blood after that embarrassment. It took the lawyers most of a day to get them out, and they still faced charges for concealed carry without a permit. A guy like Jackson probably had extended family somewhere down south, an aunt or a cousin who'd put him up until better times. Still, it bugged her that he got away.

She tapped the Reply button. Maybe management had good news for a change, like dealing with Vermeulen in Vienna rather than Newark.

"Yes," she said.

"Someone flew to Kenya using Abasi's ticket and passport," the familiar voice said.

"What?" That didn't make sense. "When did that happen?"

"A couple of days ago."

"And you're only calling me now?"

"We weren't exactly looking for dead people leaving the country. According to you, some local crook took Abasi's money. Did he also take his papers?"

Jackson? Would he have done that?

"I assume so. He tried to squeeze Rosenbaum for money, so he must have found the address on Abasi."

"Stand by for a surveillance picture taken at JFK. See if it's your guy."

She noticed the designation of Jackson as *her* guy and put the call on hold. A buzz indicated that a new message had arrived. She checked the photo. It was a lousy picture, but the man on it looked like Jackson. Who else would be using Abasi's passport and ticket to fly to Kenya? The good news was that he was no longer her responsibility. But the downside was that she had to admit Jackson had slipped through her fingers.

"Yes, he's my guy," she said after reconnecting the call.

"Any idea why he's gone to Kenya? From what you told us, he's a local lowlife, no ambitions beyond hustling a few bucks for his meal ticket."

"That's what the doctor's description led me to believe."

"So you don't think he's going to make trouble for us there?"

"I can't imagine how. He knows nothing. He's got two and a half grand in cash, an e-ticket, and Abasi's passport. There isn't a whole lot he can do with that. I'm thinking he decided to leave town after a confrontation with my guys. Maybe he felt called to the motherland. I have no idea."

There was a pause on the other side. She probably sounded too flippant. But she needed to project confidence. That's what this game was all about.

"We're not so sure that he won't be a problem. What if he finds Abasi's family? Tells them what happened?"

"I agree that letting Jackson get away was a mistake." *Eat a little crow*, she thought. *Let the man know that I'm aware of my shortcoming.* "But I don't think it will have long-term consequences even if he finds the family. Sure, they're going to be upset. Can they do anything about it? No way. They're poorer than dirt. Nobody will listen. Not to them and not to Jackson. The more I think about it, the better I feel. Jackson in Kenya is good news. There, he can yell until he's hoarse. Nobody will hear it."

That was convincing, she told herself. A cogent argument presented in logical fashion. Management had to accept that.

The silence on the phone told her that she'd been successful. They were thinking.

"We agree with your reasoning … for now," the voice said. "But we are not convinced yet that Jackson is completely out of the picture. Going to Kenya seems a big step for him. Get in touch with Nairobi and tell him all you know about Jackson. Who knows? He might run into him. Stranger things have happened."

"Will do," she said and ended the call.

Getting in touch with Nairobi meant speaking with Renko. She'd met him only once and knew immediately that he was a pig who thought he was irresistible. As with all pigs, it never occurred to him that that very assumption would be off-putting to ninety-five percent of the women in the world. Add to that his penchant for settling his affairs in the most gruesome manner possible and you had a man who was doubly dangerous. Not only was he liable to tell any whore about his dealings to impress her, he also left enough destruction in his wake to attract official attention that a more suitable method would have avoided.

The last thing she needed was that animal giving her shit about letting Jackson escape to Kenya. She could already hear his words: "You let a two-bit crook get away and now I have to clean up your mess." Never mind all the times she had cleaned up after him.

Opening the freezer door of the refrigerator, she put three pieces of ice into a highball glass, grabbed the vodka bottle she kept next to the ice tray, and poured herself a drink. Better to have something to warm your belly before talking to that jerk.

Once the vodka had taken the edge off, she dialed Renko. It rang for a long time. That was partly due to the relays that made the call untraceable. Finally she heard Renko's voice.

"Hello there, this is Renko. Talk to me."

She was about to tell him about Abasi's passport when she realized she'd gotten his voicemail. She breathed a sigh of relief. Management policy was to never leave voicemails. They'd be stored somewhere, and that was just asking for trouble. She tapped the End button and finished her vodka.

CHAPTER FORTY-SIX

---◆---

T HE NEXT MORNING, JACKSON AGAIN HAD tea and white bread with the
strange paste for breakfast. The whole proposition of having Wycliff show
him this guy Renko was starting to sound iffy. Wycliff could just not show up.
Maybe the threat of violence from Abasi's family and friends wasn't enough to
keep him in line. Without Wycliff, he'd be in trouble. He wanted to scout out
the AIDS testing place and Renko before making any moves.

Anticipation. Get to know the territory. At ten, he arrived at the square
where the carpenter had already set out his bed frames. Wycliff was waiting
for him, half hiding in the shadow of a shack.

Okay. One down.

"We don't go together," Wycliff said. "Too much risk. Go behind me."
Jackson had no problem with that. Wycliff had come; no reason to assume
he would ditch Jackson now. Community pressure did its job. If he had
threatened Wycliff by himself, he'd be standing alone now. But Wycliff knew
the people who'd beat him the day before. And he knew they'd find him
if Jackson reported him as a no show. Maybe not today, but soon. Wycliff
must've figured that Renko wouldn't find out he'd squealed. Probably not a
safe choice, if Renko was as bad as Wycliff had made him out to be.

Jackson followed Wycliff at what he considered a safe distance. Close
enough to make sure he didn't lose him in the crowd. The paths were busy.
People haggled over produce for sale at every corner; touts called out to
him, displaying gaudy Chinese watches, top-up cards for mobiles, and cheap
phones to go with them.

More clearly than the day before, he noted that even though everybody
was African, they didn't treat each other as equals. It was an angry glance a

man gave to another when they accidentally bumped into each other, a larger-than-necessary detour a woman made around a dark-skinned man. Some underlying tension that was almost palpable. Except for the folks so dark, their skin was almost blue—he'd dubbed them the Nubians—he couldn't see any difference between the people he'd encountered. Yet he had a feeling that it wouldn't take a lot for the tension to erupt.

The burner phone he'd gotten in Newark didn't work in Kenya. Something about a different system. He'd used one of the phone ladies who offered phone service to call Vermeulen the night before, but had only gotten voicemail. A local phone might be useful, if only to call Vermeulen again and the U.S. embassy the moment he'd found out what he needed about Renko. The prices weren't too bad, but since he'd given the money to Abasi's wife, he had to be careful with what was left.

Wycliff kept going. He turned here and there. Jackson had lost any sense of where they were. He couldn't have found his way back to the guesthouse if his life depended on it. It didn't seem like the smartest move—following a crook to find an even worse crook, with all his money in his pocket, without a way to get home, without anything, really. He'd never felt so up in the air, so disconnected, so alone. The little coffee shop on Bleeker with Tami, the cute waitress, came to mind. She'd be sweet to talk to and get to know. She might even go out with him. As soon as this crazy thing was over.

They'd reached the railroad tracks again. It was a different part of Kibera, but Jackson relaxed a little. He could follow the tracks back to the big square with the bed frames, and from there, find the guesthouse. On the other side of the tracks, in a hollow, sat a large white tent. A white van with an air conditioning unit on its roof was backed up to one side. The opposite side was open, the tent fabric stretched high by two poles and held in place by guy-lines. The other sides were down and marked with the symbols of the sponsoring organizations. Jackson could make out a red crescent, a red cross, and several blue logos—one of which spelled UNAIDS. Women in white outfits sat at a desk under the canopy, processing the people in line. As Wycliff had indicated, the line wasn't long. Whatever activity was going on inside the tent wasn't visible.

Wycliff stopped. Without looking back, he signaled with his hand that Jackson should stay where he was. Jackson stopped and watched. Wycliff approached the tent and walked right past the people in line. He said something to the nurses at the table, who nodded to him. Then he disappeared inside.

A couple minutes later, he came out with a white man dressed in the usual safari clothing Europeans somehow thought was appropriate for Africa. It had to be Renko. They walked toward the end of the line. Wycliff seemed to be doing all the talking. They stopped. Wycliff looked in Jackson's direction, searching. He found him, raised his arm, and pointed. Renko looked at Jackson with a stare that felt like a laser.

Fuck! He'd just walked into the most obvious trap. How could he have been so stupid? Here he thought Wycliff was too scared to double-cross him. But the guy was a much better hustler. He figured that turning him over to Renko would leave his hands clean and save him from the wrath of Abasi's family and friends. Jackson thought of running. But he knew it was useless. Wycliff would find him in no time. Despite his blackness, Jackson stood out. He was well fed and had decent clothes.

Wycliff waved to him, motioning him to come and join them. This was it. Turn and run or face the music? Every muscle in his body said, "Run! You can make it, you can disappear." But his brain knew better. Even if he could disappear for a while, what would he do to stay alive? No. There was only one way out of this. Face Renko and find out what the hell was going on. Whatever Wycliff had told Renko, it was his word against Jackson's. He ambled toward the two men.

"Renko, this is Earle Jackson," Wycliff said as if he were the host at a party.

Renko stuck out his hand. "Pleased to meet you. I'm Renko. Earle Jackson, huh? Not a Kenyan name. Where are you from?"

Jackson swallowed. A crucial moment.

"Here and there," he said. He could feel the hustler in him asserting himself. "Been moving around a lot."

"But you're from America. You got that accent."

"Originally, yes. Been seeing the world. Pleased to meet you, too, Renko. You aren't Kenyan either."

"No, I come from a place that doesn't exist anymore."

Jackson nodded.

"Wycliff here thinks you'd be a good candidate for the study."

Jackson's mind went blank. "Uh ... what?"

"The study. A large study on a new drug. Revolutionary. We need test subjects."

Jackson looked at Wycliff. That man was one great hustler. Introducing him to Renko got Wycliff out of the line of fire. If anything went wrong now, Jackson was Renko's problem.

"You look very healthy, but we'll have to test you," Renko said. "You know, safety precaution. If it all checks out, you stand to make a pretty penny. And get a trip to America. Unless you have a problem waiting for you there."

"No problem," Jackson said. "No problem at all."

CHAPTER FORTY-SEVEN

———◆———

THE HIV TESTING STATION WAS OPERATED by some Scandinavian non-governmental outfit for UNAIDS, although there were enough logos on the tent to rival a race car. A blond man seemed to be in charge. The rest of the staff was African, mostly women.

The scrubs had to be for show. As if they needed sterilized outfits in Kibera. All kinds of germs were floating in the air that wafted through the tent. Not that it mattered. They were only drawing blood. They could've done that in jeans and T-shirts. Maybe they thought the white outfits looked more impressive, part of persuading suspicious poor people to trust some foreign medical scheme, the benefits of which seemed as uncertain as winning the lottery. As Wycliff had said, if you tested positive, you had a death sentence, except that it was dragged out for a long time.

Wycliff had faded into the background. He hadn't run away, but hovered near the edge of the line, ready to take off if necessary. Renko wasn't paying attention to him anymore. He was talking to one of the nurses. Then he went inside the tent to speak with the blond man.

Drug testing. That didn't sound right to Jackson. They wouldn't fly people to the U.S. to test drugs on them. Or pay them a lot of money. The brothers who did that in Newark sure didn't get much for it. That's why he'd never participated. Maybe it was different for a revolutionary new drug. Or maybe they finally realized that they had to test drugs on a whole lot more people than the poor who needed the money. Whatever. He wasn't going to do it anyway. Once he was off the plane, he'd disappear for good. And if Renko paid for his ticket, he'd have plenty of cash left to do it right.

The crew had their method down pat. First intake, then instructions on what was going to happen, then the blood-letting and then another set of information about how to get the results. The intake nurse looked up and did a double take. Jackson's clothes were too good for someone standing in this line.

"Name?"

Jackson stated his name. The nurse looked at him again and frowned. Jackson could tell she was wondering whether this guy was worth interrupting her routine. Apparently not.

"Where do you live?"

"Kibera."

She regarded him with one raised eyebrow.

"Where in Kibera?"

He remembered the rail stop and told her so.

"Laina Saba?" she said.

Jackson nodded.

"Age?"

"Thirty-one."

"Have you ever been tested before?"

"No."

"Any diseases or infections you know of?"

"No."

"You have a mobile number where we can reach you?"

"No."

"Check back with us in two days for the results. Now wait over there and someone will draw your blood."

The blond man pulled Jackson out of the line and brought him straight to one of the nurses. Jackson looked at Renko hovering near the door to the van. The man was obviously connected to this outfit, but how? He wasn't a medical professional, that much was clear.

The nurse pushed Jackson's sleeve up, twisted a thick rubber band around his bicep, and told him to make a fist. She probed the crook of his arm until she found a vein, which she rubbed with a cotton ball dabbed in alcohol. Then she peeled a syringe from a plastic bag, snapped a vial into the housing, and stabbed into his vein without any warning. He yelped in surprise. He watched the vial fill with his dark blood. At first there was just a few drops. Then, as he relaxed, it filled faster. He looked over to the man whose blood was drawn by the other nurse. The color of his blood was the same deep maroon.

The nurse snapped the vial out of the syringe and popped another one in. One of her colleagues had scribbled something on a label, which she stuck to the vial. When the next one was full, the nurse handed the container to the woman with the labels. But she didn't add another label. Instead she handed it to Renko, who disappeared inside the van.

"You are all done," the nurse said and grabbed a new bag with a syringe. She was ready for the next customer.

Jackson wasn't sure if he should wait for Renko or find Wycliff. He knocked on the door of the van. Renko opened it. A wave of cold air came from the inside.

"What?" he said.

"You want me to wait?"

"No. Working up the complete blood picture takes a while. Come back tomorrow. We'll talk then."

Jackson didn't want to leave. If his blood test didn't work out, if there was no match, Renko had no need for him. But Jackson needed to find a reason to hang around.

"What will happen next?" he said.

"We'll talk about it tomorrow."

"I don't want to wait that long. I need to know what's gonna happen. Either way."

Renko got an annoyed expression and sighed. "Listen," he said, "if your blood test comes out well, I'm sending you back to the U.S. of A. I'll give you an address, you go there. They'll take care of everything. When you are done you get paid."

"How much?"

"Plenty. Probably more money than you've seen in a long time."

"And what if the test isn't good?"

Renko looked at Jackson as if he were dimwitted. "Then you go back to whatever you were doing before Wycliff found you."

"No money?"

"Listen, Jackson. This isn't charity. We pay for services rendered. If you don't render any services, you don't get paid."

"But I already rendered a service. You got my blood. You could pay me for that."

"Your blood is the price of admission."

CHAPTER FORTY-EIGHT

———◆———

VERMEULEN WAS BACK AT THE CLINIC, waiting for the other shoe to drop. Gaby was asleep again and Tessa had a meeting about her organized crime story. He was sure her information about the women forced into prostitution by Kurtz was going to figure large. There was nothing else to do or investigate. The mills of Austrian justice were grinding away and he had too much time to think and worry.

He had no regrets. Gaby was safe again. That was all that mattered. Still, he wondered how Suarez would react to Oserov's complaint. Not that he was worried. Any halfway competent investigation would exonerate Vermeulen. He had no doubt about that. Of course, that presumed there would be an investigation.

Everything at the UN was political. More often than not, facts became an obstacle to the need to assuage the concerns of the hierarchy. The Under-Secretary-General or even the Secretary-General might laud him for cleaning up this mess, but the important decisions were made at far lower levels. There, the petty grievances and conflicting personalities often played a more important role than the facts. By the time three o'clock rolled around, Vermeulen's thoughts had retreated into a mean corner of his mind. He waited for the inevitable call and the bad news from Suarez in New York City.

He was on his second cup of coffee. Unlike the public hospital, the clinic offered excellent coffee to its guests, served in porcelain cups rather than cardboard beakers. He had half a mind to turn off his phone until he finished his cup.

His phone rang at four.

Suarez seemed calm. "Just explain to me what happened," he said.

"The principal of the ring behind the fake invitation letters in New Jersey contacted her counterparts in Vienna. They found the hospital where my daughter was being treated and left a threatening note on her bed. That's when I got involved."

He explained how he met with Dufaux, interviewed Frau Waldmüller who obtained the signatures, and followed her as she handed them to one of the crooks.

"I needed to find out who was threatening my daughter," he said.

"I understand. Continue."

Vermeulen told him about the confrontation with Kurtz on the Ferris wheel, finding his address, and following him to the apartment building where the armed confrontation happened. Suarez let him lay out the story without interruptions, which surprised Vermeulen, who knew the choleric temper of the man. He proceeded gingerly to the details of the gunshots fired, stressing the threat to the lives of innocent people.

That's where Suarez abandoned his quiet listening.

"You attacked a man—"

"Who was threatening me!"

"Took his gun and then shot a ranking UN employee."

It wasn't a question, it was a statement of fact. Vermeulen cringed at that description. Yes, it was true, but the context was missing.

"Yes, but—"

"You are aware that you have absolutely no authorization to do that?"

"It was self-defense. My life and an innocent victim's were saved."

"It's not your job to save lives. How often have I told you that you are an investigator, not a cowboy? It's that attitude that gets you into such situations in the first place. It was a mistake to bring you back to New York headquarters. Maybe you can get away with those stunts out in the boondocks, but you have no temperament for working at the center of an international organization."

Vermeulen had any number of choice answers to that accusation, but he held his tongue. This wasn't the moment to pick a fight. He was in a hole. Better to stop digging.

"How is your daughter?" Suarez said.

"She's getting better. The coma seems to be ending. Today, she spoke with me for the first time since my arrival."

"Good. I'm glad to hear that. I assume you'll be coming back to New York soon, then? I'm placing you on unpaid leave pending the outcome of an investigation that has already begun. That suspension starts now. It's in your best interests that the investigation comes to a quick conclusion. That means you should be out in front, telling the committee all it needs to know. So call me as soon as you are back."

"Yes, sir."

He ended the call and sank into the chair. He wanted to rant and swear, but his bones had melted. What energy he'd had dissipated in the stale air of the room. Or so it seemed because Gaby's voice caught him by surprise.

"Hi, Dad."

He turned to her.

"You look sad," she said. "Is everything all right?"

"It is, sweetheart. It is."

"Don't lie to me, Dad. I know when you're down. D'you want to tell me?"

"Maybe someday, but not now. You need rest, not trouble."

"Then come here. You can lie on the bed next to me. Maybe you need a little rest, too."

There was no reason to argue. He went to the side of the bed that didn't have all the medical apparatuses and crawled atop the bedding. She stretched out her arm. He rested his head on it. As she pulled him a little closer, he smelled a faint remnant of shampoo in her hair. The orderlies must have given her a bath and washed her hair.

"Good idea, Gaby."

She murmured something and stroked his hair. Vermeulen didn't notice. His exhaustion had already pulled him into a deep sleep.

CHAPTER FORTY-NINE

———◆———

ANOTHER MORNING AT THE GUESTHOUSE. THE same tea and white bread with Vegemite, that strange paste. Jackson had finally asked about it. Apparently, the British brought it to Kenya and his host thought that all foreigners liked it. He would have killed for a fried egg and some bacon. Overall, though, he couldn't complain. The supper of *nyama choma* and moonshine had been better than the night before, and he'd gotten braver about eating street food during the day.

Jackson was itching to get back home. He was still marveling at how well Wycliff had played his cards. He'd stayed out of trouble and Jackson was on his way home. If the test turned out good, he'd be okay. As long as Renko thought he was a wandering American ready to earn some cash, he was safe. If not? He didn't want to consider that alternative. Having met Renko, he understood why Wycliff was afraid of him. The man had a ruthless streak. Dealing with him was going to be tough.

That left Abasi's wife. He felt a pang of conscience remembering how he'd told her and the neighbors that he was going to press Renko for some compensation. That wasn't going to happen. It came down to him getting home or being stuck in Kenya. It was a no-brainer. He was going home one way or another. And for that, he needed to know the results of the test.

Wycliff was waiting for him outside the guesthouse. Which was odd. There was no reason for him to be there. Jackson knew how to get to the clinic where he was to meet Renko.

"What are you doing here?" he said.

"I bring you to Renko."

"I know how to get there."

"He's not at the clinic. You go to his house."

That was seriously off. Renko had definitely told him to come to the clinic. "Why?"

"He calls me and tells me to bring you. Is all I know."

That could be true, but Jackson didn't trust Wycliff.

"Hold on a minute. Just realized I forgot something inside," he said and went back into the guesthouse.

It took a while to find his host out back, washing sheets.

"Someone is waiting for me out front and I need to get away without him seeing me."

She looked at him with curious eyes. "You in trouble?"

"Not yet. But the man outside is trouble, I think."

She shook her head as if to say, *Men, what are you going to do about them?*

"Come," she said and went to a corner of the fence that surrounded the postage-stamp yard. She twisted two pieces of wood and lifted a sheet of corrugated tin like a flap.

"Turn left and go straight until you reach a corner, then go left again and you'll get to the railroad tracks."

"Thanks a lot. I really appreciate it."

"You won't get back in that way. So you better lose the man out front."

JACKSON MADE HIS WAY ALONG THE tracks back to the general area where the tent and the truck had been the day before. Wycliff had spooked him, and he wanted to be extra cautious, whatever that meant in this strange place. Back in Newark, he knew how to disappear, blend in so that no passerby would notice him. Here, that was impossible. Although his clothing was looking worse for wear and the sporadic access to water made him smell like everyone else, the kids still stopped and eyed him. He knew that kids saw things adults didn't, but that wasn't a notion he'd base his life on.

The tent was already in operation. The van with the air conditioner on top stood backed against the rear. A small line of people waited to be tested, about the same as the day before. The nurses worked with the same efficiency; the doctor drifted between the testing stations and the van. The only thing different was the absence of Renko.

For a moment, Jackson thought he'd been too paranoid about the whole thing. Maybe something really had come up that kept Renko from coming to Kibera. That thought sent him down a different route. What could have come up to keep Renko from checking on the test results? It had to be something important. Something more than an upset stomach or a hangover or not feeling like it. If Renko's job was to recruit participants for a drug study, he should be at the testing station. But he wasn't.

Not that his absence was an obstacle. Jackson could ask the doctor or the nurses what his role at the station was. That might give him some insight into how the scam operated at this level. Since the doctor was probably part of the scam—who knew there were so many crooked doctors?—he had to be careful. Anticipation.

He approached the tent from the opposite direction, weaving carefully in and out of the stream of people, stopping here and there to check on the situation. But nothing indicated anyone lying in wait for him. He noted no telling glances from the nurses, no pretend carefree banter meant to hide the nervousness, only observed a group of healthcare professionals doing their job.

The nurse who took his information the day before recognized him and smiled.

"Hullo, Mr. Jackson. Back to check on your results?"

"Yes, I am, ma'am. You have them?"

"They should be in the database. Check with Doctor Agnor."

"Where's Renko? I expected to see him here."

"I haven't seen him today. He was still here when I left last night. Maybe he overslept."

He stepped under the tent and caught the doctor.

"Dr. Agnor?"

"Yes?"

"I'm here to check on my test results."

"You were here yesterday afternoon, right?"

"Yes."

"Then let's look. What's your last name?"

"Jackson."

Agnor did a double take. "Right." He looked left and right to check if anyone was nearby.

"So, do I have AIDS?" Jackson said.

"No, you don't. You're as healthy as can be." He looked around again. "Usually Renko discusses the remaining results with the test subjects. But I haven't seen him."

"What remaining results?"

"If a subject is HIV-free and looks promising, Renko orders a whole other battery of tests. Just a few days ago, he gave me a very specific set of criteria to check against. So I checked your blood from every which angle."

"What kind of extra tests?"

"Blood type, of course, a whole panel to check for other diseases, and HLA."

"What's that?"

"I don't know if I should tell you this. Renko usually does that."

"Well, if he's going to tell me anyway, you can give me the preview. I promise to look surprised when I hear it from him."

"I guess there's no harm in it. The HLA test tells me about your immune system—human leukocyte antigens, to be specific."

"Human leuko … what?" Jackson said. "Why would anyone need to know about that?"

"For all kinds of reasons. But I think Renko is looking for a very specific person. At least on the basis of the parameters he's given me. Almost as if he was looking for an organ donor."

"An organ donor? He told me it was for drug trial."

"Yeah, that's his story. I guess if they were testing a drug for an autoimmune disease, like regular diabetes …. But he gave me very specific values. If they were testing a drug, they'd want a variety of subjects. You don't develop a drug for such a narrow group of recipients."

"So what's the result?"

"You aced all tests. If they are looking for, say, a kidney, you'd have the perfect specimen."

Chapter Fifty

———————◆———————

KIDNEY TRANSPLANTS. OF ALL THE POSSIBLE medical schemes Jackson had imagined, kidney transplants had not been in the picture, not even in the vicinity. It all made sense, though. The amount of money involved, finding people hard enough up to consider giving body parts for cash. Made much more sense than drug testing. The distance involved puzzled him. Even with the potential money involved, it seemed like a complex operation. There were a lot of ways a scheme like this could go sideways. Even getting to America would be difficult.

He looked at the people in line to be tested. Any one of them might be a candidate. It struck him. These folks were dirt poor. They were scared. They didn't know squat about Newark or the U.S. If they got into trouble, they'd keep their mouths shut and be deported.

Abasi had twenty-five hundred dollars in his pocket. Jackson knew that was too much for participating in a drug test. But it seemed pretty low for losing a kidney. He knew people could live fine with only one, but what if that one failed?

He had to find Renko and get back home. There he'd disappear. No way was anyone getting near his kidneys, no matter how much they promised. The easiest way to find Renko was to just stay here at the test clinic. He was bound to show up eventually.

A hawker had set up a makeshift stall, selling cold drinks to the people waiting in line. He bought a Coke and a bag of peanuts and walked back to the railroad tracks. He picked up a piece of cardboard, put that on the gravel bed supporting the tracks, and settled against one of the ties. Far enough from the clinic to be inconspicuous, close enough to keep an eye on things. He opened the Coke, took a sip, and waited in the sun.

The wait lasted an hour. First Jackson heard the car horn. A few minutes later, a four-wheel-drive vehicle pushed its way through the crowd. The incessant honking didn't seem to have any effect. The people kept walking where they were walking and didn't move out of the way until the car almost touched them. It had to be a white guy. Nobody else would be so stubborn.

Eventually, the car stopped. The door opened and Renko got out. He scanned the clinic and its immediate surroundings. His glance missed the tracks where Jackson lounged. Renko even stepped on the bottom of the door frame to get a better view. No difference. Finally, he marched to the clinic and shouted something.

Dr. Agnor came out, looking concerned. Renko gesticulated and shouted some more. Agnor shrugged, pointed toward a different part of the tracks, shrugged again as if to say, *Nope, I don't know where Jackson went.* Agnor returned to the tent and Renko marched back to his truck and drove off.

Jackson considered this. Wycliff had probably spent some time looking for him. He wouldn't have liked going back to Renko and admitting that he'd lost Jackson. When that didn't help, he must've gone to Renko and reported the bad news. Renko was mad and figured that Jackson had come back to the clinic. Had he known that Jackson was a perfect match? Maybe he'd called the doctor. That would explain his rush and his anger. Jackson was a prize he couldn't let slip through his fingers.

He hiked to the clinic. If his kidney was really the perfect match, Renko would come back.

* * *

RENKO EASED HIS SUV THROUGH THE throng of people. He'd given up leaning on the horn. It had no effect. The phone call from the Broker had shaken him more than he cared to admit. Jackson had come straight from the U.S. on Abasi's passport. Not some expat, floating around East Africa, as he'd claimed. He'd found Wycliff and made contact within a day of his arrival. What was he after? According to the Broker, he was a small-time hustler from Newark. He sure didn't act like one.

To make things worse, the man turned out to be the perfect match for the special order the Broker had relayed only a couple of days earlier. None of his other candidates fit the requirements. The very man to make them a lot of money turned out to be the one who knew enough to be trouble.

It was a real conundrum. His first instinct had been to eliminate him. That's why he had rushed to the clinic, his SIG 9 mm in his pocket. But now that he sat in his car unable to go anywhere fast, he was figuring out a way to cash in on the match. The best solution would be to harvest the kidney and have Jackson expire during or after the operation. But that required getting him to the U.S. and onto the operation table. And Renko had a strong feeling that Jackson wasn't going to do that without resistance. One way would be to harvest the kidney here, put it on ice in a cooler, and bring it to the U.S. But there were no direct flights. Even with dry ice, the kidney would be worthless by the time it got to Newark.

Nope, there was no way around it. Jackson had to go back to Newark. The only question was how. Of his own free will or under duress? The more he thought about it, duress wasn't going to work on Jackson. So he had to persuade the man to get on the plane. Once on it, the people in Newark could figure out how to deal with him. The best solution was kicking the problem back to Newark. He turned the car and headed back to the clinic.

Jackson stood there with a grin on his face.

"Mr. Jackson, am I glad to see you here. Thought for a moment I'd lost you. I have good news. You earned yourself a trip back to the U.S. of A. If you're ready, we're gonna put you on a plane tonight. A quick stopover in Dubai and then on to New York City."

"Good deal. I'm looking forward to seeing the home country again. It's been a long time."

It was the reaction Renko had hoped for. But he didn't feel much better. He couldn't figure out Jackson's angle. The man shows up and tracks him down in only two days, but then he's happy as can be to go back to the U.S. Why'd he come in the first place? What if he ran? There was little chance of him staying in Dubai. There was nothing for him to do. But in JFK? That was a different story. Too many ways to escape. But that was the Broker's problem. Not his.

"Let's go to my office and get you the paperwork for the flight. You've got your passport?"

Jackson nodded.

"Great. You won't believe what we have to do to get a visa for some of the locals."

CHAPTER FIFTY-ONE

———◆———

THE GOODBYES HAD BEEN DIFFICULT. VERMEULEN had wanted to stay another week, explore Vienna with Gaby and Tessa, maybe even have a quiet dinner with Marieke as a start to getting back to a relationship that wasn't based on anger and accusation. He had vacation days he could've used. Going back to New York City was his last choice.

Tessa had been the voice of reason. *You want to keep your job?* It was her only question. After a lot of hesitation, he'd answered in the affirmative. Despite the aggravation working for OIOS generated, he liked the work and was good at it. He also liked the ethos of the UN, even if the organization didn't always live up to it.

"Then you've got to get back there now," she'd said. "Your boss was doing you a favor by urging you to come back as soon as possible. If he wanted to get rid of you, he'd have encouraged you to stay away as long as you like."

That thought hadn't even occurred to him.

"He wants you to beat this rap, and the only place you can do that is at UN headquarters. So listen to his advice."

He booked his return flight and spent a tearful evening with Gaby and Tessa at the clinic. Gaby was able to walk a bit but had little stamina after lying in bed for so long. The doctor assured them that it was simply a question of physical therapy and regaining strength. They'd do another brain scan to make sure that everything was as it should be. The rest was up to Gaby. "Human bodies are incredible healing machines," the doctor had said. Vermeulen believed him.

At the airport, waiting for his flight, he finally listened to the voicemail messages on his phone. The last one had arrived merely four hours before he got to the airport. Both came from long, unfamiliar numbers. The first one was from Jackson. He had to listen twice to understand that Jackson had gone to Kenya. It wasn't quite clear why he'd gone. As far as he could make out from the garbled recording, he'd been in trouble in Newark and took Abasi's money and passport to go to Nairobi. "I'm doing the right thing" were his last words before he hung up.

Good for you, Vermeulen thought and wondered what kind of trouble he'd gotten into. If it was related to the Broker, it probably was wise to put as much distance between himself and that woman as possible. But Nairobi was one of the organization's centers of operation. Jackson was likely to end up in even more trouble.

The second message was also from Jackson. The connection was much better. The background noises sounded like an airport. Jackson sounded excited.

"Hey Vermoolen. I found out what they're up to. It ain't drug tests as they told me. It's kidneys. They're after kidneys. They get 'em from poor folks in Kenya. They fly 'em to America for the operation, pay 'em a little, send 'em back, and cash in. Man, what a racket.

"I'm in Dubai. Never thought I'd get around this much, did ya? Here's the deal, they were looking for a very special kidney, and guess what? I got it. So I got myself a free trip back home. Don't worry, I ain't going through with the operation. Once I get to JFK, I'm gonna skip town. Renko—he's the one who runs the show down in Kenya—didn't know who I was. Told 'im I was a world traveler, looking for some cash. He was happy to send me. So long, man. Don't think I'll be seeing you again."

* * *

CAMILLE DELANO SAW THE WORD "PRIVATE" on her phone's display after the ringtone had woken her. A call from management at five in the morning meant trouble. Management never called this early. In a normal month, they'd call her twice with updates and orders and she'd call them as needed with results. But this month had been far from normal. An early call like this meant things had gotten bad. And worse, that management wasn't on top of it. When management wasn't on top of things, the trouble usually landed in her lap.

"Yes," she said, answering at the last possible moment.

"Three things," the familiar voice said. "One, Vermeulen exposed the Vienna operation. We've been working on containment for most of a day. The UN office there has been playing ball, but the Vienna police have not. Kurtz and Popescu are in jail. Two, Vermeulen is on his way back to JFK. Three, Jackson is a perfect match for the client and is also on his way to JFK. He's a serious flight risk, so make sure you get him as soon as he clears customs."

"What happened in Vienna?" she said.

"We are still reconstructing the events. We tried to talk to Kurtz by posing as family but weren't let in. Our regular legal counsel is out of town; we are looking for a suitable substitute. None of this is your concern. You must focus on Vermeulen. He's the only one who can make the connection between Vienna and Newark. If he goes public with it and involves the authorities, you'll be the first to go down."

That threat was unnecessary. She knew how dangerous Vermeulen was. She also knew that Rosenbaum would be a far juicier target for the federal prosecutors. A famous surgeon always beats an unknown woman when it comes to the perp walk. Sure, he'd lawyer up. That would make it even more interesting. In the meantime, she'd be long gone. Bonaire sounded more tempting than ever.

"Are you there?" the voice said.

"Yes."

"We'll rely on you to keep this mess contained to Vienna. Vermeulen must be eliminated. He is on Austrian Air Flight 19 and will arrive at JFK at noon. Jackson is scheduled to arrive at eleven on Emirates Flight 59. Grab him, drug him, whatever. Just make sure you get his kidney, then get rid of him. A lot of money is riding on your getting this done."

That gave her less than six hours to put her plan in place.

First, she started her coffee machine. Then she called Gergi. By the time she was sipping from her second cup, the outlines of her strategy were clear. It was an iffy plan. It depended on the two flights arriving on time. And on her crew performing without a flaw. Two conditions that weren't necessarily a given.

At seven, she called Rosenbaum and told him that the kidney for Woodleigh had been found and that the donor would arrive that morning.

"That was fast," Rosenbaum said. "I'll set everything up for tonight."

"There's a small complication. This donor is likely to resist. We'll have to sedate him the moment he comes off the plane."

"He isn't one of the usual candidates?"

"No."

"Inject him with Narcozep. I'll tell my staff to have it ready for you. Just stab the needle into his arm and push the plunger. That should make him docile enough to get him to my office. Make sure you tie him to the bed. We don't need him walking off like the other guy."

CHAPTER FIFTY-TWO

———◆———

VERMEULEN STOOD IN THE VISITORS' LINE at JFK, moving at a snail's pace to the passport control booths. Since he wasn't a permanent resident and didn't have a diplomatic passport, he had to bear the long wait. Not that he minded. It wasn't much of a homecoming. Being the object of an investigation had soured the joy of returning to his apartment.

The line moved a little.

During the flight, he'd reviewed each decision he'd made during his time in Vienna. By themselves, none of them were grounds for dismissal. Only his decision to stake out Kurtz's house and follow him to that apartment building could be interpreted as reckless. But he'd explain that by recounting his fear that his daughter might be harmed. They had to take that into consideration. Best case scenario, he'd walk away from this with a commendation for uncovering a bad apple in the organization. Worst case, he'd get a slap on the hand for being a "cowboy." No big deal. He'd gotten a few of those.

The line moved again.

Jackson's last message reminded him of all the unfinished business awaiting him. The Broker wasn't going to care about the UN investigation. He was certain that she had orders to deal with him. Her organization had taken a serious blow in Vienna. Their next steps would be protecting the other branches of their network. And he was the only one who could establish the link between them.

Protecting Gaby had been his only concern in Vienna. It made him go after Kurtz and Popescu. The fake invitation letters were just the means to find them. But those letters were also central to the case waiting for him. Human trafficking to harvest organs. Why hadn't he thought of that? It explained the last piece of the puzzle that hadn't fit—Rosenbaum. But that wasn't his concern anymore. Not when OIOS was putting his conduct under a microscope.

The people in front of him were directed to the booths. An officer motioned him to stop.

The more he thought about it, the more he didn't believe Tessa's argument that Suarez was in his corner. Why would he want to help Vermeulen? Bad employees reflected poorly on their managers. Rule number one was to disavow them. The best he could hope for was Suarez not making things worse for him. Having solved the origin of the fake letters would help. He would recommend that Suarez turn over the human trafficking investigation to the FBI. OIOS had channels to the Bureau. That might get both Suarez and the Broker off his back.

The officer sent him to Booth 8. He rolled his bag over to the booth and waited again. There were three visitors ahead of him.

It sounded just like Jackson to get himself hired as a kidney donor for a free ticket home. Once a hustler, always a hustler. He still couldn't understand why Jackson had gone to Kenya in the first place. The *do the right thing* story didn't sound like him at all. More likely, he'd run from the gangsters. They'd be out for blood after he got away from them once. He'd better be careful.

He made it to the booth. The officer checked his passport and visa. He saw the UN credentials and went about his job with a quiet efficiency. Right thumb on the green glass, right four fingers, left thumb, left four fingers, look into the camera, thank you, next.

He rolled his bag through customs and emerged into the public concourse. There were the usual array of limo drivers holding up signs. He was tempted to pretend to be Mr. Miller or Mr. Perlmutter and snag a free ride to Manhattan. Better not. It'd be his bad luck to get into a limo headed to New Jersey or Connecticut.

The whole Vienna excursion had made a serious dent in his finances. Which meant taking the subway to Manhattan. He followed the signs for ground transportation. Halfway across the arrivals hall, he saw something that made him stop.

Two white men were shepherding a black man toward the exit. The black man seemed unsteady on his feet, like he'd had too much to drink. He also looked like Earle Jackson. That couldn't be. Vermeulen was about to continue on his way to the exit when one of the men holding Jackson's arm turned his head. Vermeulen knew him. He'd accompanied the Broker at the Azure Lounge. The black man was Jackson. His plan to give them the slip had failed. *That dumb kid. What was he thinking?*

He ran after them, dividing the mass of people with his left arm while dragging his bouncing bag behind him. People yelled at him for bumping into them; others stared as if he were the Wolfman. He didn't care, because he knew that Jackson wasn't going to come out of this alive. Once they harvested his kidney, they'd kill him. When he reached the doors, he saw the two men push Jackson into the rear of a black Chrysler.

He raced to the taxi stand. The dispatcher saw him and shook his head.

"Go inside, get in line. No hailing from the curb."

There was a cop on the sidewalk. Making a stink would just delay him more. He ran inside, looked for the taxi dispatch. The line reached around a support column. He turned around, saw the limo drivers with their signs. This was the moment to impersonate a "Mr. Smith." But that wasn't necessary. To his considerable surprise, one of them was holding a sign that said, "Vermeulen."

Of course, there was a more than even chance that some Dutch or Belgian businessman was the expected client. He knew of no one who'd send a limo to pick him up.

The driver holding the sign had noticed him stopping. "Are you Mr. Vermeulen?" he said.

"Yes, I am."

"Mr. Valentin Vermeulen?"

The likelihood of that being someone else grew much smaller. He nodded.

"And you are with the UN?"

Okay. There was no one else.

"Uh … yes, that's me."

"If you'd come with me. The car is waiting outside."

The man turned toward the door. Vermeulen followed.

"Who ordered the limo for me?"

"I just got the call to pick up Mr. Vermeulen, arriving from Vienna."

"Where are you supposed to bring me?"

"The East Village, Gansevoort Street."

That was his apartment. And it didn't make sense. If Suarez had sent a limo, it would take him to the UN, not home. But then, Suarez would never in a million years send a limo.

"And you really don't know who ordered the ride?"

"No. I just get the call and drive."

They arrived at the curb where a black Lincoln stood. The driver popped the trunk and reached for the roller bag. Vermeulen was about the hand him the bag when he saw that the plate wasn't a T&LC license. This wasn't a real limo.

The Broker knew he'd come back.

Even worse, she knew which flight he'd be on. There were only three people with that information: Tessa, Gaby, and Marieke. He hadn't told the

Vienna police, since he didn't want to deal with them. He hadn't told Suarez. Hell, he hadn't known himself until Austrian Airways confirmed his seat late in the evening the day before.

There were only two ways the Broker could have found out. She, or someone connected to her, had called the clinic, asked for him, and Tessa or Marieke had told the caller. Extremely unlikely. The only other possibility was that someone in the Broker's organization had access to passenger lists of incoming flights. That required access to Homeland Security computers. And that was deeply unsettling.

Vermeulen ripped his bag from the driver's hand and ran back into the terminal. It was too late to follow the car that had taken Jackson. But its destination wasn't a mystery. They'd bring him to Rosenbaum's office in Newark.

The name-brand rental car counters were crowded. He chose a no-name company because its counter had no line. An hour later, he crossed the Verrazano-Narrows Bridge and raced across Staten Island toward New Jersey.

Suarez and the investigation would have to wait. It wasn't his choice, and it might well mean the end of his job. But a confrontation with the Broker was inevitable. She had made sure of that. Better it was on his terms than hers.

The Broker had wanted to keep Jackson's transplant separate from dealing with Vermeulen. That's why she'd sent the fake limo. And it meant her crew was split. Two were dealing with Jackson and at least one, probably two, were supposed to deal with him. That meant Rosenbaum was alone. He was the weakest link in the whole operation. He was the one Vermeulen could pressure for the truth.

Jackson's role was an added complication. He'd tried to take advantage of the scam and got caught. But Jackson was Exhibit One in the case against the Broker's organization and Rosenbaum. Jackson provided the link to Kenya. And there was something likable about that man. Maybe he *had* done the right thing in Nairobi.

He crossed Goethals Bridge and merged onto the Jersey Turnpike north, then wove his way through the Newark traffic until he reached Rosenbaum's office on MLK Boulevard.

CHAPTER FIFTY-THREE

───────◆───────

THE OLD BROWNSTONE ON MLK BOULEVARD stood quiet amid the mid-afternoon bustle around the hospital. The sign still announced Dr. Rosenbaum and his medical specialty: surgery. Vermeulen circled the block once and didn't see the black Chrysler anywhere. Either they had already delivered Jackson or they'd stashed him somewhere else. He parked on Summit and went around the block to the entrance.

Nobody answered his first buzz. He knocked on the door. Someone ought to be in the office at three thirty in the afternoon in the middle of the week. He pushed the button again.

Finally, he heard steps and the door opened a crack. Vermeulen could see the chain securing the door. The face of a middle-aged woman appeared in the crack.

"Good afternoon," he said. "I'd like to speak with Dr. Rosenbaum."

"The doctor isn't here."

"Hmm, that's too bad. Do you know if he'll come back today?"

"No, the doctor is out for the day."

That was odd. According to Jackson's last message, Rosenbaum should be expecting a very special kidney. Not the day on which you'd knock off early.

"Well, I'd better make an appointment then. Can I do that?"

"Of course."

The woman closed the door to release the chain and let Vermeulen in. The inside was decorated like every medical office Vermeulen had ever entered—off-white walls and prints of peaceful landscapes on the walls. There was a small reception area with a desk and two chairs. A hallway led to rooms in the back, a staircase to the upper floors. The woman settled into her chair behind the desk and began typing.

"Where are you keeping him?" Vermeulen said.

The woman looked up as if she'd misheard.

"Excuse me?"

"Where have you put Jackson?"

"I'm not sure I understand."

"Oh, you understand just fine. I'm talking about the black man who'll be donating a kidney against his will."

"I don't know what you are talking about. There is no black man here."

Her face had turned white. Her gaze shifted from Vermeulen to the phone on her desk and back.

"You're thinking about calling for help, aren't you?"

The woman shook her head.

"Good. What's your name?"

"Eileen."

"You don't want to do that, Eileen. I know enough of what's going on in this office to put you behind bars for accessory to murder. What you want to do right now is get in my good graces. You got that?"

Eileen nodded.

Just to remove any lingering temptation, he unplugged the cord from the phone and yanked hard. Plastic snapped somewhere under the desk and the other end of the cord flew out. Wrapping it around his hand, he looked at her.

"Your cellphone."

She didn't move.

"Listen, you people have messed up my life so thoroughly, I'm beyond cranky. Hand me your phone or I will find it myself."

She dug through her purse on the desk and handed him her phone. He stuck it into his jacket pocket.

"Come over here. Turn around. Put your hands behind you."

He tied her wrists with the phone cord.

"Now show me where you've put Jackson."

She headed for the stairs.

The second floor looked as institutional as the first. The contrast to the clinic in Vienna was stark. Given how much money Rosenbaum had to be making here, he sure hadn't put any of it into creating a pleasant space. But then, the patients here weren't meant to linger. The recipients of the kidneys had plenty of money to recuperate elsewhere, and the donors didn't matter.

There were three doors along the corridor. She took him to the last one. He opened it. Inside stood a hospital bed, a chair, and a small cupboard with a cup. On the bed lay Jackson, eyes closed and breathing slowly. His wrists and ankles were strapped to the bed.

"What did you give him?" Vermeulen said.

Eileen shrugged.

"Eileen, this whole operation is going down. You know that. One of your donors died. Do you want to be an accessory to murder?"

She shook her head.

"So tell me. What did you give him?"

"I didn't give him anything. I assume the doctor gave him a sedative before he left."

"Does that knock him out completely?"

"I don't think so."

Vermeulen walked to the head of the bed and shook Jackson.

"Hey, Jackson. Time to wake up."

Jackson didn't respond. Vermeulen kept shaking him. "Come on, Jackson, let's go. You don't want to end up under the knife."

A groan emerged from Jackson's mouth. His eyes stayed closed. Vermeulen unbuckled the straps around Jackson's wrists and ankles and moved the arms. More groans. He slapped Jackson's cheeks gently.

"Come on, Jackson. Rise and shine. Time to go."

Jackson's eyelids fluttered, then opened. His pupils were the size of nickels, black and unfocused. Vermeulen pulled his torso to a sitting position. Jackson was no help at all. He plopped back to the bed the moment Vermeulen let go. His eyes closed again.

Vermeulen sampled the liquid in the cup with his pinky. It was water. He dumped it on Jackson's face. It had the desired result. Jackson's eyes opened again. He sputtered, raised his head, and opened his mouth. Nothing came out.

"Jackson, we've got to get out of here. I can't carry you. So you're going to have to get up."

"Wha …?"

"Get up, man."

Vermeulen tried to shift the legs over the edge of the bed. Jackson wasn't much help. It took several tries to get him to sit, and then he could do so only with Vermeulen keeping him upright.

"Listen. We've got to get out of here. So you have to work with me on this."

"Okay."

Vermeulen draped Jackson's arm around his neck and tried to lift him to his feet. It was like lifting a sack of potatoes. He struggled, lost his momentum, and ended up sitting on the bed next to Jackson, who looked at him with an expression that said, *Do I know you?*

Before Vermeulen could give it another try, the door slammed.

Eileen.

She'd waited until Vermeulen was immobilized with Jackson's deadweight and made a run for it. He jumped up to run after her. Too late. There was no handle on the inside.

The door wasn't a cheap hollow-core thing you could punch through. It was wooden, installed when the brownstone was built, solid and fit properly into its frame. But it was also a panel door. Nice to look at, but not as sturdy. Vermeulen maneuvered Jackson into the chair and moved the bed aside to make more space. He stepped back and aimed a kick against the lower right panel. The door made a loud creak and a crack appeared. Another kick, and the wood splintered. With the third kick, half the panel flew into the hallway. He reached through the hole and opened the door.

That was the easy part.

He ran downstairs and found the front door open. Eileen had run away. The police were only minutes away.

Back upstairs he roused Jackson, put his arm around his waist, and slung the man's arm over his shoulder. They managed to make it out the door and into the hallway. Jackson must have realized that this was important. He tried to keep upright, moved his legs, but he was wobbly. The stairs were worse. Twice, Vermeulen had to pull Jackson back and sit him on the steps or they would have fallen down the stairs headfirst.

The temptation was to go out the front door. It was nearest. But it was also where the cops would come in. He coaxed Jackson through the office to the back door and down the steps into a neglected yard. As he closed the back door, he heard voices at the front. No time to rest.

A ramshackle gate in the rotten wooden fence didn't put up much resistance. In the back alley, he pulled Jackson forward until they reached Summit, where he'd left his rental. Jackson still couldn't stand on his own. Coaxing him into the car took more time than he had. The cops could show up any moment. After levering Jackson into the passenger seat, Vermeulen lifted his legs inside. The seatbelt kept Jackson halfway upright. They drove off.

Passing the brownstone on MLK Boulevard, he saw two black-and-whites double-parked. Eileen stood by the second car and talked to another cop. She didn't look his way.

Three blocks farther, he stopped. With all the tumult, he'd forgotten to get Rosenbaum's home address from Eileen. Damn. He reached into his jacket for his phone and found Eileen's. Sure enough, it had Rosenbaum's home address in Millburn, about a half hour away. Her phone's calendar also indicated that

Rosenbaum was scheduled for eight that evening. He entered the doctor's address into the map app of his own phone and tossed Eileen's out the window.

CHAPTER FIFTY-FOUR

———◆———

VERMEULEN DROVE PAST ROSENBAUM'S HOUSE, WHICH bordered a wooded area next to a small lake. Past the lake, he saw more mansions. He turned around and nosed the car into a small dirt lot next to the water. It was empty and the far end wasn't visible from the street, a perfect place to keep Jackson without attracting unwanted attention. He left the car keys on the driver's seat, just in case. Jackson dozed in the passenger seat.

"I'm going to visit the doctor, Jackson. Stay in the car. Don't go anywhere. If I don't come back in an hour or two, take the car to Newark and call the police."

Jackson's response was unintelligible. Not a reassuring sign, but Vermeulen couldn't wait for Jackson to recover. The Broker could show up any moment.

The house was a single-story sprawl built in a U-shape, and it just kept on going. Its wings were surrounded by gardens. A semi-circular driveway connected the road to the portico. Everything about it was pompous, even the doorbell, which sounded as if it were only a fraction smaller than Big Ben itself. It rang out the entire sequence of the original. Vermeulen half expected it to count out the hours as well. People must not ring doorbells much in this part of New Jersey. Otherwise any sane person would have disconnected the button a long time ago.

A small Latina opened the door.

"Yes?"

"I'd like to speak to Dr. Rosenbaum. It's an urgent matter."

"Who are you?"

"Valentin Vermeulen."

"Please wait."

She closed the door. A moment later, it was opened by another woman. She was the exact opposite of Rosenbaum. Her face looked peeled, scrubbed, the skin as tight as a drum. If Rosenbaum's face had a life of its own, this woman was in complete control of hers. Everything was exactly where she and her surgeon had determined it should be. Her age was a mystery. Older than thirty was about all anyone could guess.

"Can I help you?"

Her voice had a tinge of reproach, as if he should have called at the service entrance.

"I need to speak with Dr. Rosenbaum. It's very urgent."

"This is a private residence. If you have business with my husband, you should call his office and make an appointment."

"I did go to his office and was told that he'd gone home. It's a private matter."

"I doubt that very much. I know my husband's private circles, and you aren't part of them."

"I didn't say I was his friend, I said it was a private matter. It's imperative I talk to him now."

"Who do you think you are, coming to my door, looking like something the cat dragged in? Whatever it is you have to talk about, I'm sure my husband isn't interested. Leave now, or I will call the police."

Vermeulen wasn't surprised that the threat of the police came so quickly. The police would be on Mrs. Rosenbaum's side. No doubt about it. And Vermeulen needed to keep them away for a little longer.

"That would only postpone the inevitable," he said. "Your husband is involved with some nasty characters. I've tracked them from Newark all the way to Vienna, Austria. That end of the operation has already been rolled up by the police. The Newark end will follow soon. Your husband's fate depends on whether he cooperates with me or not."

"Who are you again?"

"I'm Valentin Vermeulen, senior investigator for the United Nations Office of Internal Oversight Services."

"Senior investigator of what?"

"The UN Office of Internal Oversight Services."

Repeating the information had no discernible effect on Mrs. Rosenbaum.

"Is this a joke? Why does the UN concern itself with my husband?"

Vermeulen pulled out his wallet and showed her his ID. "It's far from a joke. Given the international nature of the crimes in which he's participated, the involvement of the UN is routine."

It was a lie, of course, and ordinarily he'd be loath to add to the pervasive ignorance about the UN. But in this case, it was the easiest way to keep Mrs.

Rosenbaum from calling the police. And it worked. Her demeanor changed from haughty to worried.

"My husband is a surgeon. What is he supposed to have done that warrants the involvement of the UN?"

"He's part of a human trafficking network that smuggles people to the U.S."

She shook her head, breaking into a peal of laughter. "My husband is smuggling people to the U.S.? Have you met my husband?"

Vermeulen nodded.

"Then you should know he's incapable of anything except surgery. It's ludicrous."

"He works with a woman who's known as 'The Broker.' She supplies him with his victims."

"His *victims*? Are you crazy? Do you know what my husband does? He's a transplant surgeon. And a very busy one at that. He's so busy, he only takes private patients. The demand for kidneys is insatiable, and there are legions of grateful patients who've gotten a new lease on life. Those are his," she made air quotes, " 'victims.' Get off my property now, or the police will be here faster than you can spell your funny name."

"Where do you think all those kidneys come from?" he said.

She shrugged. "I don't know and I don't care. I'm sure it's all proper."

Vermeulen was about to explain how improper it was, when Rosenbaum appeared behind his wife.

CHAPTER FIFTY-FIVE

———◆———

"THEY SAID YOU WOULDN'T COME HERE," Rosenbaum said, his face doing that odd dance again.

"They were wrong, weren't they?" Vermeulen said.

"You should hear what he says about you," his wife said.

"Stay out of this, Mitzi," Rosenbaum said.

"The hell I will. If only a fraction of what he says is true, I'm going to be part of this conversation."

"I'm here to offer you a deal," Vermeulen said. "Cooperate with the investigation in exchange for leniency."

That was the second lie. Vermeulen was in no position to offer anything. But he couldn't think of any other way to coax Rosenbaum to his side.

"Marvin, tell me. Is it true what he says?" Mitzi said.

"What did he tell you?" Rosenbaum said.

"Something about an international human trafficking ring that brings you your victims."

"Nonsense. There are no victims."

"But are you involved with something illegal?" she said.

"Uh …" he hesitated before adding, "no."

"That does it," she said. "I want to hear what Mr. Vermoolen has to say."

"I don't think that's a good idea," Rosenbaum said. "He's blowing things out of proportion."

"That's what I want to find out. If you're right, we'll call the police."

Rosenbaum's face reflected his internal struggle. The tics were painful to watch. How could Mitzi put up with that? Maybe she appreciated that her husband could never lie to her.

She opened the door wider. "Come in, Mr. Vermoolen."

Mitzi closed the door after her husband.

The foyer was expansive, with a tall ceiling. An armoire and two chairs were the only pieces of furniture. The floor was tiled with marble slabs the size of coffee tables. Scattered rugs indicated paths leading to the interior. Mitzi headed into the left wing.

Rosenbaum's phone rang. He checked the display. Once glance at his face told Vermeulen it wasn't a call he wanted to take. "It's the Broker, isn't it?" he said.

Rosenbaum looked at him, trying hard to get his face under control. He nodded.

"Take the call. If you know what's good for you, you won't tell her I'm here."

Rosenbaum nodded. He tapped on his phone.

"Yes," he said.

Vermeulen could hear a voice but not what was said.

"Yes, I'm home. What's the problem now?"

The voice squawked again.

"Yes, later this evening. What?" He hesitated, then said, "No …" he hesitated again. "No, he isn't here."

Rosenbaum looked at Vermeulen as if to say, "See, I didn't say anything." But the pause had been the tell. Not that it mattered. The Broker had already figured out what happened. Why else would she have called? There wasn't going to be a lot of time to persuade Rosenbaum to cooperate.

"Yes, I know," Rosenbaum said. "No need to come here. I'll meet with you tomorrow. I've got to get ready for surgery tonight."

He listened some more. It didn't take much imagination to figure out the gist of the conversation. Vermeulen's sudden arrival back in the U.S. had stirred up the Broker and her gang. Add Jackson's kidney, which sounded like a very special case, and the stakes were higher than ever. Like Vermeulen, she knew that Rosenbaum was the weakest link in the operation. His turning Rosenbaum around had to be her nightmare scenario.

"Good, tomorrow at my office, then," Rosenbaum said. "Ten in the morning. Good, I'll be there."

Vermeulen knew he had very little time.

Mitzi Rosenbaum waited for them in a room that had probably been labeled "Library" on the builder's plan. Except that no one coming into this room would assume anyone actually read here. The yards of books with leather spines were the giveaway. Who actually sold books with leather spines except for fake libraries?

A low table, an assortment of chairs, and a chaise longue were the sole furnishings. On the table stood bottles of Hendricks Gin and Q Tonic, an ice bucket, and a small bowl with lime slices. Apparently, happy hour had started before Vermeulen arrived.

"I want to get one thing straight," Rosenbaum said. "I'm not going to say anything without talking to my lawyer first."

"Then I have no reason to stay here," Vermeulen said. "You'll be talking to the FBI next."

"The FBI?" Mitzi said. "You didn't say they were involved."

"Human trafficking across state lines is a federal crime. The FBI has a special task force for it. They'll be eager to hear what you have to say. Your lawyer won't make a difference."

"They can't make me talk," Rosenbaum said.

"You're right, probably not, especially with your lawyer by your side."

"You'd better leave now. There's no use in you being here."

"Dr. Rosenbaum, let me tell you something about the Fifth Amendment. Sure, you can't be forced to say things that incriminate you, but it doesn't stop the FBI from investigating you. They'll subpoena your hospital records, they'll delve into every transplant you ever performed. They'll talk to every donor. Can your practice withstand that scrutiny?"

Rosenbaum swallowed and wiped his forehead with his handkerchief.

"I didn't think so," Vermeulen said. "Once they have a case—and trust me, they'll find enough to make one—you'll wish you'd have cooperated from the beginning. The feds don't take kindly to rejection. The way I see it, cooperation with the investigation is your best option."

"What makes you think you can take down the Broker?" Rosenbaum said. "That woman is ruthless. What if you and the FBI screw up? I'll be sticking out my neck and she'll be coming after me. I can't afford that."

"You're in no position to bargain. I'm going to the FBI with this, no matter what you do," Vermeulen said. "If you're not with me, I'll personally make sure that you bear the full responsibility for your starring role in this operation. Remember, you were the one who performed the operations. Did the Broker force you to do those?"

Rosenbaum shook his head.

"I didn't think so. Without your greed, none of this would've happened."

"Don't talk to my husband that way," Mitzi said.

"Why shouldn't I? Aren't there guidelines, waiting lists, procedures for kidney transplants? He ignored those because he was paid a lot of money. And what about the poor people who were coerced into donating a kidney?"

"Nobody was coerced," Rosenbaum said. "They were paid for it. It was a legitimate exchange."

"There's nothing legitimate about this business. Rich people want to jump the queue and you were more than happy to help them in exchange for cash without regard for the consequences. I spoke with one of the potential donors in prison. The gang had threatened to kill his family. He was so scared, he wouldn't even tell me why he'd come."

"I don't know anything about that. I never threatened anyone."

"No, you let the Broker do the dirty work for you. That's not much of a defense."

"Leave Marvin alone," Mitzi said. "He only wanted to help."

Vermeulen shook his head.

"You wouldn't want me to leave him alone. Alone, he'll be serving the next several years in a federal prison. I'm his only hope right now. Cooperate with the investigation and I'll put in a good word for you."

Rosenbaum's body shrank as if collapsing onto itself. He fell into one of the chairs, breathing heavily.

"Enough," he said. "I'll cooperate."

That's when the Big Ben doorbell rang. Time was up.

CHAPTER FIFTY-SIX

———— ◆ ————

CAMILLE DELANO DIDN'T PLAY GAMES. SHE didn't do sneak attacks, scale walls, or cut through windows to gain access to a house. In her experience, just ringing the doorbell got her inside ninety percent of the time. For the remaining ten percent, she had Gergi and Andrej.

Gergi stood behind her. She'd sent Andrej around the back to make sure Vermeulen didn't skip out that way. He'd better not make a mess of it. She didn't trust her crew much. They were just muscle. The concept of improvising was foreign to them. Gergi, behind her, was no better. But he had one redeeming quality: he didn't ogle her when he thought she wasn't looking.

Vermeulen had to be at Rosenbaum's; there was no place else he could logically be. If she were in his position, she'd have targeted Rosenbaum, too. The one unknown that worried her was how much Rosenbaum had told Vermeulen after he got here. He had a lot to lose if this thing blew up. That ought to put some steel in his spine, but she'd seen plenty of people with stronger dispositions crumple. Hope for the best, prepare for the worst.

The endless Big Ben sequence of Rosenbaum's doorbell made her wonder why anyone would put up with that much noise. The door opened. Rosenbaum's fluid visage appeared. She'd seen it in enough states of flux to no longer be taken aback by its gyrations.

"I thought we'd meet tomorrow," he said.

"A slight change of plans. Where is he?" she said.

"Where is who?"

"Vermeulen."

"What makes you think he's here?"

"Because he's intent on destroying everything we've worked to build, and let's face it, you are the weakest link."

The door opened wider and a woman who'd been through a serious maintenance regime appeared.

"You must be Mitzi," Delano said.

Mitzi didn't say anything.

"Just tell me where Vermeulen is," she said. "He's obviously been by. Is he still here or has he left?"

"The whole thing has blown up," Rosenbaum said. "I can't afford not to cooperate with him and the FBI."

"The FBI? Did he tell you the FBI was involved?" the Broker said.

The Rosenbaums nodded.

"That man is too much." She laughed. "Vermeulen has been telling you tall tales. He is on his own little crusade. He's just arrived from Vienna. He hasn't had time to contact the FBI."

"He could have called from the plane, or the airport," Mitzi said.

"Yes, in theory, but remember, the man has no standing. Why would the FBI work with some investigator from the UN? Hell, they don't even work with the local cops. But even if they were involved, do you think you could walk away from this? You're going to be on the hook. I'm just the broker. I didn't cut people open and take their kidney. I didn't put it into another patient who paid big bucks. Guess who's going to be paraded on TV cameras? Not some unknown woman, but the famous rich surgeon who was so greedy he broke the law to make even more money. The public will just lap it up."

Rosenbaum looked at Delano. Whatever anchor had kept him moored had just been ripped loose. The tics and twitches of his face kicked into high gear.

"But it's never going to get that far because Vermeulen is lying," she went on. "Vermeulen is the only one who knows anything about our arrangements. With him out of the way, there is no reason it cannot continue. Just think about Mr. Woodleigh. We have the perfect donor for him. After the surgery tonight, we'll get a million dollars, four hundred thousand of which are going into your pocket."

The Rosenbaums looked at each other.

"I don't know," Rosenbaum said. "Are you sure that nobody but Vermeulen knows?"

"One hundred percent. I'm betting my future on it."

"What do you propose to do with him?"

"That's none of your concern. So don't ask."

Mitzi's eyes flickered. She probably imagined Vermeulen disappearing in the concrete foundations of some high-rise. Whatever she thought, it didn't change her mind. She looked at her husband, who nodded. The money had done its trick.

"Okay," Mitzi said. "We're listening. But I have to tell you, we're not going to be involved in murder."

"That's why I said you're better off not knowing. So, where is he?"

"I've put him in one of the guest rooms."

CHAPTER FIFTY-SEVEN

---◆---

THE GUEST ROOM COLOR SCHEME WAS a cloying shade of pink. It contained a king size bed, a large bathroom en suite, a flatscreen TV, and an abstract print on the wall. It was the type of room you'd expect to find in a two-star hotel. The interior decorator must have figured that adding a hundred pillows to the bed made up for the lack of ambiance.

Vermeulen had no illusions about the Rosenbaums. They were the kind of people who checked the direction of the wind and adjusted their convictions accordingly. The Broker—he had no doubt she had arrived—would warn them against going to the FBI. She'd tell them that Vermeulen couldn't offer them any deal. And she'd be right. Rosenbaum would flip-flop in a second.

He sidled next to the sliding glass door and peered into the garden. The sun had already sunk behind the trees. A landscape architect who must have been a big fan of Louis XIV had dragooned nature into a grid. The beds that would eventually be full of blooms were still just brown shapes on the yellow lawn. It'd take a bird's eye view to discern what form was being represented. The formal garden reached as far as the woods Vermeulen had seen from the street. Somewhere beyond that was the lake and the spot where he'd parked his car.

A man came around the corner of the house and took up position in the garden. He made no attempt to hide the pistol in his hand. It was the guy who'd sat at the bar in the Azure Lounge. The Broker had definitely arrived.

He left the room. In the hallway, he heard distant voices to the right, no doubt the Broker explaining to the Rosenbaums the value of giving up Vermeulen. To his left, near the end of the corridor, were two doors opposite each other. He tried the one to the left and found another guest room. Same décor, but in a more masculine tan. It faced the same direction as the pink room. He could see the man standing outside.

The other door led to yet another guest room—again the same décor, except in light blue. The decorator must have gotten a serious quantity discount on pillows. It faced away from the garden and toward the other wing of the house.

Vermeulen checked the map on his phone. Not a promising direction for an escape. He'd have to walk past the house to get to the car. The best way out was through the garden and toward the lake. Which meant luring the man to this side of the house.

He grabbed the chair. It was oak, just the right heft for what he needed. He threw it as hard as he could against the sliding glass door. It shattered in a loud crash. He ran back to the pink room and saw the man hurrying around the corner of the house. Vermeulen opened the sliding door and slalomed past the flowerbeds and toward the woods.

Once in the trees, he stopped, panting. The man had come around the corner of the house again. He stared at the woods. The leafless branches didn't provide any cover, even in the fading light. Vermeulen knew he'd be spotted. Sure enough, the man raced across the garden. Fortunately, his pursuer didn't know the first thing about gardening; otherwise, he would've avoided the raised beds. His feet sunk into the loam, and he stumbled and fell headlong to the ground.

Vermeulen used his head start to push his way deeper into the forest, toward the edge of the lake. The brambles were hard going. Crashing through them also made a lot of noise; his pursuer would have little trouble following. He stopped fighting with the twigs, dropped into a squat, and listened. The noise of breaking branches told him the man had reached the woods, too.

Change of plan. He saw a dip in the terrain that had filled with dead leaves. It was a better option than trying to outrun the man. He pushed the leaves into a small berm, lay in the hollow, and swept the leaves over his body.

The sound of breaking twigs and the snags of thorns tearing on clothing came closer. Shoes dragged through the leaves. The man stopped. Ragged breath. A mumbled curse. Feet shuffling around. Vermeulen held his breath. The man was very close. The urge to raise his head and look was almost overwhelming.

The breathing slowed. Had he seen Vermeulen? Was he taking aim with his pistol? A cold sweat covered Vermeulen's body and seeped into his shirt. Another step. Probably raising the gun just about now. Ready for the kill shot. Like an executioner stepping behind his kneeling victims, pointing the gun at the neck, firing.

A shot echoed through the woods.

Except, it wasn't a shot.

It was a branch breaking with a loud crack. The man stumbled. A desperate "Fuck."

A heavy body fell across Vermeulen.

The chances of that happening had to be right up there with winning the lottery. But Vermeulen didn't waste any time calculating the odds. He'd been hyper alert, his muscles tensed, ready for action. He levered the body to the side. Jumped up. Grabbed the broken section of the branch that stuck up from the leaves. The man scrambled onto all fours. Vermeulen hit him with his makeshift bat. A groan told him he'd connected. It wasn't enough, just a glancing blow. The man rolled sideways, ending up on his haunches. Still in a crouch, he raised the pistol with both hands. Vermeulen swung. The branch batted the gun from the man's hand. It flew into the leaves. His pursuer rose to his full height. He was build like a truck.

Vermeulen was tempted to swing again, but didn't. The close combat rules for sticks were the same as for bayonets: you don't swing, you stab. The man expected a swing and raised his hand to grab the bat. Vermeulen used the opening to ram the end of the branch into the man's gut. The rotten wood broke into two pieces. The man doubled over. But not for long. Without a weapon, Vermeulen had to resort to using his hands. That meant stepping forward. The man was prepared. His right hook connected with Vermeulen's ribs like a grenade. He stumbled backward.

The man followed with a roundhouse. Vermeulen dodged that one by stepping back. The momentum pulled the man toward him. Vermeulen took a step forward and head-butted the man against the bridge of his nose. The man stumbled back. His heel struck a rock under the leaves. He fell. Vermeulen grabbed the rock. The man rose again, and Vermeulen threw the rock at his head. It knocked him out cold.

Vermeulen rubbed his forehead. It felt as if he'd run into a wall. He searched the man, found a billfold, car keys, a handkerchief, a spare magazine for the pistol, and a bundle of zip ties. The zip ties were not like the plastic cuffs police carry, but still useful. He rolled him onto his belly and tied his wrists and ankles. The handkerchief served as a temporary gag. Eventually the guy would spit it out and start yelling. Hopefully that would be after Vermeulen had dealt with whoever else had come along with the Broker. There were at least two of them. As if on cue, a voice sounded from the edge of the woods.

"Hey, Andrej. Where are you?"

In the failing light, Vermeulen crawled in a circle through the leaves, feeling for the gun.

"Come on, man! I don't want to play hide and seek."

Vermeulen widened his circle. The dampness from the leaves was seeping through the knees of his pants. By now he had to look like a hobo. The sounds of someone stumbling through the woods in the dark came closer. He kept searching. At last his right hand found the cold metal of the gun.

"Andrej, don't be an asshole. Where are you?"

The voice was too close. No time to develop a strategy. Vermeulen had to rely on surprise. He crept away from the body and stood behind an old oak. The light was fading fast.

The second man almost fell over Andrej's cuffed body. He teetered at the edge of the hollow, then bent down and shook his partner.

"Andrej, what happened? Where's that dude?"

There was more rustling. He was probably feeling for an injury. Vermeulen took his chance, ran forward, and hit the man with his best rugby tackle. It wasn't as hard as in the old days, but it did the job. The guy rolled onto his back. Vermeulen jumped on top of him, clamped his hand over the man's mouth, and pinched his nose with his other hand. The man bucked like a crazed bronco but couldn't throw off Vermeulen. He struggled, grasping, kicking, bucking. It wasn't enough. Lack of oxygen did the rest. The legs stopped kicking and the arms fell to the ground as the man passed out.

Vermeulen rolled the body over and tied it up with the remaining zip ties. He found a pistol in the man's shoulder holster and stuck it into his jacket pocket.

That was when his phone rang.

CHAPTER FIFTY-EIGHT

———◆———

"HEY, MAN. WHERE THE FUCK AM I? What'cha doing driving me into the woods and leaving me? Where're you at?"

"Listen, Jackson. I just got you out of a load of trouble, so pipe down. I'm in the middle of something. Sit tight and I'll be with you before long."

"How did I even get here?"

"How much do you remember?"

"I got through customs and that's about it."

"Do you remember the two guys who were more or less dragging you through JFK?"

"Nah. Oh ... wait. Yeah. Two guys. Right. They poked me with something."

"Yes, they injected you and brought you to the doctor's office. I followed them and got you out."

"Wait, I thought you were in Australia or something."

"Austria. I got back this morning. My flight was late. I saw you on the concourse."

"Shit, man. Really?" Jackson said. "Thanks. I mean it. You got me out from under the knife, you know that?"

"Yes, I figured."

"So where are you now?"

"Close by. At the doctor's home. Listen, I've got to deal with the Broker. Wait in the car, please."

"Don't you need any help? That woman is serious trouble."

"You're in no condition to help. So sit tight. Don't stumble into this mess. They've got guns."

Vermeulen ended the call. Hopefully the mention of guns scared Jackson enough to stay out at the car. He needed Jackson. Jackson was the only one who had actually been recruited. He was the only evidence for the case against the doctor.

There was only one problem. Who would listen to his case and arrest the Broker and her gangsters? Not the local police. The Rosenbaums had already gone back on their deal. They'd convince the local cops that Vermeulen was an intruder. The FBI had jurisdiction in a case like this, but he didn't know any agents. Where would he even call? Headquarters? The Newark office? Once he called, he'd have to explain the whole story, and then what? Tell them to come and arrest the suspects? It didn't work that way. By the time they made up their minds, the Broker would be long gone. No, he had to get the Broker. Once she was tied up like her guys, he'd have leverage with the Rosenbaums, and then he'd have a case.

Vermeulen ran across the garden and around the wing of the house to the sliding door he'd smashed. The room was lit up. The maid was picking up large pieces of glass, putting them in a trash can. Her movements were slow. Bending and straightening were clearly painful. The door from the guest room to the corridor was closed to keep the cold out.

He stepped inside the room. She gasped, her eyes wide. He clamped his hand over her mouth.

"Shhh, quiet," he said. "Don't scream. You understand me?"

She nodded.

"Here's the deal. The woman and the men are gangsters. They are working with Dr. Rosenbaum. I'm with the police. I'm trying to arrest them. I need your help."

She nodded again.

"I need you to be quiet. You hear me?"

Another nod.

"Are you going to scream?"

She shook her head.

He released his hand slowly.

"What's your name?" he said.

"Rosita," she said. "I want no trouble, mister. Please."

"You're undocumented, aren't you?"

Rosita nodded. "Please, don't report me," she said. "I have two kids. They are American citizens, but I'm not. They are still little. If I get deported, who will look after them?"

It sounded just like the stories Alma had told him.

"Don't worry. But I need your help. How many came with the woman?"

"Two men. They had guns."

The Broker's crew was small, just as he'd expected. His mood improved.

With her muscle taken care of, the Broker would be easy.

"Okay. You'd better leave. I don't know what's going to happen, but it's best you don't get mixed up in it."

Rosita nodded again, dropped the broom and dustpan, and stepped outside. She knew how to get away without being seen.

"Oh, one more thing," he said. "Do you know about *Unidad Latina*?"

"Yes."

"Contact Alma Rodriguez. Maybe she can find someone who can help you. You know, get the right paper."

Rosita crossed the patio and disappeared in the dark.

Talking with Rosita reminded him that he did know one of the feds. Fred Sunderland at Immigration and Customs Enforcement. Of course. He could call him. The man had to have connections to the FBI.

Vermeulen opened the door to the hallway. Voices sounded from the library. He stepped back into the room, closed the door, and racked the slide of the Beretta. Never assume anything about an unknown gun. A cartridge flew onto the carpet. He released the magazine, inserted the round, and pushed the safety down.

Back in the corridor, he proceeded carefully. The mumbles grew louder. The Broker was talking. Mitzi Rosenbaum said something. Vermeulen stayed close to the wall until he reached the end of the corridor. Around the corner was the library with its unread books. Across was a large leather sofa occupying a back corner of what had to be the living room.

"What is taking so long?" he heard Mitzi say. "Your men should have caught him by now."

"Are you sure there is no way out from your yard?" the Broker said.

"Yes, on one side is the lake and on the other side are neighbors and a tall fence. They have the most awful Great Danes. We had to put the fence in to keep them from prowling on our property."

"Then they should be back shortly. Although I've learned Vermeulen can be resourceful."

"What does that mean?" Rosenbaum said.

"Only that he isn't a pushover." The Broker let that linger for a moment as if to point out the difference between Rosenbaum and Vermeulen. "But Gergi and Andrej are armed and Vermeulen is not. So it's not really a contest."

"There'd better not be any shooting in the garden," Mitzi said. "The police would be here in a minute and we'd never hear the end of it from the neighbors."

"If there's shooting, the neighbors are going to be the least of your worries."

"What does that mean?" Rosenbaum said for the second time, his voice pitched even higher.

"Forget it. It's not an issue. There won't be any shooting. Gergi knows what's at stake."

Vermeulen heard steps coming closer. He pressed against the wall and raised the Beretta. A woman's arm in a black sleeve appeared in his field of vision, then a shoulder. The Broker. She stopped.

"Let's hope you're right," Mitzi said.

The Broker turned back to Mitzi. "Don't worry, I'm always …."

Later, Vermeulen wondered if their physical proximity had sent invisible signals back and forth. There was no other way to explain why the Broker sensed that Vermeulen was standing around the corner. Or that Vermeulen knew she knew.

He spun into the library, pointing the gun at her. She reached inside the black linen jacket she wore. He lunged toward her. Giving up on her gun, she shot a fist at his solar plexus instead. He danced sideways. Her fist missed, and she stumbled forward. He flung his arm around her throat and pressed the Beretta against her temple.

"It's time to start worrying," he said.

CHAPTER FIFTY-NINE

———◆———

THE ROSENBAUMS STARED AT HIM, FLABBERGASTED. Vermeulen pushed the Broker into the library. The Beretta in his hand had given her enough of a shock. She walked willingly.

"I ought to have you all locked up and the key thrown away," Vermeulen said. "But I'll give you one more chance to redeem yourself. Come here, Doctor, and give me a hand."

Rosenbaum didn't move.

"Listen. I don't give a damn how good you are with your scalpel. All I know is you killed Abasi, and that's enough for me to see you go down."

"I didn't kill him," Rosenbaum said. "He didn't follow my instructions."

"Oh, shut up. He was probably doped. How could he have followed instructions? What I say to the FBI all depends on how you act now. Help me and I'll reconsider."

Rosenbaum stepped forward.

"I have zip ties in my left pocket," Vermeulen said. "Take one out and put it around her wrists."

Rosenbaum reached into the jacket pocket for one of the ties.

"Now put the skinny end into the opening, from the bottom."

"I know how to use zip ties," Rosenbaum said.

"Good for you." He turned to the Broker. "Stick out your hands, palms together."

"You'll be sorry," the Broker said. "If you think this ends here, you're sadly mistaken."

"Of course it doesn't end here. It ends when the jail cell is locked behind you. So put your hands out."

"Or what?" she said.

"Or I shoot you. You know Mr. Kurtz in Vienna, don't you? He'll never use his hand again. I think you'd want to avoid that."

She stuck out her hands and Rosenbaum looped the zip tie around her wrists.

"Now tighten it," Vermeulen said.

Rosenbaum reluctantly tugged at the skinny end of the tie. When it was tight enough to prevent her hands from slipping through, Vermeulen put the gun in his pocket, grabbed the broker's wrists, and gave the plastic strip another good yank. It zipped as tight as the wrists allowed.

"Have a seat," he said, and gave her a little push.

She plopped awkwardly into the low chair. Before she could recover, Vermeulen knelt down, grabbed her feet, and tied another zip tie around her ankles.

"You don't know who you're up against," the Broker said.

"I'm not worried. I'm going to deliver you to the FBI. They have a whole task force on human trafficking."

"And how are you going to get me there?"

"I assume you didn't walk here."

"You'll have to get the keys from my men."

Vermeulen pulled the keys from his pocket. "Way ahead of you."

"Where are they?"

"Tied up in the woods, ready for the police to arrest them."

That shut the Broker up.

"You two, behave," he said to the Rosenbaums. "This is going to end soon, and you can still end up in a cell next to the Broker. Don't do anything you'll regret."

Mitzi took a chair next to Rosenbaum. She looked defeated, but below the strain, Vermeulen could see anger. He hoped that it was anger about the way her husband had led her into trouble. He took out his phone and dialed Sunderland's number. Sunderland answered on the fourth ring.

"Is that you, Vermeulen?"

"It is. I'm back from Vienna."

"Did you stop the letters?"

"Well, that wasn't the primary purpose of my journey, but yes, I did manage to stop them."

"Some UN employee did it?"

"Yes. Listen, I need your help. The visa scam was part of a trafficking scheme to harvest kidneys from poor people. The Vienna end of that operation is already locked up. And I've rolled up the Newark end, too. Could you call the FBI for me? I'm sure you have connections."

"You've what?"

"I've found the people who ran the organ trade here in Newark."

"What do you mean, you've found them?"

"I've got them right here. Cuffed, ready to deliver to the authorities."

"Where are you?"

"In Millburn, New Jersey."

"Millburn?" There was a pause. "Give me the address."

Vermeulen recited it.

"Wait where you are," Sunderland said. "You're right. I do know the right person at the FBI. Don't call the local police; they'll just get shooed away when the feds show up. I'll call them now. Their team will get there as fast as possible."

Sunderland ended the call before Vermeulen could say anything else. Not that there was more to say. Sunderland had reacted quickly and exactly as he'd hoped. But that was the rub. In all the dealings he'd had with the man, he'd never been cooperative. Maybe he'd come to appreciate the larger picture Vermeulen had drawn for him a week earlier.

He turned back and faced the library. Rosenbaum and his wife were whispering something. He didn't really care what they were talking about. He was more concerned about the hint of a smile playing around the broker's mouth. What did she have to be happy about? She knew her crew was out of commission. Unless she had more goons hidden away somewhere, this would be the end of her career as a human trafficker.

His phone rang again. He turned toward the corridor to answer. It was Jackson.

"What d'you want now?" he said.

"Man, I'm getting bored. How long is this going to take?"

"You could practice some patience. I'm almost done. Hang in there. The feds are on their way to collect the Broker and her gang."

"The feds? I don't know if I want to be around when they arrive. Medicare is a federal program, you know."

"You are the prime witness. I need you ...."

He heard the pad of feet on the carpet behind him. He turned. All he saw was Mitzi swinging a heavy candelabra, then the side of his head exploded like a Roman candle.

CHAPTER SIXTY

———◆———

THE PAIN SEEPED INTO VERMEULEN'S CONSCIOUSNESS like a toxic cloud. His brain pressed against his skull like an overinflated balloon. The thumping sound echoing in his ears turned out to be his own heart, pumping blood. There was a tingling in his hands. He tried to move them but couldn't. Something cut into his wrists. He opened his eyes and saw a white ceiling and bookshelves filled with leather-bound volumes. His hands were tied behind his back. He remembered the candlestick and Mitzi. Damn. He rolled to his other side and saw the Rosenbaums and the broker sitting around the table. A sight worse than the pain.

Mitzi saw the movement. "He's awake again," she said.

"Welcome back," the Broker said. "Funny how quickly circumstances change."

"And they'll change again once the FBI arrives," Vermeulen said. "There won't be any deal for the Rosenbaums. I can promise that."

"You're in no position to promise anything. And the FBI won't be coming."

That statement didn't compute. Sunderland had told him that the FBI would be here as soon as possible. There was no way the Broker could have called that off. Unless she'd spoken to Sunderland. But she couldn't know about him. His phone. Of course. The Broker only had to go through his call history to find the number. But then what? She couldn't just call Sunderland. He wouldn't know who she was. And he wouldn't call off the raid just because some woman called him on his phone. Which left only one other option: the Broker knew somebody inside the FBI who could cancel a raid. It wasn't too much of a stretch. A global racket like this couldn't work without some corrupt officials looking the other way.

The headache got a lot worse. He closed his eyes.

"I see you agree with my assessment," the Broker said. "You might as well. Your role in this undertaking has come to an end."

"My superiors know exactly what I'm working on, and they know who the suspects are. You're not getting away, even if you kill me."

"I doubt that very much, but who said anything about killing? We have far more efficient means at our disposal."

"Such as?"

"I'll leave that to management to explain."

"Management is coming here?"

"In a manner of speaking."

A loud banging sounded from the front door.

"Police, open up," a muffled voice shouted.

"With pleasure," the Broker said, more to herself.

She walked to the door and opened it.

"He's in there," the Broker said, pointing. "We managed to immobilize him."

Three men and a woman in blue warm-up jackets and trousers, guns drawn, hustled into the library. They came straight to Vermeulen and rolled him onto his stomach. One of them put his knee on his back and shouted, "Stay down!" A silly demand, since there was no way he could have gotten up. The other cops took up positions around him, one facing him, his gun ready, the others looking toward the entrance. Their jackets said "ICE" on the left front and "Police. Immigration and Customs Enforcement" on the back.

None of this made any sense to Vermeulen. Why would immigration cops show up at the Rosenbaums' house? He thought of Rosita. That couldn't be it. Besides, they weren't searching the house. They'd come for him. And then he saw Sunderland walk into the room.

Vermeulen did a double-take. Sunderland? The surprise lasted only a moment; then the missing pieces fell into place. Sunderland could have gotten word to the gangbanger at the Elizabeth detention center who killed Odinga. He could have issued the threat to Luca at York Prison. He had access to Homeland Security computers and could have known about his flights to and from Vienna. His involvement provided the simplest explanation for everything that had happened in the past two weeks. Well, almost. Sunderland's involvement didn't explain why Odinga and Luca had been detained in the first place. But then he realized that Sunderland was with ICE, not Customs and Border Protection. Different bureaucracies, different chains of command. It all made sense. William of Occam would have approved.

"Is this man trespassing in your house?" Sunderland said.

Rosenbaum nodded.

"Can you speak up?"

"Yes, he is trespassing in my house."

"Did he enter with a weapon drawn and threaten your guest?"

"Yes, he did."

Sunderland turned to Vermeulen, who was watching the charade with increasing incredulity.

"Mr. Vermeulen, criminal trespass is an aggravated felony. The 1996 Illegal Immigration Reform and Immigrant Responsibility Act lists aggravated felonies as cause for mandatory detention and deportation."

"This is utter nonsense," Vermeulen said. "You have no evidence that an aggravated felony occurred here. Besides, I work for the United Nations."

"That doesn't make any difference. Your G-4 visa doesn't give you diplomatic immunity. And Dr. Rosenbaum says you trespassed with a drawn gun. That's all we need."

The four immigration cops grabbed Vermeulen and pulled him up, ready to drag him out of the house.

"Wait," Vermeulen said. The cops stopped. "First, the Rosenbaums invited me into their house. We stood outside and discussed several matters. Then Mrs. Rosenbaum invited me inside. So there is no trespassing. Second, I didn't bring any gun. She," he pointed to the broker, "and her gangsters brought the guns and attacked me first."

The cops were looking at each other, then at Sunderland.

"I see no gangsters," Sunderland said. He turned to the Rosenbaums. "Are there any other individuals in the house?"

They shook their heads.

"That's all I need."

"This is an outrage. Even if this were trespassing, it's not an aggravated felony," Vermeulen said.

"That's where you are wrong. The 1996 law gives broad leeway to ICE officers. I can declare shoplifting an aggravated felony, and there's nothing you can do about that."

Sunderland turned to the woman cop. "Linda, bring him to Elizabeth and book him."

Turning to the Rosenbaums, he said, "He'll be out of the country in no time. You have nothing to worry about."

CHAPTER SIXTY-ONE

———— ◆ ————

JACKSON HAD HAD IT. WAITING IN the car for hours on end wasn't his idea of a good time. The first couple of hours were okay; it gave him a chance to shake off the hangover of whatever drug they'd pumped into him. He'd paced around the car for a while. But now he was getting antsy. He walked toward the street.

The silence was eerie. There was nothing like it in Newark, with its hum of traffic, people shouting, fighting. Hell, there was life. This place sounded like a graveyard.

He reached the tarmac and looked left and right. There were some lights to his right, woods to his left. He walked toward the lights. They turned out to be the gate lights of an estate he couldn't even fathom. Somewhere in the dark there had to be a house, but he couldn't see it.

This wasn't a place where a black man should be walking at night. No Siree. Vermeulen had said that he was close by, at the doctor's house. Only, which of these mansions was the doctor's house? Vermeulen hadn't said anything about a mansion. He walked back to the parking area by the lake. Maybe the house was on the other side of the woods.

He walked quietly past the wooded area, staying in the shadows of the shrubbery. Ahead of him a branch broke with a crack. He froze. Somebody was sneaking in the dark. There was another sound. Like someone shuffling in place, keeping warm in the cold air. Somebody watching? He eased forward. One step. Another. Even though it was pitch dark, he thought he could see something ahead. A mass even darker than everything else. It had to be the other watcher.

"What're you doing here?" he said in a quiet voice.

The body whirled around. A person much smaller than he.

"Please, Mister, I do nothing," a female voice said.

"I can see that. What are you watching?"

"Please, mister, I want no problem. I go now, okay?"

The woman sounded really scared.

"I'm not gonna give you any problem, lady. Just tell me what's going on at that house."

"*La migra*. They come to the doctor's house. I got away just in time."

"You work there?"

"Yes."

"What's your name?"

"Rosita."

"I'm Earle Jackson. Is that Dr. Rosenbaum's house?"

"Yes."

"All right. At least I'm at the right spot. So why's immigration here?"

"They come for me. The nice man told me to get out, that there'd be trouble."

"That nice man, he's like six feet and blond with a funny name? Vermoolen?"

"That's him."

"Okay, let's get a little closer. I wanna see what's going on."

"Not me. I stay here."

"Suit yourself."

Jackson tiptoed forward until he found a place behind a large prickly bush that gave him a view of the doctor's house. There were three cars parked in the driveway. In the bright porch lights, he could tell they were Crown Vics, cop cars. Like Rosita had said, immigration.

The front door opened and two cops came out. Behind those cops walked Vermeulen. He was cuffed. Two more cops followed. They brought Vermeulen to the first Crown Vic. The lead cop opened the back door and his buddy shoved Vermeulen into the rear seat. They took their seats up front and started the car. The other cops got into the remaining Crown Vics, and the three cars made K-turns and disappeared toward the town center.

That just didn't make any sense. Vermeulen, the guy with the funny accent, working for the United Nations, hauled off like those sorry-ass Mexicans he'd seen lined up in Newark. Those immigration cops hadn't come for Rosita. That was for damn sure. They'd come for Vermeulen. But why?

He walked back until he found Rosita again.

"They're gone," he said. "They took Vermeulen, the guy you talked about."

"They took him? Why?"

"Beats me. Well, I gotta get home. You need a ride anywhere?"

"Yes, please. To Newark."

"You're in luck. That's where I'm headed."

CHAPTER SIXTY-TWO

———— ◆ ————

IT WAS FIVE FIFTEEN THE NEXT afternoon. The loudspeaker attached over the door of the cell crackled. There was a cough. Then a distorted voice said: "Vermeulen, visitor."

Vermeulen rose from the thin mattress. The last twenty hours were right up there with the worst days he could remember. Being hauled off by ICE and dumped unceremoniously at the Elizabeth detention center was bad enough. But the worst was that they'd stuck him in solitary confinement. There were four cells; his was the only one occupied.

He'd banged against the door and demanded to see a lawyer until his fists were sore and his voice hoarse. Twice, a guard came to the door. Once to tell him to shut the fuck up and once to tell him they'd put him in restraints if the racket continued.

When they'd brought breakfast at five thirty, he'd told the guard that he wanted to speak to a lawyer.

"This ain't a police station, buddy," the guard had said. "Unless you already have a lawyer, we ain't getting one for you."

"How could I have gotten a lawyer? They just picked me up and brought me here."

"Ain't my problem."

"Can I call someone?"

"No."

"And why is that?"

"No idea."

The conversation at lunchtime was no different. His attempts to speak to a supervisor were rebuffed with vague excuses. They were busy. Wait until after the shift change. They were still busy. Just quit hollering.

At four in the afternoon, somebody who seemed in charge finally came.

"I don't know why you are making all that noise. You are held here pending your voluntary departure."

"Voluntary what? I'm not leaving voluntarily. I want to speak to a lawyer."

"The paperwork says that you asked for voluntary departure instead of being removed by court order. If you ask me, that's the wise choice. Don't change your mind. If a judge orders you removed, you can't apply to come back for ten years. If you go voluntarily, you can come back again very soon."

"I didn't say I wanted to leave on my own."

"Says so in my paperwork."

"Somebody forged it."

"Whoa. Hold it right there, buddy. My paperwork says you agreed to it. I didn't forge anything. It came from the top. Listen to me." He leaned forward and lowered his voice as he spoke. "It's the better way. Get on that plane tomorrow, sort things out, and come back. You go before the immigration court, they'll throw the book at you. Ten years is a long time."

The supervisor left Vermeulen stewing until the loudspeaker announced that he had a visitor. He couldn't imagine who might come to visit him, but getting out of the cell was a reward in itself.

The guard brought him to the visiting room. There was a long wall with small booths. Each booth had a plexiglass window with a plexiglass grating in the middle. The guard brought him to a booth near the center of the room. On the other side of the glass sat the last person he expected to see. Alma Rodriguez, the immigration activist and ice cream lover.

She smiled at the stunned expression on his face.

"I must admit, I didn't expect to see you here," he said.

"I could say the same thing. But we don't have much time. Tell me what happened."

"How did you know I was here?"

"Rosita Torres called me last night. Thanks to you, she missed the ICE raid. She was very grateful."

Vermeulen gave her the broad strokes outline of how he'd ended up in the detention center.

"This tops all the abuses of immigration law I've seen," Alma said. "An ICE official involved with a criminal gang? It's usually the other way around. What did you say about voluntary departure?"

"The supervisor said I had agreed to it. Which I did not."

She scratched the top of her left hand. "I guess it makes sense. It's the only way they can avoid immigration court. Even the worst judges would have wanted to check out the story."

"But why am I still here? If I agreed to voluntary departure, shouldn't I be allowed out?"

"Not necessarily. ICE distrusts all aliens, no matter what their status. Even if you agreed to leave, they can still stick you in detention to make sure you don't change your mind and disappear."

"How do I fight this?" he said. Her calm demeanor set him on edge.

"I'm thinking. This is different from anything I've ever been involved in. This is organized crime."

"Call my boss, Suarez." He gave her the number for OIOS. "And the FBI."

"I'll call your boss, but I don't know what he can do. And the FBI? I don't know."

"But there's got to be a way to stop this," he said.

"You'd think, but immigration law in this country is so screwed up, they can ship you out of the country and even charge you for the flight. I'll also call one of our pro bono lawyers. I'm sure he'll have to call someone else."

"What can I do in the meantime?"

"Sit and wait. It's what all our clients do. Don't get into fights. Don't harass the guards. Don't do anything that gives them a reason to transfer you. Hopefully one of our lawyers will visit you tomorrow."

"That might be too late," Vermeulen said.

"Why?"

"Because the supervisor I talked to said that I'd be put on a plane tomorrow."

"What? Tomorrow?"

"Yes."

She blew out a breath. "I've never heard of someone being deported so fast. That's crazy."

"Tell me about it. What's your phone number, in case I get phone privileges anytime soon?"

She recited the number twice.

"I'd better hurry and make those calls," she said. "The van with the deportees usually leaves between eleven and two. If they are coming to get you and you haven't seen our lawyer yet, forget everything I've said about being nice. Whatever you do, don't get on that van."

CHAPTER SIXTY-THREE

---◆---

THE NIGHT OOZED ALONG LIKE HOT tar on a cold roof. Sleep was out of the question. So he paced.

Eight steps. Turn. Eight steps. Turn. Stop.

Nothing had changed.

Eight steps. Turn. Eight steps. Turn. Stop.

Still no change.

He kept up the pace, but didn't stop anymore. The rhythm soothed his mind. Better than banging on the door and yelling for a guard who wouldn't come anyway, or worse, would put him in restraints.

Sunderland.

The man had lied to him from the moment he told him that Abasi had been the victim of a street robbery. No coroner would have overlooked the missing kidney. But it showed Vermeulen that rank, status, or position had no impact on whether a person followed their criminal instinct. The rich and well connected just chose different methods. Sunderland was in the perfect position to turn human trafficking into a racket to benefit himself. Sometimes opportunity was the only necessary condition.

Vermeulen couldn't sort out if Sunderland or the Broker was in charge. The Broker had all the makings of a leader. But she was also on the frontline, dealing with day-to-day problems. That alone would make Sunderland the boss. However, Sunderland was a fed, part of a vast bureaucracy with people below him and people above him. Any one of them could've tripped him up. Would the boss be in such a vulnerable position?

At eleven that night, Vermeulen decided that Sunderland was the boss.

Not a brilliant insight, really. But it kept him from hammering on the door and calling for the guard.

Pacing kept him sane.

Eight steps. Turn. Eight steps. Turn.

What about the Vienna operation? Or Kenya? Jackson said he was recruited as a donor in Nairobi. Was Sunderland in charge of those operations, too? That didn't seem possible. A mid-level bureaucrat didn't have the leeway to put together and maintain such a network. There had to be somebody above him. Maybe not. What if Kurtz in Vienna and whoever handled Nairobi were independents? They'd get the orders, supply the victims, and get paid. It was possible. But not likely. It required more trust than Vermeulen believed existed among crooks.

By two in the morning, he decided to call it a tie. There was a good chance of someone running the whole thing. But he had no evidence to support that. It could just as well be a loose network. If someone failed to keep their end of the deal, a hit man could always remedy the situation.

Eight steps. Turn. Eight steps. Turn.

Breakfast came at five thirty. "Hey, aren't you the guy who asked about that African fellow who got himself killed?" the guard said.

Vermeulen recognized him as the man who'd stormed into the reception area two weeks ago and blurted out that Odinga was dead.

"Yes, I am."

"Then what are you doing in here?"

"Someone at ICE is a crook and got me locked up here."

"No shit?"

"Really. Listen, I need to make a call. They didn't let me make one last night."

"I don't have a key to let you out."

"Could you call for me?"

The guard looked left and right. "I don't know, man. It's a shit job, but it's the job I got. I don't need any trouble."

"Nobody needs to know."

"What do you want me to do?"

"Call the first number. Tell them you are calling for me and that they should call the second number."

"That's it?"

Vermeulen nodded.

"Okay."

Vermeulen gave him the number for the OIOS office and Alma's number. It wasn't that he didn't trust Alma. He couldn't think of anything else to do.

He wished somebody would call Tessa, but there was nothing she could have done.

They came for him at eleven thirty. Four men in ICE uniforms.

No lawyer had materialized. Nobody had talked to him. Alma's plan had failed.

He retreated to the farthest corner of the room. *Whatever you do, don't get on that van.*

The head ICE cop grunted, "Let's go."

"I'm not going," Vermeulen said. "I demand to see a lawyer."

"You're not entitled to see a lawyer; besides, you are going voluntarily. So let's make this quick. The plane isn't waiting."

"I'm not going."

The other three ICE officers came to take him out of his cell. Vermeulen let himself slide to the floor. He wasn't leaving the cell. That was for sure.

Two cops pulled him up by his arms and carried him to the door, his feet dragging behind on the linoleum. He grasped the doorjamb, clamping his hand as hard as he could around the metal frame. The head cop peeled his hand off, one finger at a time. They were calm and methodical. Vermeulen was not their first deportee.

In the end, all four carried him out of the detention center, two holding him by the shoulders and two by his legs.

"Does this look like voluntary departure?" he shouted.

He could see other detainees flocking to the windows of their dorms, staring, afraid. This was their future.

"I'm not leaving voluntarily," Vermeulen said again. "This is a criminal setup. You are committing a crime."

The officers didn't care one bit. They carried him through a double door into a loading area. A windowless gray van, its side door open, waited for them. They shoved him into the van and cuffed him to a rod welded to the partition that separated the rear from the cab. The door slid shut with a bang. It had no handle on the inside. Two of them got in the front. The van drove out of the loading area, crossed the employee parking lot, and turned into the street.

Almost immediately, it came to a stop. Loud shouting.

"Fucking protestors," the cop behind the steering wheel said.

Vermeulen craned his neck to peer through the window in the partition. A crowd of people occupied the street. Their signs were the same he'd seen during his first visit to Elizabeth. "Not One More Deportation."

There was one difference.

Ten or so protesters had formed a human barrier across the width of the street. They had chained themselves together and to the lamp poles on either end. There was no way the van could pass. Still, the cop drove forward until the front of the van touched a woman at the center of the chain. The cop revved the engine. The woman didn't budge. Instead, she smiled. Despite the hat and scarf, Vermeulen recognized the smile. It was Alma.

On the other side of the human chain, several Elizabeth PD cruisers had parked. The cops were attempting crowd control. It didn't work very well. A supervisor with a bullhorn kept shouting for them to disperse or be arrested for trespassing, but nobody moved. A police van arrived and two cops came with bolt cutters. The protestors booed them and flocked to the street to form human shields around the chain. The cops began to drag people away. Ear-shattering whistles accompanied the process. The protestors already shoved to the sidewalk tried to run back to the human chain. More cruisers arrived. The officers put up a temporary pen to keep people away from the human chain.

It took a half hour before the officers with the bolt cutters came close enough to cut the chains.

"Finally," the ICE cop at the wheel said. "We're gonna make the flight after all."

Once the first chain was cut, the police just pushed the two ends of the human barrier off the road until there was a gap wide enough for the van to pass.

The cop at the wheel revved the engine. The van jolted forward.

That's it, Vermeulen thought. *The end.*

Except it wasn't. Three black sedans came to a squealing halt and blocked the road. Behind them, a blue Corolla stopped in the middle of the street. A man jumped from the Corolla and ran past the Crown Vics toward the van. Six men in FBI jackets followed him. He knocked at the driver's window and pressed a piece of paper against the glass. The ICE cop cranked the window down.

"This is an injunction issued by a federal judge. You are to release that man immediately."

CHAPTER SIXTY-FOUR

———— ◆ ————

"MORE COFFEE, HON?" SANDY SAID. THERE weren't many patrons in the diner. It was the afternoon lull, and the waitress had been hovering near their table.

"Yes, please," Alma said.

Sandy poured from her thermos. She eyed Vermeulen, who nodded. She poured again.

"You made a decision about the pie yet?"

Vermeulen said, "Blueberry."

Alma said, "Apple."

"À la mode?"

Both nodded.

"We really can't make a habit of this," Alma said.

"What? Meeting or eating pie?"

"Eating pie, of course. You really didn't have to, you know."

"There isn't enough pie in the world to thank you for what you did for me."

The two had just come from another protest against deportations. Nothing like the one a week earlier that had sprung Vermeulen from the clutches of ICE. Alma had invited him to join them. The protest only involved holding up signs. There was no van leaving the Elizabeth detention center that day. Nobody was carted off to the airport for deportation. But *Unidad Latina* came out anyway. Reminding everyone that just because it was quiet didn't mean there weren't people stuck inside the prison.

Since his release, Vermeulen had a new appreciation for the work done by Alma and her organization. He wanted to thank all those folks who'd braved the police and faced arrest to save him. He couldn't think of a more humbling experience. Cynicism was an occupational hazard in his job. What they did for him was the perfect antidote. Supporting their cause seemed the best way to thank them. And eating pie with Alma was a pleasant conclusion to the afternoon.

"So, what happened after the FBI whisked you away?" she said.

"They took me to the Newark FBI office. The Special Agent in Charge and my boss were waiting for me. I told them what I knew, they interrogated me, went over everything three times. That took a long time. They let me go at five."

"Did they clear you?"

"Eventually, two days later. I had to leave my passport with them and was lucky to be allowed to go home."

He forked a bite of pie into his mouth and chewed slowly. What a simple pleasure! As nice as being back in his bed that first night after leaving the detention center.

"What about you and your friends?" he said. "Did the police hassle you a lot?"

She put down her fork, and brought her thumb and index finger close together. "Just a little. One of the FBI agents spoke to the lieutenant and explained the situation. After that, the cops let us go. They usually do. We're all trained in non-violent protest. They know we won't do anything to harm them."

They savored their pies quietly.

"What about the trafficking network?" Alma said. "They caught the guys, no?"

"They arrested Sunderland at his house, suitcase in hand. The ICE agents called him after the FBI took over and he tried to leave town in a hurry."

She smiled. "I know the next Special Agent in Charge won't be any different when it comes to deportation, but I was happy to see a crooked one be arrested."

"I can see why. The investigation is still ongoing. We at OIOS don't get the details, but the FBI sent us an update, sort of a courtesy for having brought the network to their attention. According to that report, Sunderland was the man in charge."

"What about the doctor?" Alma said, putting down her cup.

"I don't really know. I saw him come into the FBI office the next day. He had two people with him. They looked like lawyers. I have no doubt the three already had a strategy to weasel out of it. The FBI update didn't include any information about him."

"And that woman? What was she called?"

"The Broker. Her real name is Camille Delano, the daughter of a dead New

Jersey mobster. But this doesn't seem to be an operation of those gangsters. She had her own crew. Not the brightest bulbs in the chandelier. The police found them a day later. They were the ones who gave up her name. The police put out an APB, but Delano had disappeared."

"Aren't you worried? She sounds dangerous," Alma said.

"She certainly is. She is also smart. I bet she's left the country. She struck me as someone who's prepared for all eventualities. She'll surface somewhere. People like her never just retire."

He took another bite of pie and washed it down with a swallow of coffee.

"The oddest character in this whole thing was Jackson," he continued. "His story was the key evidence against the whole network. He'd actually been recruited as a donor under false pretenses. He gave them the name of the contact in Kenya and the FBI forwarded that to the Criminal Investigation Division in Nairobi. But Jackson disappeared after the first interview. Just didn't show up for the second one."

"He's the African-American man who found the other victim at Broad Street Station, right?"

"Yes. We never really talked much, but I knew right away he was a hustler. He had some kind of racket going that made him afraid of the FBI, said something about Medicare being a federal program. He changed, though. Brought some of the money Abasi had back to his family in Kenya. At least that's what he said. He probably kept enough to stay afloat for a while. The FBI wasn't too happy. He would have been the prime witness. Now they're interviewing Mihaly Luca at York Prison. With the network destroyed, he should be willing to testify."

His phone rang. He checked the display. It was Gaby.

"I've got to take this," he said to Alma, stood up, and walked toward the door.

"Hello, Gaby. What a surprise. Where are you?"

"Hi, Dad. I'm back in Düsseldorf. You can't imagine how nice it is to be in my own bed again."

"I can, believe me, I can. I spent two nights in jail."

"What? When? Why didn't you call?"

"A week ago, and I didn't want to bother you. You were still recuperating."

"Whose nose did you bend this time?"

"It wasn't like that at all. Once I got back to New York, the gangsters there were already waiting for me. I had no choice but to confront them."

"Oh, talking to the police was out of the question, eh?"

"There was no time."

"Yeah, I know. There never is," she said.

"Do you want me to tell you the story or not?"

"Better not. You can tell it to me in person."

"What? How?"

"Well, my doctor at home told me I needed another two weeks of rest and relaxation before going back to work. So I thought I'd come and visit you?"

"Should you be flying?"

"He didn't think it would be a problem. So, I'll be there the next weekend. Is that okay?"

"Sure it is. How long will you stay?"

"A week. I can't wait to see New York City. You can show me around?"

"I sure will. Can't wait either."

"And don't worry, I know you'll have to work. I can do things on my own, too."

"No worries. I'm still on unpaid leave, remember? They're still investigating my conduct in Vienna. I may have to pop into the office once or twice."

"I can't believe they're still doing that. They ought to give you a medal."

"I know, but the wheels of bureaucracy turn slowly, and it's not always assured the truth will emerge."

"I'll be there to support you."

"Thanks, darling."

"Oh, Tessa says 'hi,' " Gaby said.

"Anything else?"

"She said you two need a good talk. I think she's right."

"So you're giving relationship advice now?"

"Dad, I know you care for each other. But a relationship doesn't thrive unless it is tended. So use your time wisely."

"What do you mean?" Vermeulen said.

"Oops. My big mouth. I promised not to tell, but Tessa has an assignment in Thailand. She decided to take the long way there."

"The long way?"

"Via New York. She'll be there tomorrow evening. You didn't hear it from me, so pretend to be surprised. I'll email you my itinerary. Love you, Dad."

She ended the call before he could answer. He had to smile. Having your daughter back in your life was amazing. That she also got along with your lover was icing on the cake.

"You look like you're in a good mood," Alma said when he got back to the table.

"Yes, I've got some wonderful company to look forward to."

Photo by Joanna Niemann

MICHAEL NIEMANN GREW UP IN A small town in Germany, ten kilometers from the Dutch border. Crossing that border often at a young age sparked in him a curiosity about the larger world. He studied political science at the Rheinische Friedrich-Wilhelms Universität in Bonn and international studies at the University of Denver. During his academic career he focused his work on southern Africa and frequently spent time in the region. After taking a fiction writing course from his friend, the late Fred Pfeil, he embarked on a different way to write about the world.

For more information, go to:
www.michael-niemann.com
www.facebook.com/MichaelNiemannAuthor/

A Valentin Vermeulen Thriller, Book 1

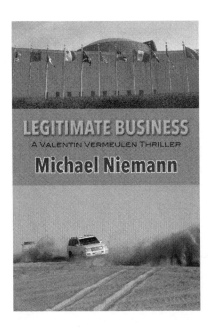

A constable with an all-female United Nations peacekeeping unit in Darfur, Sudan, has been shot dead in an apparent random shooting. The case remains closed until Valentin Vermeulen arrives to conduct a routine audit. As an investigator with the UN Office of Internal Oversight Services, his job is to ferret out fraud. It will soon be clear that he has stumbled onto a major criminal operation.